Sea Glass Hidden in Plain Sight

Serenity
Book 2

Stacey Wilk

Sea Glass Hidden in Plain Sight by Stacey Wilk

Serenity, Book 2

This is a work of fiction. Names, characters, places, and incidents are either the product of the author's imagination or are used fictitiously, and any resemblance to actual persons living or dead, business establishments, events, or locales, is entirely coincidental.

Sea Glass Hidden in Plain Sight

Cover Art by *Diana Carlisle*

Published in the United States of America

For Hannah

Chapter One

Organizing an extravagant wedding for a famous baseball player and a social media influencer should have been a cakewalk for Maren Russo. She planned major events for some of New Jersey's wealthiest. Except tonight's wedding had tested her endurance. The uphill battle from day one had finally worn her out. She no longer wished to chase around an entitled, spoiled woman wearing pounds of tule and hairspray.

She only had to hang on for another hour or so and then she would be free of the bridezilla extraordinaire. Sixty minutes wasn't so bad. She could handle another sixty minutes. Hell, labor had lasted longer than that.

Maren stood off to the side, out of the way of guests, assessing the evening. The magnificent ballroom with crystal chandeliers dangling from a twenty-foot ceiling reflected prisms from all the diamonds worn in the room. Everyone seemed to be having a good time. The band

1

played an upbeat song. They were due to slow it down soon and allow the guests to enjoy their dessert being placed on the tables by the competent staff.

Some of these women in their high end dresses and shoes were her clients and she was grateful for their business. *Glass Shoe Events* had not taken off the way she had hoped. Only no one knew that.

Maren pushed a long breath over her lips. She tried—but failed—not to glance across the crowded room and find Shane Sutherland, brother of the groom, leaning against the wall by himself with a whiskey glass in his hand and looking better than he had in decades. Her body wanted to remember Shane. Her mind did not.

The band downshifted into a Sarah Vaughan tune. Paris, the bride, decked out in her ten-thousand-dollar dress and the groom styled in his custom-made navy-blue suit swayed on the dance floor.

Paris looked up at her new husband. Maren expected the typical expression of love and adoration sculpted into Paris's makeup. Instead, Paris's mouth curled into a snarl. Her Botox filled brow attempted to furrow.

Maren took a step forward. She needed to get a hold of Paris before she threw one of her tantrums in front of all the guests. Maren pushed through the crowd of warm bodies, but the center of the dance floor moved farther and farther away with each step.

Paris pulled her arm back and in one quick, fluid move slapped her groom across the face. The smack echoed off the tall centerpieces dripping with white flowers loud enough to stop the band. An audible gasp traveled across the room in an outraged wave.

Paris hiked up her gown and ran off the dance floor as the guests parted to allow her to pass. *Sure, now they get out of the way.* Evan reached for his cheek—*was that a handprint*—with shock painted in crimson across his face as if to say, he couldn't believe that had just happened.

Maren couldn't quite believe it either. She didn't know if she should run toward the injured groom or the upset bride. All eyes were on her, as if she had the answer to the million-dollar question. *What the hell was that all about?* She might be the wedding planner, but she never had a bride slap a groom before. She was fresh out of answers on that one.

Shane pushed off the wall and plowed through the crowd. Somehow, he made eye contact with her and tilted his chin in the direction Paris had run. Maren understood. Shane would take care of his brother—like always. Maren needed to find Paris.

The venue, which was situated at the beach in her lovely Serenity by the Sea, had hallways darting in several directions like the arms of an octopus. Paris could have run down any of them. But Maren had an idea and hurried to the ladies' room. The locked door fought against her grip on the knob.

"Paris, are you in there?" Maren knocked, nicking her knuckles on the dry wood.

"I hate him." The words were muffled, but clear enough.

"Paris, you don't mean that. What happened? How can I help?"

The door swung open. Paris stood before her with mascara running down her face in long black streaks. That was supposed to be waterproof mascara. Paris's headpiece had slid from the top of her head to the side, becoming a crooked point of crystals.

"This is all your fault." Paris's mouth puckered.

"Excuse me?" She had heard Paris just fine but needed some time to figure out how to respond to the latest ridiculous comment.

"This whole night is a disaster because of you." Spit flew from Paris's lips, nearly hitting Maren.

"We've had a few hiccups, but we took care of those. Why were you and Evan fighting?" She didn't think for one second an actual argument transpired because Paris often found things to complain about when nothing was wrong. But Maren wanted to keep the battlefield as safe as possible to navigate.

"He told me not to make such a big deal about the cake falling over in the kitchen and having to serve cupcakes from the grocery store instead. He said I should focus on just him and ignore the pork loin that no one ate."

"I tried to—"

"You never should've allowed me to pick pork loin. Why did I listen to you? You're the worst wedding planner ever." Paris's face turned an interesting shade of raspberry. The color would look lovely on bridesmaids' dresses.

Maren forced the disloyal laughter down.

"Paris, I didn't encourage you to hit your new husband. Why don't we go back out there and have some fun."

"Fun? Fun? You call this day fun? I can't breathe in this dress. My feet are killing me. I'm starving because I haven't eaten since last night and that was just a cube of cheese. You haven't been any where that I needed you. The photographer won't stop putting his hand on my shoulder, my mother has drunk enough vodka to sink a ship, and three other brides on social media are wearing my gown."

Maren had tried to tell Paris not to choose pork loin as a dinner option and not to buy the hottest wedding dress of the season because a celebrity actress had worn it. But pointing all of that out now would do her no good. She needed to focus and get the bride back out to the reception. The band wouldn't play if she wasn't present, and they cost a fortune.

"Is that what you're upset about? Some brides on social media?"

"Of course, I am. I've been following that designer for ages now. I should be the only one in her dress. I'm also upset because I've had to tell you how to do every step of this. I don't know why I allowed Evan to talk me into using you. He only felt sorry for you, you know. He didn't think you had any skills, but you needed the charity, and you had dated Shane like a hundred years ago." Paris rolled her black-stained eyes.

Maren forced her lungs to work. All of that couldn't

be true. Well, the dating Shane part was true, but the rest couldn't be. Could it?

"I was mad at my husband because he said I wasn't nice to you, and you needed me to be nice to you. He said I had advantages you don't. Can you believe him? As if I haven't suffered for what I have. I have worked hard for every second of my success. Someone should feel sorry for me because it's my wedding day, and I have the worst wedding planner ever. I'm going to ruin you. I promise you that. I will be telling all my followers how you didn't know what flowers to pick or what color my girls should wear or what time the damn rehearsal dinner started." Paris's headpiece slid off her head from all her yelling and clattered on the floor.

"And now you made me break my crown." Paris burst into tears and slammed the door.

Maren startled. This night had to go well because she needed more business. Maren hated the fact Paris had the power to influence others to hire her, but nothing could be truer. Maren had been banking on a good recommendation for the past six months.

She knocked this time with a little more force than necessary. "Paris, we need to go back to the reception." And pretend that Paris wasn't a self-centered entitled brat.

"Go away. I hate you and I hate Evan. I want a divorce."

She couldn't help with that. Trying to convince this woman to come out and play nice with her guests, maybe apologize to her husband seemed like a fool's errand. But she knocked one more time.

"Please come out."

"Go. Away."

Maren returned to the reception defeated and with a sharp pain behind her eye. Most of the guests had disappeared while she was talking to the bride. Maren envied them.

The banquet room grew vaster with its emptiness. The waitstaff wandered around offering more coffee to the few stragglers. The band played a sour tune. Evan and Shane stood at the bar. Evan held a bag of ice to his cheek.

"You'll never work in this town or any other again." Paris's father pointed a meaty finger in her face. "You should have watched how much Evan drank. When he's drunk, he gets belligerent and demanding."

"Evan?" This old, wealthy, affluent man could not be serious. Evan was a lot of things, she knew because of her time with Shane, but hostile or aggressive he was not. Shane on the other hand...

"That's right. He said or did something to hurt my baby and you should have kept the booze out of his hands. That's what I paid you for."

"Sir, you paid me to plan a wedding not be a babysitter."

"Other duties as assigned. Ever heard of that phrase? Now, if you'll excuse me, I have to check on my baby girl." He brushed past her, almost knocking her over.

She was ruined.

Maren headed for the French doors that opened to a large balcony, expansive enough for the cocktail hour to be held on while a harpist had played in the corner, and the guests mingled in and out while enjoying the ocean's salty breeze. That balcony was her favorite thing about this venue. That was one thing Paris had loved as much. She had squealed when she saw it and told her very wealthy, professional baseball playing fiancé she had to have it.

From the balcony a guest could take the steps down onto the sand. Maren grabbed a half-empty bottle of champagne discarded on the tray of dirty plates and glasses. She crossed over the threshold onto the balcony and followed the stairs to the beach.

She didn't even like champagne, but she sure had earned this drink. She kicked off her pale rose-colored high heels with opalescent crystals covering the top and stepped onto the cool sand where her feet sank with each step. Sand sprayed against the back of her legs as she pressed forward.

With her shoes in one hand and the champagne bottle in the other, she moved toward the surf and plunked down right before the waves could grab her and ruin the clothes she couldn't afford. Her clothing budget had cost her almost as much as her property taxes, but she couldn't wear the same outfit to more than one wedding.

Her phone blew up in her pants pocket. She ignored it. Nothing good would come from looking at the texts and missed calls. Maren downed the champagne and grimaced against the sour taste.

When a social media influencer who could do no wrong in the eyes of her followers slapped her handsome and famous husband across the face during what should be the happiest day of their lives, who else was there to blame except the wedding planner? Clearly, even the father of the bride planned on using Maren as the scapegoat too. After tonight, her reputation as the up-and-coming premier event planner was over. No one would work with her now.

She flopped back in the sand and stared up at the star-filled night sky. The beautiful evening was perfect for a wedding, during the last weekend of the summer at the shore, but the ocean's constant whisper could not soothe what was aching her.

She had divorced her husband, come back to Serenity by the Sea to live near her sisters, started a brand-new career as a wedding planner to some of New Jersey's wealthiest, and had sent her only daughter off to college. She had believed she actually nailed it—that she was a success. That all her hard work and sacrifices had paid off.

Foolish. She had nailed nothing except maybe the seashell sticking in her back. She reached underneath and pulled it out. Only it wasn't a shell. She held the brown piece of sea glass between her fingers. This one was larger than most she could ever find here. She held it up to the moon and let the white light filter through the worn and smooth stone.

She was a lot like sea glass when it started out. Broken. Tossed aside. She had believed she had become restored, older, different, and maybe even better.

Her phone buzzed again, drawing her attention toward the vibrations. This time she pulled it out and glanced at the long list of notifications. Plenty of missed calls. And plenty more that were texts all reading *you're fired* in one form or another. Just like she suspected.

"What have you got there?" Shane stood above her. He had removed his shoes and rolled up his pant legs, revealing his muscular calves covered in dark downy hair. He always had great legs. He had unbuttoned the top two buttons of his white dress shirt and rolled up the sleeves too. His gold watch winked at her.

"Champagne." She turned to him and arched her brow on purpose to convey her utter surprise at his decision to be cordial. She might have avoided him during the past few days, but he had kept a good distance too. Maybe Evan had only hired her because of her past with Shane.

She held out the bottle. Any other night, she would avoid him. Their breakup had cost her. But after tonight, she didn't care much who she spoke to or how.

"No, thanks. I've had enough. Do you mind if I sit a minute?"

"It's a public beach." She couldn't stop him. The professional athlete was used to getting his way. She took another swig of the champagne to give her something to do besides look at him.

He pulled his knees toward his chest and wrapped his arms around his shins. His biceps bulged against the fabric of his shirt. Even at his age, the man was solid as stone. She should find out what supplements he used. She now had plenty of time on her hands to workout. No money to join a gym, but who's complaining? She took another swig.

"You planned a nice wedding."

She didn't want compliments from him, didn't need him to take pity on her because the night combusted. "Until the end. How's Evan?"

"His pride is bruised worse than his face. He and Paris are probably already making up."

She didn't understand their strange relationship at all. Love should be built on trust and honesty. Two people should be able to talk out their problems, not assault one another.

"Are you okay?" His gaze searched her face.

She glanced at him over the champagne bottle, still baffled by his appearance on the beach. "Why did you follow me out here?"

They had nothing to say to each other. Their relationship had ended a long time ago, before she had met her husband. But it had ended unfinished, at least for her. At one time, she had more to say about their goodbye, but he had walked away without giving her the chance to be heard.

"I overheard what Paris's father said to you. I wanted to make sure you were okay."

She had almost forgotten how chivalrous Shane

11

could be. Not all his qualities were bad. "Well, I'm just fine. You don't have to worry about me."

"If you say so, but it looks like you're trying to get drunk."

"Maybe I am. It's been a long day." The last two years had been long, getting divorced, starting a business, falling behind in her property taxes. She was six months past due with no way to dig out and the tax collector breathing down her neck.

"Can I give you a ride home?"

"Absolutely not. Is there something I can help with? Is the banquet manager looking for payment?" As if she'd get in a car with this man like nothing had occurred between them. She might be more mature than the last time they spoke in both age and knowledge, but she wasn't ready to share close space with Shane Sutherland.

"Don't worry about what's going on in there. They'll figure it out. How about you?"

"How about me what? I already said I was fine."

"You don't seem fine."

"I can take care of myself. Thank you." Maren glanced at the sea glass still in her hand then chucked it into the ocean where the white foam sucked it up and dragged it out to sea.

She had to admit... she was slightly jealous of that little piece of garbage.

Chapter Two

The Crew Chief screamed at Shane. They stood nose to nose, dancing around each other, spit flying from both their mouths. The Crew Chief reeked of sweat and aftershave. Shane wanted to step away just to get a breath of fresh air, but he would not give the ump the satisfaction. The call was wrong. Plain and simple and a coach didn't back down when his player needed him.

Fans cheered from the stands as he fought for his player. Their jeers and chants pulsed in his head. The pitcher had thrown a ball, not strike three which ended the top of the ninth inning. His team couldn't sit now. They had a chance to win, and they needed this chance. They were behind in the game count and weren't likely to win the series if they didn't win tonight.

"Coach, you're out of here. Leave the field." Donny, the Crew Chief and head ump, stepped back and signaled as if he threw a ball. The crowd yelled louder, some in favor of the ump's call and some against.

Shane threw his hat on the field. If he hadn't been thrown out before, he would now. He stepped back into Donny's personal space again. This fight wasn't over for Shane.

"You're wrong, Donny. You're wrong and you know it. You're trying to screw with us."

"Get off the field, Shane. Now." A vein pulsed in Donny's neck as he bumped into Shane.

Shane had taken away Donny's space, leaving little chance they wouldn't bang into each other. Players ran onto the field as if that collision was the fight bell, which it kind of was in his world. The first base ump tried to push his way in between him and Donny without touching Shane. He made sure to hold his ground, making it harder for the first base ump to do his job. He wasn't leaving the field without his money's worth.

He kicked the dirt and his hat.

Matt, his batting coach, gripped Shane's shoulder. "Shane, let's go. Drop it. What's done is done. We'll get it next time."

"There is no next time." He didn't have the luxury of time. If they didn't make the playoffs, he was gone. The GM had said as much in a recent meeting. He couldn't get fired from another team. No one else would hire him.

"You need to cool down," Matt said, following him off the field.

"Don't tell me what to do." He hadn't meant to bark at Matt. Matt was a good guy, a good coach and friend.

He stopped half-way down the tunnel to the locker rooms. "Sorry, man. No excuses. I'm just pissed because we needed that call."

"You have to let it go. The team needs you to stay in the games."

He was starting to wonder if the team did need him. Maybe his team would be better off with another coach. He loved this sport, but he wasn't sure it loved him anymore.

"I need a favor. Can you do the press conference? I need to go for a drive or something. Cool down. Get my head straight before I prep for the next game."

"Yeah, sure. Go out the back door. I'll take care of the rest." Matt stuck out his hand and Shane shook.

He hurried to the underground garage where he had parked his car. The leather seats practically curled around him like a good woman. He pictured Maren Russo lying on the beach, staring up at the sky with her hair spread out around her the night of Evan's wedding and pushed that thought away faster than a ninety-mile an hour ball.

His phone pinged. He should ignore it, but his gaze betrayed him. The general manager had already sent a text.

You're fired.

Shane resisted the urge to throw his phone. He shouldn't be surprised. He'd been warned, but those two words stung as if he had been hit in the head with a broken bat. Fired. Again.

He couldn't think about it, had to get out of there and

put space between him and the team. He needed a distraction that didn't involve booze.

Roads uncurled before him. Streetlights blurred in his peripheral. He had no destination in mind. He turned left and right, took on-ramps and off-ramps without much thought to his destination. Music blared through the speakers, thumping in his head much like the crowd's shouts from earlier. Everything rode on those games. Each one was more important than the last. If they were going to be champions, he had to fight for every bad call.

But the energy it took, and the drain it left on him, game after game after game, became a sum he struggled to total. Was it time to walk or was he in a slump?

The screen on his dash lit up with an incoming call. He didn't recognize the number and was tempted to hit end, but his finger pressed the green button instead.

"Shane Sutherland."

"Evening, Shane. This is Barry Solomon. How ya doing tonight?"

Barry Solomon owned the New York Warriors. They were the number one team in the East League and untouchable with what looked like all the best talent. Shane's team was a mix of rookies who complained about the press wanting to interview them and the lack of attention they got from management and veterans who injured one thing or another every time he turned around.

The Warriors were also the team he always dreamed of playing with since he was a kid in Little League.

"Hey, Barry. If you saw tonight's game, then you know how I'm doing." He couldn't fathom what Barry

Solomon could want with him at this hour, or any hour. Solomon didn't waste his time with calls to managers who clawed their way to the wild card position in the playoffs. Not when managers of first place teams were on speed dial.

"I did see that. Sorry about the call. You were robbed."

"Glad you think so."

"You fight hard for your players."

"I try." Damn straight he did. "What's on your mind, Barry? It's kind of late for a social call." The press conference must have begun. That would explain how Barry knew Shane might take a call. Shane wasn't sitting in the hot seat with the networks, getting slammed by their endless questions.

"I'll get to the point. I'm offering you a job. I want you to come and coach for me. As my manager."

"Me?" Rumors had run long and deep about the Warrior's manager retiring. Shane hadn't given the rumor much thought. Winning had been the only thing on his mind, of late. Winning and Evan's wedding, that was.

Every day that had led up to the wedding put him closer to Maren, a place he hadn't wanted to be, but when Paris had slapped Evan and her parents had immediately blamed Maren, a knot had formed in the center of his chest. He had wanted to protect her and didn't understand why. She didn't need him, never had. Didn't stop him from following her out on the beach and sitting next to her.

"Yes, I want to hire you." Barry's soft chuckle filled

Shane's car and derailed anymore thoughts of Maren. "You're the kind of manager I need for my team now that Earl is leaving. The players respect you. You get them to perform under pressure."

"We're losing." He should not point out the obvious. Working with Barry Solomon and the Warrior's would be a step up for him and something he had secretly coveted because only two people ever knew how much he wanted a spot on that team.

The Warriors were the team with almost a century of baseball history no other team had. As a kid, he and Evan used to wear those jerseys, pretending to be Rocky Crosby at short or John Flynn at third.

The Warriors were the one thing he and his dad could talk about without arguing right up until he passed. The Warriors bridged the gap between father and son when his dad questioned all Shane's decisions from marrying his first wife to his short-term use with steroids. Steroid use was a mistake Shane regretted and wished he could erase from his past, along with breaking up with Maren, but looking over his shoulder never did him much good.

"I'm aware of your stats," Barry said, bringing Shane back to the present. "You have a few things working against you. Your lineup. Those boys are a motley crew. Your general manager who has been gunning for you since you put on that uniform because we both know he never wanted you on his team, and... well, honestly, your temper, Shane."

"I prefer to think of it as passion." He'd been hearing

about his outbursts since high school ball. Every coach had told him to simmer down, not let so much bother him. He could admit sometimes he went too far. He had with Maren all those years ago.

Shane took exit 100 off the Garden State Parkway and followed the highway.

"Passion. Anger. Either way, between you, me, and the night sky, the job is yours for next season. I want you at the meetings after the Grandstand Series ends in October. I'll have my people call your agent in the morning, if you say yes now. But before you do, I need to make one thing clear if we're to work together."

He would agree to about anything to work on this team, but his agent might strangle him if he couldn't negotiate a good contract, one that he and his agent would benefit by. But Shane didn't care about the money. He wanted to wear that uniform.

"What's your request?"

"Clean up your act. Get that temper under control. No more outbursts—anywhere. Not on the field, not in public. No media that shows Shane Sutherland losing his cool. I run a tight ship on my end and there's no place for bad reputations on my team. I've booted men and happily paid out their contracts if they break my rule. Morality is a number one priority for us."

"Are you sure you want me with my history?" He had tried countless times to control his outbursts on the field. The attempt hardly ever stuck. He could be setting himself up for failure, but since he lost his job about an hour ago, he didn't see he had a whole lot more to lose.

Shane stopped at a red light. He had been up and down this road that led to the shore a million times, would know it with his eyes closed. He hadn't planned on coming this way, but his car had taken him as if he had no control over the wheel.

"If you're talking about the steroid use, I know you were young and dumb. I also know you weren't juicing like the others. I know about Evan too. I don't hold mistakes made in the past against anyone. But you kicked that dirt tonight. So, get yourself together. I'm giving you a month to show the world you're a changed man."

"How would you like me to do that? I don't have any more games to avoid getting thrown out of."

"You'll find a way. You're resourceful. If you can't show me a man with his head and heart in the game and not in the boxing ring, the offer goes to someone else. Can you handle my request?"

He could try. "Yes, of course I can keep my mouth shut. I appreciate the opportunity."

"One more thing. My management team thinks I'm off my rocker, offering you this job, but I believe in you. You're right about your passion for the sport. I see it in your eyes. Just keep it out of your mouth and off the field."

"Thank you, sir. You won't be sorry." He hoped.

"Don't make me, Shane." Barry ended the call.

Shane passed small houses tucked alongside one-story businesses that had been there for generations. Traffic thinned out as he headed east until he was the only car on the two-lane road. The hour was late. Only a few days ago, he was out here at Evan's wedding.

He should turn around and go home. Barry Solomon had given him plenty to think about. His life could change for the better. No more putting up with the spoiled players on his team. No more dealing with his pain in the ass general manager who made demands that were impossible to meet. He had a chance to be a part of baseball history. If he could take the team all the way to the Grandstand Series next year, they might talk about him for decades—centuries. His name would be engraved in the Winners Section where fans passed at every game. He could see it now—.

He slammed on the brakes and jerked the steering wheel hard, but it was too late. Metal crunched against metal. The airbag deployed with a bang, and the guardrail folded like aluminum foil right outside his windshield, but at least he missed the deer. He hadn't seen it charge in front of him. Thoughts of a winning legacy had distracted him.

"Strike three. You're out, Sutherland." He didn't think he was hurt, but the car was undrivable.

The dashboard screen read eleven o'clock. This end of the highway was all commercial and at this time of night, all closed. Not a single car drove by, and why would one? The entrance to Serenity by the Sea was just across the street. If someone didn't live in that town, not likely they'd be coming in and the residents would be all tucked in for the night. Serenity wasn't known for its night life. On the upside, no one was around to ask questions or worse ask for a selfie. But the silence also meant no one was there to help.

He clamored out of the front seat. His back and his knee expressed their dissatisfaction with his collision. He debated on calling for a tow, but he wasn't in the mood for any questions. If the tow truck driver was a baseball fan, Shane would be less in the mood to hear opinions about his coaching choices or the overzealous pat on the back as the fan touted off Shane's stats when he was a player. He never liked being reminded of his career as a player.

He could call Evan for a ride. Paris and he had bought a home in Spring Lake, not far from Serenity. He could crash on their couch and in the morning deal with his car, but the idea of seeing Paris gave him a headache.

Maybe he would walk to the beach and sleep under the boardwalk like he did when he was a kid. No one was home looking for him, not a wife or any children. No one would miss him if he didn't return tonight.

"You're a real prize," he said to himself and the empty road.

His shoes grinded the dirt on the side of the road with their wood soles as he headed toward Serenity.

Warm, thick air put its hands around his neck and squeezed. Getting that call from Barry Solomon was like a dream come true, but keeping his temper in check on the field was an impossible task. And how the hell was he supposed to change his image as one of baseball's most hot-headed managers in a month? Even when he wasn't getting thrown out of games, the announcers, umpires, and sportscasters expected him to throw a fit.

If he had help, staying focused, then he might have a chance. But who would he ask for help? Evan was no help in that area.

He took a deep breath of salt and seaweed scented air. He didn't want to miss this town or the beach or the ocean. He wanted to forget it all. But he couldn't, not after seeing Maren over the wedding weekend.

The ocean called to him like it used to when he was a kid. Once he got out of Serenity and had made it in the big league, he thought that call was just the musing of a child's mind, but he soon realized it was more than that.

He should go back to the car and call for a tow. He could be home in a few hours, wash the night off him, have a drink, and enjoy the possibility of real success.

Instead, his feet took him down the cement sidewalks and tree-lined streets. Each step was burned in his memory. As he approached the ocean, the trees dwindled down, but the houses continued to nearly touch. Every road was parked up with cars because no one had a driveway.

If he went to the left, he'd soon be at the Topside Community. If he went right, he would pass the old tennis courts, the baseball field, the mansion that had been converted to an orphanage, and if he was lucky, The Blue Dot bar.

He turned the corner and stopped short. The Blue Dot was gone. The building was still in the same place, but it had a whole new look.

Instead of the old tired dark tavern, large windows faced the full parking lot. People mingled inside and sat at high-top tables. The marquee announced a band playing tonight, which might explain why so many people were still around at this hour. The building was painted like a modern beach house. The business's white sign read Sea Glass.

Sea Glass? Shane's heart sunk. He needed that dark, brooding tavern tonight. He could have slipped into a table in the corner where no one would notice him and nurse a beer.

This place was alive and vibrant. Its pulse pounded across the street and reached out for him. He backed away. He could walk into the next town. There had to be some dive bars still open there.

But he stopped again. If the Blue Dot was now Sea Glass, did that mean that Mr. Russo no longer owned it? Maren's father was always kind to him.

Shane had checked on her from time to time through the years. He never told anyone he did that. But he had found out, thanks to social media, she had moved across the state away from Serenity several years ago, married a nice man, and settled down. Exactly what he wanted for her and what he couldn't give her. Or what she hadn't wanted from him because of his temper.

Wasn't Maren the real reason he had driven over an hour after getting kicked out of the game? Serenity wasn't the only thing pulling him. His memories of Maren were just as strong and after being in her company he wanted to be in the last place he had seen her. He also kind of hoped she might be in this new place. She had moved back to Serenity. Evan had told him that after he dropped the bombshell Maren was his wedding planner.

Sea Glass would be safe. He could grab that beer and maybe no one would recognize him. If they weren't baseball fans, they usually didn't. His prime was a long time ago. Few fans wore his number on their backs at games and those people were becoming less and less each year.

Unless someone was a tried-and-true baseball fan, the managers weren't as well known as the young hot-shot players stationed around the diamond. The ones who hit homeruns and smiled for car commercials.

But he was infamous. The coach who repeatedly got thrown out of the game. The manager who fought with the umps. The manager who got fired more than once. He still didn't understand why Barry Solomon wanted him. Could his offer be as simple as straighten up and fly right or did Solomon think Shane was incapable of such a task? Was he being taunted for someone's amusement?

The restaurant's entrance faced a freshly tarred parking lot. Last time he was here, potholes crated the ground and risked an ankle. From his view by the door, the new back patio jutted out to the side. Tables filled with people eating, drinking, and roaring with laughter. This was definitely not the Blue Dot.

He pulled open the door and more raucous voices washed over him. Light oak tables were filled with people inside too. A bigger stage was carved out in the corner than the small one that used to be there.

The walls were bright and decorated with a nautical

theme. Pendant lights hung from the ceiling. He thought he might have walked into the middle of the afternoon on the beach. Whoever had designed this knew what they were doing. The place was great. Even if he preferred dark and gloomy tonight.

A television hung above the bar in the corner. The station was tuned to the local news. His fight with the Crew Chief flashed across the screen. Shane couldn't hear what the announcer was saying, but the screen switched to his last fight with an umpire when Shane grabbed homebase and walked off the field.

The room stretched out before him as if he were in a long tunnel and he had no way out. People watched him, but he couldn't focus on anyone in the room. Sounds became muffled. He was almost certain someone said his name and a few choice words after, but when he looked, he couldn't tell who had spoken.

He had to get out of there. But he couldn't move.

Chapter Three

Maren couldn't hide forever. She wanted to, but she had to leave Sea Glass's bathroom before her sister Bailey came looking for her. She hadn't been in the mood to socialize, but Bailey had dragged her to the restaurant, spouting words about one door closing, face her fears and other life coach rhetoric always on Bailey's lips.

The door swung open, and a woman entered, offering Maren a smile. Sea Glass was packed tonight with people enjoying their food and the band that had stepped off the stage to take a break, giving her the excuse to go to the bathroom. She struggled to believe she had been the one who designed the interior of this place. Where was that ambitious woman now?

She was glad for the noisy crowd that had drowned out her errant thoughts tonight about losing her business and her pride, but she was ready to go home to her quiet townhouse. The townhouse she would lose soon if she didn't come up with the money to pay the back taxes.

She tossed the paper towel in the garbage, tugged at the hem of her shirt, and on a deep breath headed back to the table to inform Bailey she was leaving.

A television played on silent above the bar. The sports station showed a replay of tonight's game and sure as the sun rose in the east, Shane Sutherland fought with one of the umpires, standing toe to toe with him and getting red in the face. She couldn't hear what they were saying, but she could guess. *Typical Shane.*

The umpire only took seconds to throw him out. Some of the Sea Glass's patrons hollered at the television.

Maren used to have a front row seat to Shane's behavior on the field for years and after they broke up, she still watched it happen when she caught one of his games. She could only think of one time off the field when his anger got the best of him—the time they broke up.

She had followed his career though, as he blossomed from a gangly young man with a strong arm into a power-house full-grown athlete that broke records still incapable of being conquered.

She watched every season as his haircut grew shorter and streaks of gray highlighted his soft brown strands. He had matured nicely. She wanted to hate him for that as her hips widened and her belly softened. The bags under her eyes could carry clothing for a week's vacation, but the lines around his ice blue eyes only added depth.

The last thing she needed was to be thinking about

Shane. She had real problems on her hands. With her gaze still pinned to Shane on the screen, she navigated around some tables and collided with a customer. The force threw her back. She grabbed onto the closest thing to keep from landing on her butt, and that thing was a muscular arm.

"Oh, I'm so sorry." Her brain took an extra second to catch up to what stood before her. He couldn't really be here. He was on the screen, yelling at the umpire. But that had been hours ago. That scene on the television was not live.

Shock registered on his face.

No kidding, buddy. She never expected to see Shane in person, let alone crash into him like a rogue wave.

His white dress shirt was open at the neck. Purple circles bruised the skin around his ice blue eyes as if he hadn't slept in weeks. His jaw was dusted with a salt and pepper beard he wore as well as that dress shirt.

"What are you doing here?" She put a hand to her hair. She didn't look her best. At least Bailey had made her change out of her pajamas before coming here.

"Maren. It's great to see you again." He scooped her into a hug before she knew what was happening. His strong arms wrapped around her and pulled her against him. His hard edges poked into her, stealing her breath. He smelled of oak and cedar, strong, rugged. Just like Shane.

She pushed out of his hold, needing to stand on solid ground. Her world was off-balance enough without Shane coming in here and acting as if they were

29

old friends. She had no intention of ever being his friend.

Other patrons noticed him too. They gawked. Some grabbed their phones. Their entire display of affection had caught attention. Of course, it would have. Anyone from Serenity by the Sea knew the baseball legend and anyone who knew baseball knew Shane.

"Why are you here, Shane?" She fought the unexpected tears trying to embarrass her. She and Shane were from another life. No reason existed for her crying. Except this week had been the worst she'd had in a long time and then there was a truth she would never utter out loud. Her heart had waited for him even when she had forbidden it to do so.

He glanced behind him, but didn't answer. Instead, he grabbed her by the hand and pulled her into the kitchen. Once the doors swung closed, he released her.

"Sorry about that hug thing. I can't be on television anymore tonight causing a scene. I wasn't expecting to see you and when I did, I lost my head."

"Clearly."

He smiled. His white teeth contrasted against his tanned skin. Most people believed his teeth were caps, but they were his. His one incisor was pointier than the other. She never forgot that.

"I couldn't give them anything else to record, Maren. You know how it is."

"Frankly, I don't know how it is to be videoed everywhere I go. But you can't just walk in off the street and drag me into the kitchen like you have a right to. You don't get to tell me what to do." The old argument snuck up on her. She had to push it away. Nothing that had happened then mattered now.

The bustling staff stopped and gaped at her. A silence fell over the kitchen. Shannon the dishwasher held the faucet nozzle midair above a pot. Brock who always wore a bandanna around his head while cooking paused the wrapping of meats. Dana the sous chef with her long braids held back and out of the way of food, stopped plating what would be the last dishes of the night. And Hank, the head chef, took a step forward with recognition on his face.

Maren held a hand up to stop him.

Hank nodded. "Everyone back to work."

"Yes, chef," the staff said in unison. They went back to work as if she and Shane were not in the kitchen with them. Kassidy's staff was loyal. They would not betray her sister or a member of her family with photos of Shane.

She led him into Kassidy's tiny office and closed the door. She didn't want the staff looking on even if they would never take out their phones and document them. "What are you doing in Serenity? Didn't you have a game earlier tonight?"

"My car is out on Route 33." He leaned against the corner of the desk.

"I'm not following. You left your car on the highway. Why? And why are you here?" She had asked that already but needed to ask it again to make some sense of what was happening. Or better yet, *who* was happening.

The two of them standing inches apart with the weight of his hug still tingling against her skin could not be real.

"I swerved to miss a deer and hit the guardrail. That's it." He shrugged and shook his head as if that explanation was sufficient.

"You still haven't explained what you're doing in Sea Glass." Why did she even care? His presence in town had nothing to do with her, but it still threw her. He had no right to show up in the middle of her personal crisis and turn her head upside down. If she were this disoriented in the ocean, she would drown.

She didn't bother to wait for his answer. "You know what? Never mind. What you're doing in town or in the restaurant is none of my business."

"My car isn't in any shape to drive. I didn't want to call for a tow. So, I walked. That's really the whole story. I'm not hurt. I don't need to go to the hospital, not that you bothered to ask. I will need to get my car off the side of the road soon before someone realizes that it's mine."

"You want me to ask if you're all right? I don't even know if you were in a car accident. You could have made the whole story up." He had never lied to her. Maybe if she hadn't been blind-sided by his appearance, she might've asked if he was hurt.

She hadn't seen Shane in person in years—close to twenty if she tried to do the math—before the wedding weekend. Seeing him walk through Sea Glass's doors right after he was on the television was a shock to the system.

"Why would I lie to you?"

"Why does anyone do what they do?"

He looked away before returning his gaze to hers. "I'm telling you the truth. I don't know if you were watching the game, but the ump threw me out."

"Again."

"Yes, again. I'm not proud of myself, if that makes you feel any better." He shifted from one foot to the other.

"It does not." She wasn't trying to make him suffer. Well, maybe a little, but she had loved this man once. She had never wanted anything bad to happen to him.

His lips twitched in a smile, but it didn't take hold. "I left the stadium and started driving. I needed to clear my head. Somehow, I ended up taking Serenity's exit. When I crashed, walking toward the beach seemed like a good idea. I was looking for The Blue Dot."

"Yeah... that's gone. Kassidy and Bailey own Sea Glass now."

"Where's your dad?"

"He passed." She wasn't about to go into the whole story about their father's passing or how she sold her part of The Dot now, or ever, with Shanc. She didn't want to talk to him at all, but she couldn't make herself leave the office either.

"Oh. I'm sorry. I didn't know."

"Thanks. I still don't understand why you didn't go to Evan's if you were in a car accident." She should shut up and walk back into the kitchen, but her mouth had a mind of its own.

"I have no interest in seeing my brother or his wife

tonight, and I wouldn't have come inside Sea Glass if I'd known you were here."

"That's good to know because if I knew you were coming, I would have left." The words came out harsher than she had meant. He was just a memory to her. Why did her heart think he was so much more?

"So, you're still mad at me after all this time."

"I have nothing to be mad about. The past is the past." Now that she wasn't sitting on the beach, drinking champagne and wallowing in her demise, being near him unnerved her. Too many emotions collided. She wanted to ask him how he was doing, and she wanted to run as far and as fast as she could. She wasn't about to tell him she still had his jersey in the back of her closet.

"How's business since the wedding?" His question jarred her from her thoughts.

"What?"

"How's your event planning business since Paris went all over social media blasting you? Is business good?"

"I don't see what that has to do with anything." She wouldn't dignify his sarcastic comment with an answer. He must know the damage Paris had caused.

She never should have read the comments under Paris's post. People who had never met Maren had said vile things about her. Some said she had a bad work ethic while others wrote that she should be in a mental hospital or that her nose was too big and her eyes too far apart. They called her dumb and untalented. Each one stung even though she knew they shouldn't bother her.

"I'm sorry. That was out of line. What Paris did was cruel. This isn't an excuse, but I'm wiped out." He tilted his head back and let out a long breath.

"Thank you for saying that."

That hint of smile tugged at his lips again. "I'll get out of your hair. It's clear you don't want me here. I shouldn't have come. Like I said, if I had known..."

She held his gaze. His heavy lids hung over bloodshot eyes. The lines between his furrowed brows deepened. He might be the manager who was thrown out of more games than others, but he never liked that reputation. He hadn't enjoyed being the player known for his hot head either because the label had made him too much like his father. He had shared that truth with her in the dark under the covers.

She opened the office door. The staff scurried as if they were rats caught by a bright light. "Hank, could you make Shane a burger and some fries, if it isn't too much trouble. Pack it to-go please."

"Coming right up, Boss."

She was no one's boss.

"Thank you. I haven't eaten all day."

She suspected that was the case but left her knowledge to herself. He didn't need to be aware of the things she remembered about him. "I'll drive you back to your car unless there's somewhere else you'd like to go that's not too far."

The hour was late and she was tired too. She didn't want to drive Shane anywhere, but she couldn't allow him to walk back out to the highway for his vehicle. The road wasn't safe to walk on at any hour. She would drop him and go home, climb into bed, and pretend this night never happened. She'd like to pretend the past week hadn't happened.

"I can take care of my car with a phone call." He pulled out his phone and held it up. "I'd rather crash and get some sleep."

"Fine. There's a hotel not far from here."

"No hotels. I don't want anyone to know I'm in town."

"Then where would you like me to take you? I think you're running out of options and Kassidy won't let you sleep here."

"You're forgetting one place."

"It's late, Shane. I'm not up for guessing games."

"Your place."

Chapter Four

He didn't know he was going to suggest Maren's house until he said it and by the horrified look on her face, he thought he might've struck out with that idea. He hadn't proposed they sleep together or anything. He would take the couch. Hell, he'd take the floor. He just didn't want to drive all the way home to New York in a car service or cab.

He needed to get his head together. Seeing Maren tonight had given him an idea, and he would need some time to convince her to even listen to him because he was certain the first word out of her mouth would be a resounding no.

"Well, Maren, how about it? Let me crash on your couch tonight."

Hank stepped into the office with a white to-go container. His head spun from the aroma of grilled beef permeating the air.

Hank's wide smile and expectant expression could mean he was a baseball fan. Shane had met many people who had looked at him as if his next words held the key to the meaning of life. He was honored, but he wasn't that grand.

He would put on his best game face, but Hank's timing sucked. Maren hadn't answered him and if she had too much time to think about what he had suggested, she would tell him to take a hike. He'd be literally walking back to his car.

"Here you go, Shane. I added some fries too."

"Thanks, man. What do I owe you?" He looked between Hank and Maren.

"It's on the house," Hank said first. "I'm a huge fan. I've been following your entire career, being you're a local boy and all. I saw you in Game 4 of the Grandstand Series in 2000. Great game."

"That was some time ago. My knees worked a lot better back then. Thanks for the support. I appreciate it." He meant those words more tonight. Even with the job offer floating in the air around him, hot but untouchable, he was still fired for losing games. If he did in fact, step onto the Warriors' field, he had better be ready for some of the most difficult fans in baseball.

"If you need anything else, let me know. We're closing up the kitchen, but I can always stay later."

"That's not necessary," Maren said. "Thank you for helping out. Shane and I will be leaving."

Maren brushed past Hank and through the kitchen doors. He would be wise to follow her and did just that.

Maren grabbed her purse from the table where her younger sister Bailey still sat. He had kind of hoped everyone would be gone by now, but there were a few customers at the bar while the band packed up their gear.

"Hello, Shane." Bailey put down her phone and glared at him. He had to give it to the Russo women; they weren't always close but they never allowed a man to hurt one or the other. He had been guilty of hurting Maren. It didn't appear Bailey would be letting that one pass.

"Bailey. It's nice to see you."

"Yeah, okay." She pushed out of her chair and turned to Maren. "If he's bothering you, just say the word. But if you're good, I'm going to spend the night at Kassidy's."

"I'm good. Thanks."

"I'll buy all the fixings for s'mores tomorrow. Will you come over?"

"Will you still be staying with Kassidy?"

"For a few weeks. At least until the baby comes." Bailey hugged Maren then set her glare on him. "Shane."

"Good night, Bailey." He waited until Bailey was through the doors before turning to Maren. "Well, can I crash just for one night? I'll be gone tomorrow. I promise."

She gnawed on her bottom lip and her eyes narrowed. He needed to stay quiet while she worked out her decision. She had every right to throw him to the curb, but Maren used to have a soft spot for the underdog and tonight that was him.

"I must be out of my mind to agree with this idea. There are a thousand other places you could stay."

"Please, Maren. Just for tonight. It's late. We're both tired. You'd be doing me a favor I didn't deserve. I realize that. I just need a break from reality. Tomorrow will be like you had never seen me." He was hoping to stick around a little longer.

"I'm too exhausted to argue with you. Just one night. You need to be gone before lunchtime. We're not starting up a new friendship because we shared five minutes on the beach last weekend while I was drowning in champagne."

"I wouldn't think of it." He might think about it a little, but he wouldn't press his luck. She had agreed to put him up for the night. He had one the first round. That would have to do.

"Good. My car's outside."

"I will follow you anywhere."

She shot him a death glare.

"Okay. That was too much."

He would follow her everywhere if she would allow it. After tonight, he needed her to.

Maren *was* out of her mind. How did she ever agree to allow Shane to sleep on her couch? Her life was already in shambles. Did she really need to risk another explosion? After all, only her heart was at stake now—nothing important.

She put her key in the front door of her humble home

and had to swallow the insecurities of showing Shane her house. He probably lived in a sprawling mansion with eighteen bathrooms and ten garages. She lived in a two-bedroom, two and a half-bath house that was once part of a larger Victorian home that had been divided into a couple of townhouses. She had to share the front porch with the other tenant if she wanted to sit outside in the front. The side entrance led straight into her foyer and she was glad for the small extra piece of privacy.

"It's not much." She dropped her keys on the table and flipped on a light by the door. She couldn't remember when she had vacuumed last. A couple of dust tumbleweeds blew off the staircase runner from the breeze caused by the door as if to prove her point.

"It's really nice." Shane poked his head into the living room. "That fireplace looks original."

"It is." She went into the large dining area. Her table could seat ten without a problem and she used one end as her office. She gathered her papers into piles. "Sorry about the mess. I wasn't expecting anyone. If you want to eat your food, you can sit on the other end of the table."

"Thanks. Your place isn't messy, by the way. You should see my place and I'm hardly there half the year." Shane took a seat at the end of the table. "Do you happen to have any beer?"

"Afraid not. I might have a diet soda."

"I'm good then. Thanks."

She passed into the open kitchen that gave her access to a small deck and backyard. She wasn't as close to the beach as Kassidy's house was. Kassidy and Grant had decided to expand her tiny bungalow and stay there, Since she had such a prime location.

She grabbed a bottled water for Shane. "Here. I'll bring down a blanket and some pillows. There's a half-bath under the staircase in the foyer. That door there leads to the basement."

He glanced in the direction she pointed. "I really do appreciate this. You're saving me."

"I hardly think you need saving. You've got a pretty good life." A life that she had envied in so many ways. Even while she was married, she always worried about money. Dave never made enough and what little jobs she had held only brought in chump change. They had saved every cent for Peyton's college fund and their daughter still needed a loan and her work study job to cover the rest of the tuition. After the divorce, she didn't have much left over. Thankfully, Dave had to pay her alimony, or she'd really be screwed right now.

"Would you sit with me for a minute? I'll share my fries." He held one out and looked up at her through his thick eyelashes. She would not fall for that puppy dog look.

"What's the matter? You're not used to eating unless you have a team of men surrounding you?"

"Actually, it's nice to not to have a bunch of young guys pushing and shoving each other around the table, laughing at things I don't understand anymore. The older I get, the more I just want to be by myself. Weird, right?" He took a huge bite of his burger. Meat juice ran down his chin. He chuckled around a mouthful of food and wiped his face with a napkin.

"I like being by myself."

"Would you sit please? You're making me nervous while you stand over me glowering."

"I'm not glowering." She might be, but she refused to admit it out loud and give him the satisfaction of being right, but as a concession, she pulled out a chair and sat.

"Thank you. There's something I'd like to talk to you about."

"Are you sure it can't wait until morning?" Sitting there watching him eat that whole burger risked those pesky emotions seeping out like spiders crawling through the dark.

"Maren, it is morning. This won't take long. I promise. Then you can get your beauty rest. Not that you need it."

"Please. Spare me." She had aged ten years in the past week and every line on her face confirmed it. Once he said what he needed to, she could sleep. In the morning, she would worry about what to do with him if he was still in her house.

"Is being in the same room with me so bad?"

"You have to admit it's strange, the two of us sitting here as if nothing happened between us, and we've been friends for years." If anyone had told her even six months ago that Shane would be in her dining room she would have laughed until her side split.

"I wish we were friends."

She wasn't sure if that was a true statement. Being

friends hadn't been possible for her. She didn't know how anyone stayed friends with someone they slept with—especially the first person they slept with.

"What is it that you want to talk to me about that can't wait?"

"I have a business proposition for you." He shoved a fry in his mouth.

"I don't think so." This whole night was something out of a freak show. She pinched herself to make sure she was awake and not dreaming Shane at her table talking about a business proposition.

"Hear me out a sec, okay?"

"I really don't understand what's happening here."

"Look, I don't either. I saw you and I had an idea that I think we both could benefit by, but if you don't want to hear it, I'll stop, but I think that might be a mistake."

He was always so confident in his decisions. She had chalked it up to a lifetime of people telling him how good he was at baseball. She shouldn't be surprised that he decided at the last second that he had an idea that might include her. If he thought he was onto something, he believed he was right.

"Okay, let's hear it." Sure, she could go upstairs and pull the covers over her head, but she was curious about what he had to say. Her curiosity would probably cost her.

He told her about his conversation with Barry Solomon the owner of the Warriors. He didn't have to tell her what a big deal that call was for him. He had talked about playing for the Warriors since he was fifteen.

"That's fantastic news, but what does his job offer have to do with me?"

"I need you to help me clean up my image."

She burst out with a laugh. She hadn't expected him to drop such an absurd idea on her head. "Me? How am I supposed to do that?"

"Pretend to be my fiancé for a few months."

She hopped out of the chair, as if something bit her bottom and maybe it just had. "Are you crazy? I can't pretend to be your fiancé."

He pushed out of the chair too. "Let people see me on the town with you. If I don't get into anymore arguments, everyone will say the love of a good woman changed me and Solomon will be happy. Once my contract is signed, and my agent will make it airtight so the Warriors can't fire me without a huge payout, you and I can break up. Please, Maren. I need this."

"No one would believe us. We haven't seen each other in years." Logic had to prevail here. She could never pretend to be in a relationship with Shane, not after the way their real relationship had ended.

"We could say we were secretly dating during the wedding planning. That's believable, and since we have a past, the story holds that we would rush into an engagement." He closed the distance between them.

She needed space to get her mind straight and backed into the breakfast bar that separated the kitchen from the dining room.

Shane's eyes went wide, but he raised his hands and took a step back. "I wasn't trying to..."

"Shane, I didn't think you were going to, but I don't know you anymore." She ran her hand through her hair because she didn't know what else to do. They had been so young back then. They had both made mistakes, but she didn't know how to tell him that now.

"Will you pretend for me?" he said, dragging the conversation back onto a safer lane.

"Evan and Paris won't believe it." She moved into the kitchen.

"It doesn't matter what they believe. If we stick to the story, everyone will get on board."

"If Paris suspects we're lying, not that I'm agreeing to this insanity, she will stop at nothing to ruin us both. Sorry. Maybe I shouldn't have said that about your sister-in-law. You might think the world of her."

Shane arched both brows. "Paris is like a lit match hovering over a puddle of gasoline in a fireworks warehouse."

"So, you do think that much of her?"

"She's a loose cannon. But we can handle her."

At least Shane saw Paris for who she really was, and Maren was grateful for that little nugget of information. She had reeled hard since Paris posted the video, blaming her for ruining the wedding. To have someone say what she had thought all along gave her some hope.

"Will you do it? Will you help me keep this opportunity?"

"Why me, Shane? You could make this arrangement with a hundred different women." He could have any woman he wanted and had married two models. She had tried to ignore the click bait articles and entertainment pages, but every once in a while, her gaze would see a hint and she had to know what he was up to and with whom.

He came into the kitchen and stood inches from her. She couldn't look away from those bright eyes.

"It has to be you, because no other woman has ever understood me the way you did, not my ex-wives, not anyone I dated. Most importantly, when we were together was the only time in my baseball career that I wasn't fighting with the umps."

That much was true. He had said back then he didn't want to argue on the field to make her proud of him. She had been proud of him no matter what he did on the field. Dating Shane had been a badge of honor until he broke her heart.

"It's my dream, Maren. You remember that don't you?" He reached for her hand, but she pulled away. If the warmth of his skin invaded hers, she would not be able to tell him no.

"That's not fair. I do remember how much you wanted to play for the Warriors, but you can't waltz into my life out of the blue and ask for something so nuts you might as well be asking me to hang the moon for you."

"I know it's crazy. I didn't think it through or plan it, but it will work, and I'll make it worth your while."

"Really, how are you going to do that?" Why was she even asking this question? She would not agree to pretend to be Shane's fiancé. Her sisters would think she was bonkers, and they would be right. Bailey would never let her hear the end of it and when she and Shane did their fake breakup, her sisters would say they told her so. Shane's ask was impossible for her. Pity or guilt might be edging her to say yes, but she couldn't allow her emotions to rule the show. He had to take care of his image himself.

"I can get your business up and running again. You can start planning our wedding and we can plaster that all over social media. I can also suggest to people I know that you're the planner they want."

"No one is going to listen to you after Paris's destruction of my reputation." At least he hadn't offered something more enticing like buying her a wedding venue, and she would not take money for this transaction. Being paid for her time would be no different than cash left on the bedside table in the morning.

"I've got two players right now engaged and both of them have their fiancés nagging at them to plan something. My guys don't pay any attention to Paris. Some of them are still small-town and dating their sweethearts from back home. Let me help you while you're helping me. It's a win-win."

"I'm sorry. I can't do it. You'll have to find someone else to keep you on the straight and narrow. I'm going to bed. Sleep well." She brushed past him, and he let her go.

As she climbed the steps, she fought the urge to run downstairs and ask him more questions about how all of this would work. Because she couldn't imagine how it would and her not end up with the short end of things.

But a chance to rebuild her business... No. She would

rebuild herself. She didn't need him. She still had some options.

She stood at the top of the dark staircase. Shane moved around below her. How easy it would be to give in, but she would live to regret pretending with him. Just like she regretted the day she feared him.

Chapter Five

Maren put on a robe and padded down the stairs. She didn't have one those fancy silk ones women sometimes wore. Her robe was a Christmas gift from Dave ten or more years ago. The terry material had faded from too many washes and stained with hair dye but was still warm and cozy. If she had known she was having a sleep over party with Shane Sutherland, she would have run out and bought something a little sexier because even though she didn't want him in her bed, she wanted him to miss her a little.

Darkness still cloaked the house in shadows. She used the glow from her cell phone home screen to guide her way. Turning on lights or tripping over shoes at the bottom of the steps might wake Shane and she needed more time to herself. Maybe she should have showered and done her makeup before coming downstairs. *Nah.* She didn't have to impress him or anyone for that matter.

Without bothering to look in the living room, she

hurried through the foyer and into the kitchen. She'd let him sleep until a reasonable hour and then offer him a ride to his car, assuming it was still on the side of the road and he hadn't taken care of it after she went to bed.

As soon as he was back on the road, she could go on with her life. She dumped a coffee pod into the machine and pressed the start button. Kassidy always grimaced when Maren made coffee from a one-use coffee maker. Kassidy was all about the fancy press. Maren just wanted it hot and strong—like the man sleeping in the other room.

She flipped on the small light above the sink. The glow reflected off the jar of sea glass kept on her windowsill. The common colors of weathered and worn glass rarely drew her attention anymore. She moved the jar to the center of the sill. Sea glass was beautiful because it went hundreds of years sometimes to resurface as a better version of the broken glass that had fallen into the sea. She would call Kassidy later and see if she wanted to go hunt for some. Maybe new pieces would inspire Maren to find a new path.

With her cup of coffee warming her hand, she went out onto the back deck. End of summer mornings whispered cool breezes as the days shortened, and she was glad for the reprieve from the summer's suffocating humidity.

The holidays would be fast upon them. Autumn always raced by at dangerous speeds. Already, Labor Day had fallen behind, leaving memories of summer bashes on the side of the road, lost and soon forgotten. She would blink and October would bump into November, giving her whiplash.

How would she pay for gifts for Peyton and her sisters? She might have to make gifts this year from the left-over sea glass stash they had found in their father's attic. Everyone would understand. Only she wouldn't. She was supposed to plan three big weddings with holiday themes that would have helped grow her business and put money in her bank account.

"Good morning." Shane's deep voice, still pocked with sleep, startled her.

She spun around to find him disheveled and unfairly adorable. His hair was cropped close to his head, so he didn't have that bedhead look. But the hair growth above his normally clean-lined beard only added to his appeal. Well, she also always liked the way his ears stuck out a little. The man had few physical flaws, if any.

"Good morning." She tucked a hair behind her ear as if that would help her drop ten years and ten pounds. "Would you like some coffee?"

"No, thanks. I called for a ride. My car was towed to Ray's in town. He's going to fix it up, but it will take a week or so. I wanted to say thank you for letting me crash. I needed it."

"Sure." She didn't have much else to say. He was leaving, and she wanted him to go.

"I will assume you didn't give my offer anymore consideration." He scratched the back of his head.

"I can't pretend to be engaged to you."

"Well, if you change your mind call me."

"I don't have your number." She wanted to slap a hand over her mouth. She would never call him and now had implied she might.

He held out his hand. Seconds passed before she realized he wanted her phone. She handed it over with only some resistance, and he saved his contact info for her. He sent himself a text so he would have her number too.

"Now you do. Don't hesitate to use it. For anything."

She was careful not to touch him when she grabbed the phone and shoved it in her robe. Before she could pull her hand out of the pocket, it rang.

"I'll let you get that." He leaned toward her. Panic twisted her feet together and she stumbled, spilling her coffee in a splash on the porch.

"Oh, damn." She plopped the cup on the table and wiped her hand on the robe. Her phone continued to ring. She debated on whether to answer it but retrieved it from her pocket anyway.

"Let me get something to clean that up." Shane disappeared into the house before she could stop him.

A glance at the phone told her she needed to answer the call. "Hey, Peyton." She would never miss a call from her daughter if she could help it.

"Hi, Mom. I have a problem."

Maren stifled a sigh. "What's going on?" *Where was Shane?* And did she want him here while she was on the phone with Peyton?

"I was denied the work study job."

"How can that be?" She stepped over the coffee puddle and took the steps to the yard.

53

"I don't know. I showed up at work and they told me I wasn't on the list and after I ran around campus for two hours, I don't have a job. Someone messed up paperwork or something and all the jobs are filled for the year. The year, Mom. What am I going to do? That job is supposed to go toward tuition. Will I have to come home?"

"Let's not get ahead of ourselves. Did you go to the head of your department?"

"I went to everyone. Everyone says the same thing. There is no job for me. I'm screwed, aren't I?"

"We'll figure it out. Your next payment isn't due for a few weeks. Maybe Dad can spot the money until the job comes through."

"Dad says he doesn't have any extra money for school."

Leave it to Dave to deny his daughter. He had a good paycheck with a stable company unlike her who had none of those things. She couldn't help Peyton without taking out a loan and who would give a defunct business owner a loan?

"I'll figure something out. We'll keep you in school." She had no idea how they would do that. Maybe Peyton could live at home and commute, but Maren didn't mention that just yet.

"Thanks, Mom. I have to run to class now. Can you keep me posted? I'm freaking out right now."

So was Maren. First her business, now her daughter's job. What could be lurking behind the next corner? "Don't panic. There's a solution somewhere."

"I'm already a panic. See you." Peyton disconnected the call.

Maren hung her head. She would have to argue with Dave about putting up more money until Maren could get back on her feet.

"Is everything all right?" Shane stood on her back porch with a wad of paper towels in his hand.

"No. Yes. I don't know. I'll figure it out." She always did. This time wouldn't be any different. She had to rely on herself for everything.

"Can I help?"

"I'm not sure how you can do that." Or that she would want him to help.

"Why don't you tell me what happened." He squatted down and wiped up the mess on the deck. He didn't flinch or complain. He took care of it. A warmth flickered inside her.

"My daughter is at our alma mater. This is her first semester. Her father and I had all the money worked out. Part of that equation was a work study job that helped with that ridiculously expensive tuition. The school says they don't have a job for her any longer. I can't help her." Maren's voice hitched and she wanted to die a thousand deaths.

He jogged down the steps, the paper towels discarded on the table along with her mug. "Hey, it will be okay."

"Really? You know that how? I can't take out a loan to help her. Her father says he can't help. The campus claims there are no more jobs even though she had one.

She already borrowed enough money this year. I'm going to have to tell her to come home and go to the community college."

Shane placed a warm hand on her shoulder. She wanted to lean against him if only for a second to get her bearings and soak up his strength. But she couldn't rely on Shane. Her money troubles were her own.

"You don't have to do any of those things," he said.

She held his bright gaze. "I'm not following."

"I can get her a job in the athletics department. No problem."

"How can you do that?" She shouldn't be surprised that he had contacts, but she didn't live in a world where everything always worked out. She was the girl whose mother left her family for one that didn't involve children. Her marriage had ended. She never had a career worth speaking about.

"I've donated a ton of money to the department for baseball equipment, uniforms, stuff like that. I also happen to know the baseball coach well." His confident smile pressed dimples into his cheeks.

"Why would you help us that way?"

"So, you'll pretend to be engaged to me."

She moved away from him. "Oh, that's unfair."

"How is that unfair? We're helping each other out." He retreated to the steps, giving her more space.

"You're using my daughter to get me to do this thing for you."

"I'm not using your daughter, and I'm not offering

you any charity so you can put your pride back in its box. This is a business arrangement, a barter if you will. You have something I want, and I have two things that can help you."

The job for Peyton and Maren's business.

A horn beeped from the street, interrupting them. That honk must be his ride. He would get in that car, and she would never see him again, not in person, anyway. But she could not take him up on this crazy idea even if it did mean giving Peyton a job so she could stay at school. Maren would find another way. Maybe she could skim off some of what Dave paid her in alimony.

"Take care, Shane. It was nice to see you."

"Think about my offer. And Maren?"

"Yes?"

"You still look beautiful in the morning." He went around the front of the house without waiting for a reply.

She dropped down on the step. "You had a chance to help him and him you." she said to the empty yard. But she would need to be more desperate to accept his offer.

Her phone buzzed in her hand, and her heart sunk. The name on the screen was Dave's. What could he want at this hour? She was tempted to let it go to voicemail, but he could be calling about Peyton's new situation.

"Hello, Dave."

"Hi, Maren. Do you have a minute? I need to talk to you."

"Is it about Peyton?"

"What? Oh, the job thing. I spoke to her about it, but

I can't help right now. She'll have to take out additional loans."

Maren didn't want Peyton to suffocate under college debt. She wanted Peyton to start her grownup life with a clean slate. "It's our responsibility to help her."

"We've taken care of our responsibilities. Paying for college is not a parental requirement. I don't want to fight about this, but I did call to talk to you about money."

"We have to help Peyton."

"Peyton can take a loan, live at home and commute or go to community. Or, since you're the big-time wedding planner, you pay the difference." His voice strained each word until they twisted and broke apart.

She had no idea if Dave knew what had happened to her business, but she wasn't going to be the one to tell him. He would offer no support. He might even gloat.

"I'm not in the red yet. I expected to be by the year's end." Which had been a truth before Paris came into her life.

"Well, then Peyton will have to figure it out. Look, I really need to talk to you about your alimony."

"You have the court order. The alimony is all laid out." Her lawyer had worked a good settlement. Dave had to pay a decent amount of alimony to her. She had earned it married to him all those years and putting a career on hold to raise their only daughter. She wouldn't trade her time with Peyton for anything in the world, but if she had known her marriage was doomed when Peyton was born, she might have gone back to work sooner.

"Here's the thing. I have a new order from the judge."

"Excuse me?" She pushed off the step to stand. She must have misheard him.

"I lost my job six months ago. I've wiped out my savings to pay for Peyton's school and your alimony. I can't find a job in this economy. And let's face it, no one wants to hire a guy my age. I'm too expensive."

"You lost your job? Why? Did you do something?" Dave had never been out of work the entire time she knew him. He wouldn't think of leaving a job without having another one lined up. If the company was laying people off, he would've figured that out and made a backup plan.

"Downsizing. Look, I didn't see it coming. My department was supposed to be safe. Anyway, my lawyer went before a judge to have the alimony stopped. I wanted you to hear it from me before the papers are delivered to you today."

"Wait a second. Today? Don't I get a chance to have a say in this? Shouldn't we have discussed it?" She paced the yard. Dave had a habit of waiting until the very last possible second to tell her anything difficult. He might want to be prepared, but he never allowed her the same courtesy.

"We aren't together anymore. I don't have to discuss anything with you, but as a courtesy because of our years together, I didn't want you to be surprised by the papers when they arrived. I just can't keep paying you and afford to live too. I'm going to have to take a job at a warehouse store."

"Poor you." If she didn't know better, he might be

enjoying this little tidbit of information he could hold over her head.

"I have no choice, Maren." His voice tightened again. She could imagine the red blotches forming on his neck right about now.

"How am I supposed to live without that alimony? I earned it." She continued to pace the small yard, fueled by her frustration and disappointment. When her marriage had officially fallen apart, she had questioned every decision she had ever made. If she had left sooner, been braver, demanded to be treated like an equal and not the maid, anything, maybe she wouldn't be a divorcee living alone and without a career.

"You may have earned access to my money, but you can't get blood from a stone. I'm sorry about this. Once I have employment that pays me close to what I was making, I'll reinstate the alimony. I promise."

"Save your promises, Dave. You promised to change the backsplash twenty years ago. It never happened."

"This is not the same thing. I won't leave you high and dry. I just need to find a job."

"Your promises don't hold a lot of water where I'm concerned. I'm going to try and fight this."

"You can't. It's a loophole in the divorce laws. I had to take advantage of it. I can't end up homeless when you live at the shore in that Victorian townhouse enjoying the ocean in your backyard while you plan your silly parties all day long. If you had a real job, one with health benefits and a pension, you wouldn't need my damn money. And it is my damn money."

He hung up.

She stared at her phone, wanting to throw it as hard as possible so it would crash into something and shatter into a million pieces, giving her an ounce of relief. With all the restraint of holding back a speeding locomotive, she gripped it until her knuckles turned white.

What was she going to do without Dave's alimony? She had spent most of her own money starting her business and killed herself the past year and a half trying to build it. Now Peyton... Maren would call her lawyer once the offices were open and figure out a plan. Dave couldn't do this, could he?

Nine o'clock wouldn't come fast enough and she went inside to search the internet on her computer. Sure enough, there was a loophole in the law that allowed someone to request alimony be stopped when they had been out of work long enough.

Pain burned the back of her eyes as if someone screwed bolts into them. The townhouse was her only asset, but she owed six months of back taxes. Even if she sold it tomorrow, she'd have to pay off the mortgage and that wouldn't leave her enough to clear her tax bill. If she didn't have that bill cleaned up by the end of the year, the town would put a lean on her house.

She might have to seriously consider asking Kassidy and Grant for money. They had plenty. Well, Grant had plenty. The money would be a loan, and she would pay it back with interest. If they would even do it. Her pride would be scraped dry if she had to ask her sister for help, but that might be her only option. Shane had accused her of being prideful... But no, she could not, would not call him.

She pushed away from the dining room table and went upstairs to change out of her robe and keep herself from calling Shane.

She would need a job like yesterday to pay her bills and help Peyton, but where? And like Dave, who would hire her? She didn't have transferrable skills. If she hadn't sold her portion of Sea Glass to Kassidy, she would have that equity, and she needed it now.

Most of the stores on Main Street didn't stay open in the off-season. They didn't have enough business, and the ones that did, cut back on hours. Beach life wasn't always easy.

She dropped down on the edge of the bed and dumped her head between her knees. She took slow breaths. Having a full-blown panic attack or worse, heart attack, would be a bad idea about now. No one was around to take her to the hospital, not that she could afford a hospital stay.

She could call Shane, but she pushed the idea away. Except it rolled right back in like the tide.

She had a way out. The option might be riddled with risk and hurt and who knew what else, but she would be able to keep her home, keep her dignity as long as no one found out the truth, keep her daughter in school, and her business would get the revival it not only needed, but deserved. And maybe, just maybe, it would also be a bit of a *stick it* to Paris.

Maren shoved her legs into a pair of jeans then headed back downstairs. If she took Shane up on his wacky idea, she had a chance to come out on the other side of this a little better than going in and she had to admit—she hadn't thought about it until now—how rewarding it would be to see Paris's face when Maren showed up at the Thanksgiving table in two months. Better yet, she would insist they double date with Evan and Paris immediately. Why wait to enjoy some of the fruits of her labor?

She stopped at the bottom of the steps. But could she lie to everyone? She'd have to lie to Peyton too and that would put her mothering skills into question. Hadn't she preached about honesty and integrity? Her sisters would be much harder to convince, and Maren questioned her acting chops.

She grabbed her phone off the table. If she leapt, there would be no going back. She'd be in up to her ears and the only way out would be through. But the time together with Shane would be temporary and he was easy on the eyes. His anger was the only problem, well, and her pride being destroyed again.

Her fingers tapped at the screen, summoning the call that would either make her or break her. The call rang on the other end. She could still walk away—.

"Hello, Maren." His deep voice washed over the rough edges of her nerves. She could listen to him speak all day and had often believed he would've had a great career in radio.

63

"I'll do it." She didn't see the point in starting with pleasantries. Theirs was a business arrangement, as Shane had said.

"What changed your mind?"

"I just found out that my alimony is stopping. I don't have any money saved. My business is gone, and I have bills to pay."

"What kind of bills?"

She swallowed the pride filled knot in her throat and almost choked on it. "I'm behind six months in my property taxes."

He let out a long whistle. "In Serenity? That has to hurt. You want me to pay your tax bill." He didn't ask.

"I want you to loan me the money. I'll pay you back. And you have to get the job for Peyton." She paced the long length of the dining room table. The sky outside the window turned a steal gray as if it knew she was about to enter a storm she could not return from. "I'll build back my own business. I don't need you for that."

She would work her backside off doing any party, any odd job. She'd even wait tables again if she had to. If it meant, not owing Shane for anything.

"I'll loan you the money, and I'll make the call to the athletic department as soon as we hang up. Peyton will have a job by the end of the day." The smile in his voice came across the line loud and clear.

"Thank you." She only agreed to this because she was desperate. If Dave hadn't dropped that bomb on her, she would not be having this conversation with the one person she swore she'd never get involved with again.

"Do you require anything else of our arrangement?" The playfulness in his voice grated against her skin. He had all the power, and he probably knew it.

"I have a few requests."

"Anything. Name it."

"No kissing." She squeezed her eyes shut, waiting for his response.

"Not even on the cheek?"

He was relentless and they did have to make it look like they were together.

"Okay, the cheek, but only public displays of affection that are appropriate for all audiences. Deal?"

"Can that rule be amended at any time?" His voice dropped an octave, and she was suddenly too hot in her sweater and jeans.

"I won't sleep with you, if that's what you're getting at. This is a business arrangement, like you said." She could allow herself five minutes of a fantasy here and there, but that would be it. Anything else would be dangerous and she needed to focus on her business. She'd be busy planning weddings and parties—her fake wedding too.

"Okay, no private touching, but I can't say I'm not disappointed."

"You can handle it. You've struck out before."

"Ouch."

"I'm sure you'll have women lining up around the corner for you once they know you're off the market and getting married for the third time."

"You know I was married and divorced?"

"Everyone in Serenity knows you were married and divorced." The people of Serenity never missed an opportunity to chew on a little Shane Sutherland gossip.

"Who's running the gossip mill these days? We'll want to make sure that person sees us together."

"You didn't hear this from me, but Natalie Lowe who owns the yarn store has her finger on the gossip button. She will tell the entire county we're an item when she finds out."

"That old buzzard? I didn't think she still had any teeth to speak with."

She chuckled despite herself. She hated that he could be funny. "Now what? What's our next step?"

"Are you free for dinner tonight?"

"Um... No. I have plans." She had no such plans, but didn't want to have dinner alone with him so soon.

"Can you cancel them?"

"Why would I want to do that?"

"So we can start telling people about us. I'd rather be the one directing the story over old Natalie Lowe. Besides, the sooner my image changes the sooner you can be done with me."

"Speaking of that, how long do you think we'll have to pretend for?" She needed to brace herself for what was to come.

"A few months."

"I plan on paying you back before then." Maybe she had a few things she could hock to pay him back sooner.

"There's no rush."

She was in a rush and with no intention of dragging

this fake relationship thing out for longer than necessary. Maybe she could even see if Mr. D over at Bella Notte bakery had any hours he could give her. They had worked on many parties together. She always used him for the dessert portion of an event.

"I won't be in debt to you. I appreciate what you're doing. I really do, but once your contract is signed, I'm out. I don't want to still owe you money if we can stop pretending."

"Whatever you want, Maren. I'm only trying to help you. I'm not trying to tie you up longer than necessary. We both have lives to get back to you." His icy words bit hard.

She flinched. "I'm just trying to establish boundaries."

"Believe me, I'm well aware of the concrete wall you put around yourself. Will you meet me for dinner tonight?"

She stared out the window. The wind whipped her neighbor's flag into a frenzy. Another gust tore it from the pole and sent it tumbling end over end down the street.

If she was to be believed by the people she had to lie to, her performance must be convincing.

"I can be ready by six. I need to tell my sisters about us before they find out on social media. They won't forgive me. I have to tell them."

"Tell them whatever you want as long as you stick to our story. You can't ever tell then the truth. I can't risk that information out on the internet."

"Don't worry. I plan on taking our little secret to the grave." Her sisters would never forgive her for lying.

"Thank you, Maren. You won't regret this. I promise."

She hoped Shane had become the kind of man who kept promises. He hadn't been before.

Chapter Six

Maren shifted the tray of apple muffins from one hand to the other and resolved to stay strong. She had procrastinated most of the day by baking unnecessary treats. She should have stopped at the bakery but she wasn't ready to tell Mr. D that she wouldn't need him for a while. She was behaving like a coward, but two confrontations in one day was too many.

The sun prepared to set as she procrastinated on the street, and she needed to get home and get ready for her date. The time to tell her sisters was now whether she liked it or not and she did not like it.

Standing by her car, she mustered up the nerve to tell a huge lie to the people she cared about most. The street was quiet because the homes, that residents of Serenity by the Sea lovingly referred to as tents, were closed up for the winter and their occupants gone home.

Fall creeped into the evening air, shoving summer

aside. Maren shivered. Leaves rustled in the salt-air breeze as if to warn her she was making a mistake. Backing out now would be a problem. She had given her word and promises made were important to her, not to mention a chance to save her daughter and her home.

She had better start moving before someone looked out the window and saw her standing there. She stepped with care up to the front porch as she balanced the tray.

Kassidy's house had once been a white bungalow that had grayed from years of weather, but now it was a two-story modest sized home with four bedrooms and two and half baths. The house was lovely and cozy, exactly the way Kassidy and Grant had wanted it.

Maren knocked on the screen door that would soon be replaced with a full-view glass one, blocking out the bitter winter winds, but keeping all the beauty of a setting sun. Voices echoed inside. She hoped Grant was home too. His presence might provide a buffer for her. He could remain calm when Kassidy got wired up.

"Oh my God, I didn't think you were going to come over anymore." Bailey hurried to the door.

"I brought muffins."

"I thought we were doing s'mores. Kass, Maren is here with food. Something's up," Bailey shouted over her shoulder and back into the house.

"Do you have to yell? The whole town knows now." She brushed past her sister. This whole thing was going to be harder than she thought.

"Someone is in a grumpy mood. At least you're dressed today." Bailey swatted her butt.

"Hey." She pushed Bailey's hand away.

"Oh, good, you're here. I have some baby shower ideas for you." Kassidy came around the corner of the kitchen. Her wild hair bent and creased in all directions as if she'd had her hands shaking in it. Her baby bump stuck out a little more than yesterday. Her smile spread across her lips, but didn't reach her tired eyes. Kassidy burned the candle at both ends and, in the middle, running Sea Glass. Maren always envied her energy.

"Kass, you shouldn't be planning your own baby shower." Bailey took the plate of muffins and placed them on the kitchen counter.

"Why don't you sit down and put your feet up. I'll get us some plates and forks." Maren headed for the cabinet with the plates.

"Let me get my folder for the shower." Kassidy slipped out of the kitchen before anyone could stop her.

"Do you want an herbal tea?" Bailey held up two packets of tea leaves.

"I'll pass on the tea. That's like dish water to me. I was hoping to talk to the two of you for a minute." She searched the area, but no sign of Grant. "Is Grant home?"

"He's meeting Levi for dinner in the city. He won't be back till late. It was just going to be me and Kass unless you want to join us for dinner. I'm making pasta."

"Yes, join us, please." Kassidy returned with her pink and blue folder.

"I would like to, but I have plans." She forced her gaze to meet Kassidy's then Bailey's. The train was out of the station, as they said—no going back now.

71

"Really?" her sisters said in unison.

"I know it's hard to believe with all that's been going on, but once I tell you the whole story, you'll understand." She took a seat at the kitchen table when what she wanted to do was pace like a dog ready to give birth, but she had to appear as casual as possible if this was going to work.

"Does that mean you don't have time to run through my ideas?" Kassidy placed the folder on the table and grabbed some plates.

"I'm afraid not tonight, but I'll come by tomorrow and we can go over everything. I have some ideas too."

"I can't wait to hear this." Bailey sat cross-legged in her wide-legged pants. She reached for a muffin and tore it in half.

"I have some big news." Her throat dried out. She swallowed to moisten the words, but without success. Needing water, she helped herself to a glass and afforded herself a few more seconds of reprieve.

"Are you going to tell us? The suspense is killing me," Kassidy said.

"I've been seeing someone."

"What?" Bailey dropped her muffin on the table. "Who? When? How?"

"Give her a chance to speak." Kassidy put a hand on Bailey's arm. "Eat your muffin. I want to hear this."

"We were keeping it a secret until we were sure. But we are now and you two are the first to hear it. Shane and I are back together." She braced herself for their reaction.

Kassidy burst out laughing. "You had me there. Good one, Maren. What's the real story?"

"That's not funny, Maren. Why would you joke about getting back together with Shane of all people? He broke your heart." Bailey tossed her muffin in the garbage. Maren tried not to take that action as a metaphor.

What she said next would be important. She had to convince them. "I know it seems strange, Shane and I getting back together, but we're both different people now. We're older, wiser. We were spending time together during the wedding planning and one thing just led to another,"

"I know you're not sleeping with him." Bailey crossed her arms over her chest and set her jaw.

"I beg your pardon?"

"I'm your sister. I would know if you were intimately involved with a man. You can't hide it. I knew the second you slept with him the first time." Bailey busied herself with filling the tea pot.

"We were sixteen years old the first time, and you were what? Twelve? You had barged into my room when I was on the phone with him afterward. You overheard me."

"So?" Bailey said.

"This is different. You didn't know we were together this time. No one did." She wasn't sure if she could hold on to the greasy lies much longer. If she came clean, she could swear them to secrecy, but Kassidy would have to tell Grant and Bailey would want to tell Aunt Joanna. Maren had to keep the secret.

"I don't like the sound of this. Why?" Kassidy cut her muffin with a fork.

"Did I ask you why you wanted to be with Grant?"

"It's hardly the same. Grant and I did not have a history together. I know your life has been a bit of a roller coaster the past couple of years with the divorce ad moving back to Serenity and Sea Glass, but is getting back together with your ex a good idea?" Kassidy's question cut to the quick because she was right. Getting back together with Shane in any other capacity besides a fake relationship was a horrible idea. A smart woman would not deliberately put her heart, or anything else, in harm's way.

She needed to make them believe and stood to hold her ground. "We didn't plan for it to happen. It just did. I know what I'm doing. This thing with Shane is real. Our love never went away. We didn't know it until recently, but we've been given a second chance and we're taking it. I hope I can have your support on this."

"I think you're making a mistake," Bailey said.

"Bailey." Kassidy's tone reprimanded.

"What? I can't speak my mind? She should hear the truth. Shane is wrong for you. But it's your choice, obviously, and if you want to date him, then I'll support it. I said my piece and that's that."

"I'm glad you'll support me because there's more."

"Are you pregnant?" Kassidy asked.

"What? No. We're not just dating. We're engaged."

Bailey through her arms in the air. "You're going to marry him? Don't you want to take some time for yourself before you get married again?"

"Is this how you coach your clients, by judging them?" Kassidy pushed out of the chair with some effort. Her hand cradled her belly.

"She's not my client. She's my sister, and I don't want her to get hurt. Because he's going to hurt her again and who will be left behind to watch her stay in her pajamas all day and drown in too much sugar?"

"I'm right here, Bailey. Stop talking like I'm not. And if Shane and I don't work out, that will be on me. You won't have to worry one bit. I can take care of myself." She had taken care of herself after their horrible breakup because she had been too humiliated to tell anyone what really had happened between them.

"What about your event planning business? Shouldn't you be focused on rebuilding that instead of getting involved with Shane?" Bailey poured the hot water into mugs for tea. The water splashed over the side of one mug.

"I'm going to continue to drum up business. I'll plan any kind of party right now. I'll also plan my wedding." If this thing was real, she would ask her sisters to help with the plans. She would take them shopping at her favorite bridal shop in Red Bank and let them pick out whatever kind of dress they wanted in the color of their liking. She would include Peyton too and make her the maid of honor. But all she could do was hold her tongue and pray they would forgive her if they ever found out she had lied.

"Is he telling you not to work?" Kassidy's brows creased. Kassidy could not imagine Grant or any man telling her she couldn't work behind a bar making drinks and booking bands. Kassidy had been on her own a long time, but things would change once that baby came even if she didn't know it yet. Mixing drinks and running tabs would quickly lose its sparkle when Kassidy could finally hold that baby.

"I just said I'm going to continue to try and save my business, and Shane isn't some misogynistic caveman. He doesn't care if I work."

"As long as you're not back in the same spot you were married to Dave, unemployed with no direction. Don't let Shane take your identity." Bailey pierced her with a fierce gaze. Maren had to look away.

She couldn't do this another second. Lying to her sisters was like holding her breath under water for too long. She needed to get outside and breathe again.

"I have this under control. Shane and I are in love and happy. I hope you can be happy for us too. Now, if you'll excuse me, I have to go home and get ready for a date with my fiancé."

She hurried to the front door.

"Maren, wait," Kassidy called after her, but Maren ignored her sister and pressed forward.

She burst into the evening air and the screen door slapped shut. Tears dampened her cheeks, but she slid into the car before she could really break down.

Without another look at the house, Maren pulled away. The worst part was over. Someday, when life was right again, and she and Shane were no longer an item, she would tell her sisters the truth.

She only hoped she didn't destroy her relationship with them in the meantime.

Shane dropped his duffel bag on the hardwood floor. "Well, home at last." Except this wasn't his home. His home was in New York state on a few acres that kept him close enough to the team that he could commute back and forth.

When he began with the Warriors, he might move to north Jersey where his commute would be minutes. Even from Serenity by the Sea the drive in wouldn't be the worst. For now, the small town and the house rental with a third-floor view of the beach and walking distance to Maren's would be his home.

The rental was void of furniture and each of his steps echoed as he moved from the foyer to the kitchen. He would have to buy everything or have stuff brought in from New York. Maybe Maren could decorate it for him and that would add to their story. The idea of her bustling around his house, adding her touches, warmed his insides. He would do a better job with her this time. He wasn't that young arrogant hot-head he used to be in college.

Everything pissed him off back then. If they lost a

game, he'd be angry. If he struck out any time, mostly when he needed to advance the runners, he would throw his helmet on the ground and curse under his breath.

But when he had walked onto the college quad that day to surprise Maren with his return and what he found was her riding the back of his friend in some silly game, anger had torn him in half. He had assumed his friend had moved on his girl, even though technically she wasn't his girl any longer.

What he had seen hadn't been the real story. Only he hadn't found out until it was too late.

Shane went back outside to the car and brought in a few more bags and some staple items he had picked up earlier today. He wanted a quick shower before grabbing Maren for their date, but he had to make a call first.

He dug through his contacts until he found who he needed and hit the call button for Dillon Lynch.

"This is Lynch."

"Hey, man, it's Shane Sutherland."

"Suthers, what's it been? A year?" Dillon's big voice held the hint of a southern accent.

He had transplanted to New Jersey from South Carolina more than twenty years ago, but the accent had held on with both hands.

"Maybe a little longer. Sorry about that." His career always took precedent in his life. Each of his wives had complained about that. Maybe he should work on balancing his life. He wasn't getting any younger.

"Don't apologize to me. Hey, I saw the game the other

night. Wow, sorry to hear they canned you. You didn't deserve it."

"Thanks. I appreciate that." He stepped out onto the front porch. The ocean's sweet scent coated the air. He took a deep breath.

"So, what do I owe this call? You have another heavy check to dump in my hands?" Dillon released the hearty laugh he was known for.

"You know I'll be at the fundraiser in the spring. Whatever you need for your silent auction. Just let me know." He had donated game tickets last year in a luxury box. They were a hit with the winner.

"Perfect."

"But I do have a favor to ask." He took a seat on the top step.

"Anything for our biggest donor."

Shane wasn't sure if he was their biggest, but he had given plenty of money and sport memorabilia over the years that added up to a lot.

"I have a friend who lost her work study job on campus. Can you find her something in your department to do? It doesn't matter what it is." He would like to meet Maren's daughter someday if Maren would allow it.

"You have a friend in college? Aren't you a little old for college aged friends?" Dillon let loose his laugh again.

"Funny. She's the daughter of a friend." A friend he wanted to get to know again. He couldn't believe she had called and agreed to his proposition, but when she had he would have given her anything she asked for.

She was still as beautiful as ever and his body remembered exactly how she felt under him when he had scooped her into that hug in Sea Glass. She had smelled like salt-water and sunshine, and he had wanted to bury his nose in her neck.

"Does she play sports? Is she here on a sports scholarship?" Dillon's voice dragged him away from thoughts of Maren pressed against him.

"No and no. She just needs the money."

"Man, I wish I could help you. But work-study positions are assigned by how many students a department needs. I only need three and I have three."

"She can't work there?" He couldn't go back to Maren at dinner tonight and tell her he didn't have a job for Peyton.

"She can work here. I have plenty for a student to do, but it can't be work study."

Shane held back a long breath. He had promised Maren he could get her daughter a job. If he failed on day one, she would be in her rights to tell him to shove his hair brain idea. He couldn't lose her or this opportunity right out of the gate.

"What about a scholarship? Can I give a student a scholarship for the full tuition?" He would gladly pay the money and not just because he needed Maren. If he hadn't received a baseball scholarship to college, he would have ended up in a dead end job because college was never in his father's plans and they had no money. He never wanted to see someone miss out on an education because they couldn't afford it.

"Probably, but I'm sure there are channels you'd have

to go through. If you don't mind me saying, if you're determined to help this kid, why not just pay her tuition?"

"Her mother won't take my charity. She's the proudest woman I have ever met. What if I pay the tuition anonymously and you hire her, telling her she's a work study student. Can we do that?"

"So, you want her to work for free?"

"Isn't that what she's doing if her salary goes back to the school?"

"I suppose it is. How will we work this out?"

"I'll figure out the details. But when Peyton... damn, I don't know her last name, I'll find that out too, but when a young woman named Peyton comes looking for a job from you and that I sent her, you hire her. Okay?"

"Sure thing, Shane. I'll take care of the job part. You take care of her tuition."

"Thanks, Dillon. I'll be in touch." He ended the call. One problem solved only to create another. He'd tell Maren tonight over dinner about Peyton's new job.

He had one other surprise for her too. He sent her a text because he couldn't wait to see her.

Wear something nice tonight.

She responded almost immediately. *Are you telling me how to dress now?*

This woman was the most stubborn of all. He would never dream of telling her how to dress or if she should even dress.

He had only wanted her to be prepared for what he had planned because if he didn't, and she was under

81

dressed she would hold it against him. He had been married for ten years. He knew how that went down.

I just wanted you to know we were going somewhere fancy and not a fast-food joint.

Oh. Sorry. I'm a little frazzled. Spoke with sis's today.

Her conversation with Kassidy and Bailey must not of went well. He still had to talk to Evan, but that would happen tomorrow.

Sorry they gave you bad time. I'll make it up to you tonight. He had something for her he thought she might like and might put a smile on her face at least for a little while.

Buy me a drink and I'll be fine.

Done. See you soon.

He put his phone in his pocket and began some unpacking. After a shower, he drove over to Maren's.

Night had spackled in the cracks of dusk, covering everything in black. The street was quiet. Only a few cars were parked on the road. Serenity emptied out after Labor Day. The summer visitors were glad to wave goodbye to the beach and the ocean and return to their busy lives. The locals were glad to have their town back. When he lived here, he loved watching the tourist's tail-lights head for the town line, freeing his beach from the crowds. Even the stores on Main Street didn't bust at the seams the same way.

He took the porch steps two at a time and rapped on the glass pane. Maren didn't answer right away. He checked his watch and then his phone. He was about to send her a text when she swung open the door. His breath stuck in his throat.

Her hair floated past her shoulders in a smooth wave. Whatever glossy thing she had on her lips made them look fuller and ready for someone to come along and kiss them. That someone had better be him, if she allowed him to kiss her. He hadn't said anything to her about not dating anyone on the sly, but he hoped it was understood.

She wore a black top with thin straps over her toned shoulders. The top tucked into black flowing pants. The whole outfit gave her a look as if she went on for miles and he wanted to follow her to the end.

"Shane? Are you okay?" Her brows creased and the smile had dropped off her face.

"I'm sorry. Did you say hello?"

She laughed. "I did and you just stared at me. Do I have something in my teeth?"

"You're stunning."

"Oh, please."

"I mean it." He had to roll his tongue back into his mouth.

A pink tint spread across her cheeks. She tucked a hair behind her ear. She always did that when she was nervous. He had watched her do it when she was fifteen, and he'd loved that move from the start.

"Thank you. You clean up well."

He had opted for a white dress shirt with a navy-blue blazer and dark jeans. He hoped her comment was a compliment but would not fish for one.

"Are you ready to go or do you need more time?" He

checked his watch again. They had reservations in twenty minutes.

"I'm ready. Just let me grab my purse." She leaned back inside and grabbed her bag from the table by the door.

Her smile hesitated, but it slammed into his chest just the same. He gave her his elbow, but she waved him away and followed him to the car.

"I made reservations at the Fence and Post."

"Wow. Fancy."

"It's a special night." He held the car door open for her.

"Is this the car you hit the guardrail with? Ray works fast."

The car he hit the guardrail with was still with the mechanic. The bumper was knocked loose. His other cars were at his house in New York.

"Rental."

"Also wow. Who rents a BMW?" She folded into the passenger seat. He caught a whiff of her perfume, subtle and unnamable, but sexy and very Maren.

"Me. I guess." He ran around to the other side and slid in beside her. He had wanted the best car the rental company had on the lot. He hadn't thought about what it looked like just that it would handle well. But now he wished he had asked for something less obvious. He wanted tonight to be about them launching their agreement and not a lot of spectacle.

"Did you tell anyone where we would be at dinner so they could photograph us?"

Even though he needed this thing between them to be public as quickly as possible, he didn't want to announce them tonight. Once the entertainment stations and social media accounts got wind of his newest engagement, there would be no going back.

Maren was the right choice for this scheme, but what if he couldn't control his anger even with her by his side? What if he didn't have what it took to take a team like the Warriors all the way to the championships? What if he'd stayed too long in this industry?

"Shane, are you okay? You keep zoning out." Maren placed a hand on his arm. Her heat burned through the cotton of his shirt and seared his skin.

"Sorry. I'm good. I didn't tip anyone off yet. I wanted our first date to just be us. You know, get to know each other again without any pressure." That much was true. Other than last night, he hadn't had a full-length conversation with her in decades. He knew nothing about the woman she was now.

"Makes sense." She folded her hands in her lap and looked out the side window.

"Why did you move back to Serenity?" He snaked the car through the streets until he left the town behind and could pick up speed on the highway. He wanted her to look at him, but her gaze remained on the landscape of buildings that whizzed past.

"You still like to go fast." She turned to him with a small smile.

"It's the car."

"I think it's the driver. Would you mind slowing down?"

"Um... okay. Yeah, sure." They were coming to a traffic light anyway. He eased to a stop to prove he could do what she asked of him. "You didn't answer my question."

"Why did I move back home? It's the only place I've ever felt connected to. Dave—that's my ex—and I lived in a nice town in a nice house. We made friends, of course my daughter grew up there, but something was always missing for me."

"What do you think it was?" He had often missed Serenity when he was on the road season after season. One hundred and sixty-two games were a long haul. He had bought homes in the different towns he'd played in, but nothing really held a candle to the Serenity's charm for him.

"I don't know exactly. My roots are in that sand. After my dad died, I wanted to be where he had lived and walked and saved all that junk."

"Junk? I don't understand."

"Never mind. That's a story for another time." She played with the gold charm on her necklace.

"I'm all ears now."

She reached up and tugged on his ear. "Yes, you are."

"Hey, now. No poking fun at the ears. You know I'm sensitive about them." A warmth spread through his chest and lingered in the spot her fingers touched.

"They are your best feature." She dropped her hands in her lap, and he wanted them back on his skin.

He needed to slow down. They weren't going to bed fellows. This was a business arrangement, a temporary one at that. In a few months, he would be up to his hairline in work, helping his team be the very best they could be, and she would be planning party after party. She wouldn't need him or want him. And he had no business needing or wanting her. If she ever found out that he had paid her daughter's tuition, she would never forgive him.

He turned into the parking lot and found a spot in the corner of the lot away from the lights. She slid from the car with grace and waited for him as he came around the front.

The maître's d greeted them. They followed him to a booth in the back away from prying eyes just as he had asked.

"Thank you," he said.

Maren slipped into the booth, and he moved in beside her. They had a view of the restaurant with its paneled walls and long mahogany bar that added to the mystique of the room. Tables were tucked away, offering privacy from other patrons. No one paid attention to them, and for that he was grateful.

She studied her menu without a word. He didn't know where or how to start this conversation. Whenever he found that happening in game time moments, he just jumped and took the chance, much the way he had asked her to go along with his crazy scheme.

He had been certain when he walked out of her house this morning that he would either have to find another woman to play the role or he would have to take up meditation or yoga to keep his hot head in check.

If he lost this opportunity, another one that would allow him on the field wouldn't come along. He'd burned too many bridges, made too many important people in the organization mad at him. He needed to change, and Maren would help him.

"What are you going to have?" Maren looked at him over her menu.

"Maybe the steak. Hey, can I ask you something?"

She adjusted in her seat to face him directly. "Are we going to have to tell all our secrets? I'd rather keep this as surface as possible."

"You don't have to tell me anything you don't want to tell, but we do have to make this relationship look real. That may require us to know a few things about each other."

She glanced away then back at him. "You're right. Go ahead ask what you want to know."

"First, I spoke with the head of the athletics department. Peyton has a job."

Maren's mouth fell open before her lips pulled up into a smile. "Thank you for that. Peyton hasn't called yet."

"Give her a day. The department will reach out to her." The lie was a small one. Maren never had to know what really happened with the job and that he was the benefactor. He was glad to help her daughter. He would've done it without the arrangement.

"Okay. Now for my question." He put his hand in his

jacket pocket and pulled out the black velvet box he had been carrying around most of the day. He placed it on the table.

Her eyes grew wide.

He stifled a laugh at her complete surprise. He had always loved surprising her when they were together which was why he had returned to campus that time without telling her he'd had a break in his playing schedule. Except the joke had been on him, and she had been on a date with Phil. If he hadn't lost his temper, maybe they wouldn't have broken up. Maybe, just maybe, his crazy idea of them pretending to be engaged was a way for him to prove to her that he had changed. At least, he hoped he could change.

"Will you marry me?" He pushed the box a little closer, but it stuck on the tablecloth and refused to move as if the fabric tried to stop him from making a fool of himself.

"I don't understand." She rearranged the utensils on the table.

He popped open the box, revealing what had taken him an hour to choose. He had wanted the perfect ring for her, a ring she deserved.

"Oh my god. Is that real?"

This time he couldn't hold back the laugh. "Of course, it's real. I bought it today right after I rented a house."

"You've been busy." She glanced at him then back at the ring.

"I want this all to be right and my fiancé would have

the very best ring on her finger. I need to know if you'll wear it."

"You're already loaning me money for my taxes. You could've bought a fake thing from the internet for a hundred bucks. No one would've been any the wiser." She smoothed out the napkin.

"Don't worry about the money. I have plenty of money. I want you to know I'm taking this thing between us seriously. You're helping me in a big way, and if for any reason, I can't get you the parties I promised, then you can keep the ring and sell it. You'll be able to start another business or put it away or pay the light bill for a year or two. Whatever you want."

"Thank you, Shane. It's beautiful, truly. But I can't wear it."

Chapter Seven

The waitress, Acantha, came to take their order. The woman with the unique name stood close to six feet with flawless makeup, and her braided her pulled back low on her neck. Her white dress shirt contrasted nicely against her dark skin. Shane scooped the box back in his pocket and Maren could breathe again.

They ordered their meal and Acantha glided away with the poise of a Greek goddess.

"Will you excuse me a moment?" Maren couldn't sit a second longer and needed to get out of there. She hurried to find the ladies' room because going out the door could mean Shane would follow her.

Cooler air hit her in the bathroom. Maybe now she wouldn't pass out. The size of that diamond nearly blinded her when it caught the light from overhead. She had never seen something so spectacular. The engagement ring Dave had given her was small and barely noticeable, but it was what he could afford at the time, and she had thought she was lucky to have it because it had come from a place of love.

The ring out there was about business and extravagance and something she would never wear. Besides the fact she would always be worried about smacking it into something or getting it covered in chopped meat when she cooked burgers, a piece that screamed *look at me while I flaunt* wasn't for her.

She would have preferred a stone that suited her hand in a simple setting, and though she loved the sparkle of a good diamond like most women, she would have been just as happy with a sapphire or a ruby as her center stone because she loved those stones more.

Maren glanced at the solid wood door protecting her from the dining area and the man who could make her nerves dance and sing. Shane would do something frivolous and romantic and buy her a big ring to show off. He did like to show off too with his fancy cars and gold watch. The spotlight had gone to his head. She didn't blame him. He'd been told his whole life he was an athletic god.

She dampened a paper towel and pressed it against the back of her neck, trying to pull herself together. This wasn't a real relationship. It was a game, a gimmick and when it was done, she would stand alone.

Shane was trying to cover all his bases, like usual, by giving her something she could sell later if she needed to, and she might. He couldn't make any guarantees, not really, and no matter how hard she hustled to get out of this agreement as soon as possible, the money might not come to her.

But all that money, the loan for her taxes, the fancy rental car, he rented a house in town and now this ring. How easy it was for him to throw thousands of dollars around as if they didn't mean anything. She had scrimped and saved her whole life and lost everything because of one over indulged woman. Life wasn't fair.

The door swung open, and Acantha came in to the bathroom. She shut the door and engaged the lock. "I'm sorry to bother you, but your date is worried about you and asked me to come and check. Is everything all right?"

"Yes, thank you. I'm fine. Why did you lock the door?"

"Look, it's none of my business, but if you feel unsafe with him, I can get you a ride home or sneak you into the kitchen. Whatever you need. Us girls have to stick together."

"What? Oh. No. No. It's not like that but thank you. That's very sweet of you to come in here and make sure I'm truly okay. He's wonderful, actually. Exactly the man for me. I was taking so long because he asked me to marry him."

"That's great. Or is it? Do you want to marry him?" Acantha cocked a perfectly sculpted brow.

She had never been totally over Shane. Maybe no one ever got over their first. She didn't know. Her marriage had been fine until it wasn't, but life should be filled with more than fine. The man in her life should set her soul on fire, make her feel as if she had been struck by lightning and Shane had always done that for her until he scared her badly enough, she told him to never come near her again.

"I think so." The truth hurt.

"If you really love him, and he's not some kind of weirdo, then it's more than okay to want to spend the rest of your life with him. And for the record, he doesn't look like a weirdo or anything."

"He's not weird in a creepy at all. In fact, he's quite the opposite. I was surprised when he asked me. I think I panicked. We hadn't talked about marriage, not seriously anyway." More like not for real. They had talked about marriage plenty in the last forty-eight hours. She really might be sick after all.

"I get that. If my guy popped the question out of the blue, I might need a minute to gather myself too. I'll tell him you'll be right out."

"Thank you."

Alone again in the bathroom, she straightened her jumpsuit, tucked her hair behind her ear and took a long breath. She could do this. She could pretend to be engaged to Shane Sutherland.

He stood when he realized she was on her way back to him. His smile faltered. She must look worse than she thought.

She placed a hand on his warm cheek, wanting to reassure him they were still a go. "Sorry about that."

"Are you okay? Do you want to go home?" He laced his fingers through her cold ones.

"I'm fine. Let's sit."

"Maren, if you don't want to be with—"

"Shane, it's all good. I apologize for running off. I wasn't expecting such a grand gesture. That's all."

They found their seats again, and he took her hand. His fingers were long and thin, speckled with scars from playing rough over the years. With his other hand, he placed the box on the table.

"Will you marry me?" His bright eyes lit up, and his smile dimpled his cheeks.

He had an incredible ability to handle a situation and move forward without looking over his shoulder. He had to be able to pivot in real time when a game could turn on its head in seconds. She admired that quality in him, but for her, she wasn't so sure she was back on solid ground yet.

He had purchased a ring for her that said more about him than it did her. She was a small-town short story. If he didn't really know who she was as a person, then he couldn't have any real feelings for her.

"You know I've already agreed to marrying you." She had imagined a proposal from him a hundred times when they were together, but Shane had never wanted to settle down back then. He had dreams to catch, and she hadn't wanted to go along for the ride. She had told him to go on without her and he had.

She had never expected to see him on the campus that day that was so long ago it should be nothing more than a plume of smoke in her memory, but it was loud and clear with teeth still.

Shane also liked to spring things on her, like that ring

winking from its pretty black box, and when he saw her with that sweet young man all those years ago, he had lost his temper and hit a wall with his fist.

He had broken two fingers and was on the injured list for three weeks. He had apologized many times, but she had told him to go away.

"When I saw the ring, I knew it belonged on your hand, and I had to get it. If you hate the ring... tell me what you want, Maren. I want you to be happy during this."

"Any woman would be thrilled to wear it." Anyone, but her. She was in over her head, and it was only one date. How was she ever going to last until this was over?

"Then what's the problem?"

"You didn't have to go to the expense for me, but I think it's very sweet that you did. I'll wear it and when we have our breakup, I'll give it back."

"You can keep it."

"No, I can't." Because the man attached to it didn't understand her at all. Or maybe he did since he chose her for this charade, knowing she was plain and simple and the opposite of what he wanted, but either way the ring might be real, but the two of them were not.

"I want you to have it."

"Please, Shane. This is strange enough, us doing what we're doing. Let's not get ahead of ourselves. I'll wear your ring. It will make our engagement look real to others and it will give something for the photographers to take pictures of. All the women will want to see it. But when we're done, I don't want it."

"I wish you'd change your mind." He slid the ring on her finger. It fit perfectly.

"The loan is more than enough help. But if you can get a few players to book a party, that would be great. Or hand out some of my business cards while you're in town. That's all you need to do."

"I think I'm getting the better deal here." He kissed her knuckles.

She did too.

Maren sat on her back porch and flipped through a bridal magazine while the sun climbed out of the horizon, claiming the day for its own. She wrapped her old cardigan around her and sipped hot coffee.

Glossy pages stared back at her with their beauty and glamour. Women dressed as brides posed in exotic places with art painted on ceilings and long palms swaying around them. She tried to imagine herself in one of those elegant white gowns, but she couldn't.

Those brides were not like her. She might have been a wedding planner for women like Paris, but that wasn't who she was. If she were ever to get married again, and she doubted that she would, but if she did this time, she would do it the way she wanted and not the way Dave's mother had.

Maren had married her mother-in-law's only child and Betty Cole wanted to have the wedding she had always dreamed about. Maren had been willing to go along to keep peace and because her own mother couldn't be bothered to get involved, but her heart had never been in the floofy dress or ornate venue. She had never wanted to be a Paris Sutherland.

Maren had envisioned a wedding on the beach in her bare feet wearing a cream-colored simple dress that flowed in the breeze and draped over the sand.

She had wanted a backyard reception and Dave's mother had almost choked on her lunch when Maren had suggested it.

If she and Shane were really getting married, she would ask Kassidy for the use of her backyard because she was closer to the beach and the guests could walk there after the ceremony. She'd have Hank handle the menu right in Sea Glass's kitchen.

Kassidy. Maren needed to get planning that baby shower before the baby decided it was time to arrive. Instead of pulling up her Pinterest account, her gaze returned to the black velvet box beside the magazine. She had taken Shane's ring off the second she came into the house, but it haunted her the whole night.

The stone had to be four carats and was a radiant cut. Two smaller round cut stones flanked the sides in what was most likely a platinum setting, but she would need to see the appraisal to be sure. The piece was worth tens of thousands and if she had to sell it, would help her pay her bills for months until she was on her feet again.

She didn't want to wear it, but she would have to get used to it. She slid the ring on and tilted her hand so the morning light could catch the facets in the stone. It truly was radiant.

She had one phone call to make before she could get on with her day. This call she had been dreading more than any other, but Shane had a plan in place to announce their engagement and Maren had to tell Peyton before one of her friends saw her mother with a new man on social media.

The phone rang. Maren hoped to catch Peyton still asleep in her dorm room.

"Mom, it's early." Peyton's sleep induced voice creaked over the line like an old rocking chair left and forgotten in the corner of an attic.

Maren's heart warmed and clenched at the same time. If Peyton never forgave her for this lie, she would be in her right.

"Hi, honey. Sorry to wake you."

"What's going on?" Maren imagined Peyton throwing off the covers and sitting up.

"I missed you and wanted to hear your voice." That was true. That was always true.

"Oh. Okay. Well, guess what?"

"What?" She could also picture Peyton flopping back down and scooping her hair away from her face.

"Well, I was at work, and I overheard one of the coaches talking to one of the football players..." Peyton continued to prattle, but Maren only half listened. She wanted Peyton to share everything with her and today was no different, but she didn't have the energy to focus on campus gossip now. She heard enough to interject the appropriate agreements or expressions of awe. She'd become very good at being talked at by her child.

"You handled that like a pro." Her voice inflated with pride for Peyton. Maren was always amazed at how she had created a child who could advocate for herself and speak her mind at such a young age

"Thanks. I thought so too."

"Hey, Peyton, there's something I need to talk to you about." She glanced at the ring on her finger but turned it so the diamond was facing her palm.

"Uh oh. Is it about the tuition again?"

"It's about me. I've been seeing someone." She held her breath.

"That's great. You should be out dating. You and Dad split like what, three years ago."

"More like two." Dating wasn't the problem. Lying was. That and she had never told Peyton about her relationship with Shane. At some point, she would have to reveal their past and when Peyton asked why they had broken up, she would have to keep to the story because she didn't want Peyton to think Shane was the sum of one incident. Even if he did lose it on the field often.

"Whatever. You're hot, Mom. All my friends think so."

"That's very sweet, but I don't think I'm hot." She would never describe herself that way. Attractive, sure, but hot? Not her. Bailey was hot.

"Well, you are. Who's the guy? Is it a guy? If you wanted to date a woman, that would be fine with me."

She loved how accepting Peyton was of everyone.

Maren liked to think she had a little to do with that. "Yes, it's a guy. His name is Shane. He's a baseball manager."

"Like Little League? Does he have small children? I'm not babysitting."

She chuckled. "Professional. The Warriors want to sign him."

"Wow. That's cool. Can we go to some games?"

"Maybe." They would not still be together by the start of the new season, if Maren had anything to say about it. Promising professional baseball games that wouldn't materialize to Peyton would only let her down and Maren didn't want to do that.

"What do the aunts think of him?" Peyton valued her aunts' opinions on pretty much everything. Maren was grateful her daughter had other positive strong independent women in her life.

"Well, honestly, they're a little surprised." Did she say more? Had she said too much?

"Why? Is he a dork?"

"Shane and I dated a long time ago."

"As long as you're happy. Mom, I need to go use the bathroom and get ready for work. Can I call you later?"

Maren had run out of time and needed to get to the point before Peyton hung up. "There's one more thing."

"Okay." Peyton huffed in that fashion reserved for teenagers.

"Shane and I became engaged two nights ago. We're going to get married."

"You're marrying some guy I didn't even know you

were dating?" Peyton's voice squealed as if someone had pulled it from her tight throat.

"I realize it's quick." She fidgeted with the back of her earring.

"How long have you been together?"

"Just a few months. But we're older and don't need a lot of time to know it's right." She choked on the words and wanted to vomit on the glossy magazine.

"Does Dad know?"

And yet another conversation she would have to have. Dave would probably be thrilled because if she married someone, he was off the hook for alimony permanently.

"When can I meet him?" Peyton drew her attention away from thoughts of Dave.

'You want to meet him?" She hadn't thought about that and yet another mistake. She had assumed Peyton wouldn't care at all about her mother's love life and by the time Peyton gave Maren a second thought, she and Shane would be broken up.

"Soon. You can come home one weekend, or I can come to you and we can take you to dinner." She preferred the latter. They could find a place near the school and keep the dinner short. If Peyton came home, she might want to spend the whole weekend with Shane.

"Can Isabella come?"

"Sure." Even better. Peyton and her friend would spend the entire time talking to each other and probably forget the adults were even there. Maren could handle an hour of this make-believe relationship in front of her daughter.

"Congratulations, Mom. Can I be your maid of honor?

"Absolutely." Tears stung the back of her eyes. What was she doing, adding lie upon lie.

"I really have to go now. I'll call you later. Love you." Peyton ended the call before Maren could say she loved her back.

Chapter Eight

She hopped out of her chair and paced the deck. Her feet pounded the wood. What had she done? She was the worst kind of mother. She couldn't go through with this. It wasn't too late to back out. No one knew except her sisters and maybe Evan. She would let her sisters have a laugh at her expense and then they could go about their business like nothing had ever happened. Peyton already had the job on campus, and Maren could give Shane the money back that he had deposited into her account just last night.

So what that she didn't have the money to pay the taxes? She could walk away from the home and foreclose on the mortgage. People did that kind of thing all the time. Not that she had agreed with that method. Paying bills was a responsibility she took seriously, but she had no other choice if she was going to back out of this fake engagement. She'd just have to find a new place to live.

She grabbed her phone to call Shane.

"Good morning, you're up early." His deep timbre vibrated across the line and settled around her like warm sunshine. She imagined him still in bed with the sheets tangled around his legs and in nothing but his boxers. His muscles would flex as he put one hand behind his head.

"Stop."

"Excuse me?"

"Sorry. Not you. A crow was pecking at my bushes." No crow or any kind of bird pecked at anything. She hadn't meant to reprimand herself out loud. Her mind played tricks on her with all this stress. Imagining Shane in his underwear... what was wrong with her?

"Sounds like you have a bird problem."

She had a problem all right and he was six-feet tall and all muscles even for a forty-nine-year-old. "I can't go through with this."

"What do you mean? Do you mean us?"

"Yes, us, Shane. I just called my daughter to tell her, and she was actually happy for me. Happy. I can't believe it. She even wants to meet you. I lied to my child. What kind of an example am I setting? This will never work. We'll never convince anyone that we're in love and want to spend our lives together. I shouldn't torture Peyton with meeting you and then having you walk out of our lives just for money. What a selfish thing for me to do."

"Hey, it's going to be okay. You're not being selfish trying to take care of yourself. Paris did you wrong and for no reason. I have the power to help you and by you being engaged to me, gives your business a certain amount of legitimacy. Peyton won't get hurt."

"You can't promise that." She was determined to grow her business herself, but he was right about his influence. Maren had read about a rock star's wife who owned a flower shop that would never be as popular as it was if she wasn't married to him. The flowers weren't that amazing.

"I'll come over and we can talk."

"I'm not going to change my mind. You should find someone else before you go and make the announcement about us." She twisted the ring around on her finger. She would have to give this back too and there went any chance of a nest egg.

"I'm throwing on some clothes now. I'll be there in ten minutes. Do you want me to bring you some pastries from Bella Notte?"

"Bribing me with Mr. D's muffins and cookies isn't going to help your case any." Backing out of this relationship was the right thing to do. If they kept moving forward, she would have to tell Mr. D about her plans to marry. She couldn't lie to that sweet man who had been like a second father to her. She still had to tell him that her business was over, and she wouldn't be using him for anymore weddings.

"Plying you with the best pastries on the Jersey shore will only help my case."

Despite the fear and frustration raging inside her like a hurricane, she smiled at his joke. Shane could always find the win in any situation. He was good that way.

"Fine. Say hello to Mr. D for me, but don't mention we're getting married yet."

"So, you're not completely saying no?" His voice lifted with what had to be the help of a large smile.

"I just don't want him thinking he's making the wedding cake." Mr. D. would make the best damn wedding cake. Too bad it wouldn't be for her wedding. She could, however, order a cake for the baby shower and made a mental note to do that after Shane left today.

"I'll see you in twenty," he said.

"Thanks." She ended the call.

She had to stay strong when Shane arrived, no caving in to his charm. She had no idea how she would do it, but she could not allow this fake relationship to continue.

"Hello, Maren? Are you in the back? It's me, Jemma Klein." A female voice traveled around the side of the house and reached her at the table.

She stifled a groan before her visitor could appear in her backyard. Maren didn't want to deal with Jemma now with Shane about to show up.

"Back here." Why had she ever moved back to this small-town? Living in a big city where no one knew had to have advantages.

Jemma came around the house's corner into the backyard. She was tall and big boned with a blond bob that swung with her every step. The sum of her face made her attractive, but if her parts were picked apart, she would be unusual with her wideset eyes that always gave Jemma a surprised look and her doughy nose that seemed too big for her face, or those full lips that could be filler or genetics.

"I'm so glad I caught you at home. I was out for a

walk and took a detour down your street. I have a quick question." Jemma played the part of doting wife, mother, and business owner to perfection. Even her deep purple leggings and light pink tank top screamed put together with high-end fashion

Maren glanced at her old and faded robe. She would need to buy a new one—today.

She also couldn't imagine what this question of young Jemma's might be. She and Jemma didn't run in the same circles. Maren had a good ten years on the woman who had two small children and a New York City hedge fund husband who made more than enough money to keep Jemma home. Except Jemma owned Sweet Chocolate Haze on Main Street. The chocolate was amazing. Maren had used Jemma for party favors.

"I hope I have an answer." Maren also hoped the smile was on her face.

"Can I book you for Amelia's birthday party?"

"I'm sorry. I missed that." She needed to make sure she heard Jemma right.

"I need a party planner for Amelia's fifth birthday. I would do it myself, but I'm swamped at the store, and you know husbands. They aren't a lick of help. Don't get me wrong, I love Devon with my heart and soul, he's an amazing girl dad, but plan a party? Not a chance." Jemma wiped the air with her hand and bent in half, laughing at her own joke.

Before the Paris video fiasco, she would've been able to give Jemma a polite, but definite no way. When she had embarked on the event planning business, her plan included adult parties for wealthy clients only. She didn't want to run after little children who would do better at a ceramic studio or sports complex. She also wanted clients who were used to having their way and willing to pay for it.

Jersey was home to plenty of wealthy people which gave Maren a large population to earn business from. Monmouth County alone was home to celebs like Jon Bon Jovi and Bruce Springsteen.

"When is the party?" She couldn't believe those words came out of her mouth.

"Next weekend. I know it's short notice, but I was hoping with your recent incident, your calendar might be a little less... hectic, let's say." At least Jemma had the decency to appear uncomfortable.

"Next weekend? I will have to check my calendar." She could picture her empty planner sitting on the end of her dining room table.

"That's fine. Whatever your regular price is, I'll pay." Jemma pulled a piece of paper out of the back pocket of her leggings. "Here's the theme. My house at three o'clock. I wrote that all down for you. Amelia wants cupcakes from Bella Notte. Just tell Mr. D they're for me. He'll move me up his list. I can also give you a deposit now, if you take credit cards."

She bit back the words that of course she took credit cards because she was a real business owner just like Jemma, but the day had already worn on her and she didn't have the energy to go inside and upstairs to retrieve the device. Besides, Jemma wasn't hard to find, and

Maren doubted Jemma would stiff her. Not when it came to throwing a birthday party for one of her children.

"You can pay next week when I arrive." Now that she had a little cash in her bank account thanks to Shane, she would pay Mr. D. That was how they always did it before.

"Perfect. You're fab. Truly. I'm off. I must get to the store. We are swamped. Hope you have a fantastic day." Jemma hurried away as if she bounced.

"We are swamped," Maren muttered under breath.

She wondered if that energy came from sampling chocolate all day long. She dragged herself inside to make another cup of coffee and jot down a few ideas for the party. A little girl's birthday party wasn't exactly an extravagant wedding, but sweet Amelia didn't know that and though Maren would rather pull out her eyebrows than plan a birthday party for a child, she would still make it the best party Amelia ever had.

A knock came at the back door. Shane must be there and now she would have to argue with him about ending this hair brain idea of his.

Instead of Shane, she opened the door to Kassidy, wearing a crocheted cardigan of raspberry and orange over a white t-shirt and maternity jeans. She looked adorable with her wild hair catching the wind. Her wedding rings caught the sunlight as she waved to Maren.

Grant had bought Kassidy a diamond as beautiful and bright as the one Shane had purchased for her. Maren twisted her ring back around, allowing the diamond to face out. She couldn't let Kassidy think she didn't want it.

"Come on in. I was about to make another cup of coffee."

"I came to apologize for last night." Kassidy leaned against the counter and wiped a hand over her face.

"Are you feeling okay?"

"It's exhausting being pregnant and forty. I thought I had the stamina for this. I was wrong." Kassidy's smile matched her watery eyes.

"You're doing great. It's the teen years you need stamina for and a few shots of vodka. Sit down. I have decaf coffee if you want."

"No, to the coffee. It will only make me have to pee." Kassidy reached for her hand. "I truly am sorry about last night. I should have been more supportive about you and Shane. If you're happy, then I'm happy for you."

"Thanks. I appreciate it. It was all unexpected."

Kassidy lifted Maren's hand. "Holy cow. This thing is huge." Kassidy glanced at her and back to the ring. "Did he give you this last night on your date? Because I would've noticed it when you were at my house."

Maren swallowed the truth and stuck with the engagement story. "He gave it to me at dinner."

"It's stunning, but not what I would picture you wearing. I'm not saying that's a bad thing or judging you. It's just..."

"Big."

"Very." Kassidy smirked.

They shared a laugh and the tension in Maren's chest

eased for the first time since Shane opened the black velvet box and gave it to her.

"Grant and I would like to have the two of you over for dinner. Grant wants to fire up the new grill and we'll all get to know each other again." Kassidy dropped into a chair at the dining room table.

She wasn't ready for a family dinner. "I'll have to check Shane's schedule."

"I heard on the radio he was fired. What kind of schedule does he have to keep right now?" Kassidy plopped her feet up on the opposite chair. "You know what? I will take that coffee if you don't mind. It's chillier this morning than I realized."

"Do you want me to grab you a heavier sweater?"

"Nah. Just the coffee, please. So, tell me, what is our resident baseball manager busy with these days besides stealing my sister from me so she can't help plan my baby shower."

"He's not stealing me, and I haven't forgotten the shower. I already ordered the cake from Mr. D." What was one more lie thrown on the heap? And now she had to order those cupcakes, so she'd take care of two things at once.

"That's great. No one bakes like Mr. D. So, where is Shane going to manage next? Wasn't that some of your problem last time? He was moving to California and wanted you to come."

That was the story she had told, but it had been only part of the truth. His new schedule left no time for their relationship. He had said he needed to take a break.

Maren had left out the part where he returned to campus unexpectedly and in a fit of anger punched a hole in her dorm wall.

"The Warriors are talking with him." Which conveniently made their story more believable. The Warriors were in New York City. He could commute from central Jersey for games and when he traveled, she would stay home with her family. Too bad that wasn't going to be a true story. She never guessed she would write fiction or act in her own memoir.

"That's fantastic. You won't have to move away."

"I'm not moving. I'm not leaving Serenity by the Sea this time or ever. This is my home with you and Bailey here."

"Does he want to live in Serenity?"

"I want that, and he wants me to be happy." Based on what he said last night at dinner, at least that much was true. She kept her gaze on her task of making decaf. Looking at her hands was easier than facing Kassidy.

"Okay. Great. I'm glad you won't be going anywhere. I need my big sister to help me be a mom."

"You don't need me or anyone. You'll be just fine. You always are." Maren poured milk into the cup for Kassidy. Her sister had always made her own way and never allowed anyone to define her path.

When Kassidy's old fiancé had broken up with her because she wasn't educated, she didn't decide to go to school. Kassidy came home and ran the family tavern instead. She made up her own rules all the time. Maren was only pretending to be someone she wasn't.

"You're doing just fine too. I know the business thing hit a big bump, but you'll bounce back." Kassidy sipped her coffee.

"Jemma Klein just booked me for her daughter's party. Things are already looking up." She tried to keep the sarcasm out of her voice, but Kassidy knew her as well as anyone and would probably hear it dripping down her words.

"Maren, are you sure you're happy?"

"Of course, I am. Why wouldn't I be?" She turned away to make a second cup of coffee for herself because Kassidy could and often did read her like the stars in the sky.

"Are you feeling like Shane might be your last chance?" Kassidy gripped her arm, forcing Maren to look at her.

"Last chance for what?"

"I don't know. For anything. Love, commitment. You don't have to settle."

"Why would you think I'm settling? Let's go back outside. It's too hot in here." The room was hot because Kassidy was getting too close to the truth that Maren wasn't in love with Shane the way she should be to marry him. Falling all the way for him, would take a big push, because she couldn't know if he really had the ability to control his anger.

"You never mentioned him in all this time and out of nowhere you announce you're marrying him. I just want to make sure you're doing this for the right reasons."

"My reasons are my reasons right or wrong. I thought

you were coming over here to tell me I could count on your support. I see that's not the case."

"That isn't true."

"Hello, ladies." Shane pounded up the back steps with a tray of two cups and a white pastry bag from Bella Notte. He wore a black sweatshirt that hugged all his muscles and a baseball cap. "I brought some breakfast."

He leaned in and kissed her on the cheek. He smelled rugged and refined, like leather. She rested her head against his for the moral support she needed to finish this conversation with Kassidy.

"I didn't know you would be here, Kass, or I would've brought a coffee for you too." Shane flashed his smile.

Kassidy returned hers, but it didn't quite meet her eyes. "No problem. Maren made me one and I wasn't going to stay very long. I told Maren that Grant and I would like to have you both over for dinner. Would that work for you?"

"Absolutely. I'd love to meet Grant. This weekend sound good?" He looked between Maren and her sister.

"That's fine with me. Well, I just booked a party. I'd have to work around that." She didn't see as if she had much choice. If she tried to back out, they both would suspect something was wrong with her.

"Great. I had hoped your schedule would be a little lighter right now," Kassidy said to Shane.

"Maren has my undivided attention until February. Then it's pitchers and catchers season." He put an arm around her and pulled her close.

She wrapped an arm around him and hoped that she

looked up at him for Kassidy to see that she did love Shane.

"I'll text you the time and what to bring," Kassidy said to her. "I'm going to head home and leave you two love birds alone. Oh, and Shane, impressive ring. I'm glad to see you know what my sister is worth."

"She's worth that and more."

"See you." Kassidy waved over her head as she left.

Shane waited before Kassidy was out of sight before looking at her with wide eyes. "You kept to our story."

She flopped into a chair. "I didn't know she was coming over. She saw the ring."

"You're wearing it." Shane's smile spread wide across his face.

"I was trying to get used to it and then I called Peyton. The whole morning was too much. That's when I called you."

"So, you don't want out or you do? I'm confused." He pulled out two cannolis and set them on top of the bag. "I also got you a strong coffee, black. The way you like it."

"How do you remember the way I like my coffee?"

"I remember everything, Maren." He handed her the cup. She couldn't avoid touching him, even if she wanted to, and their fingers grazed. He wagged his eyebrows.

"Stop that. I had to touch you or risk dropping the nectar of the gods."

He choked out a laugh. "We wouldn't want that to happen." He sat beside her. "Don't leave me just yet. We can make this work."

"The more lies I tell the deeper I'm in. My sister and

her husband want us to come over like a regular couple. If I back out, and I want to, she'll be suspicious. If I say yes, then all night we have to lie to two people I care about. Probably three, because Bailey will most likely be there."

He took her hand. "Listen, I understand you wanting to shoot straight with your sisters. But what we're doing doesn't affect them directly. They will never know that we weren't a real couple."

She pulled her hand away. "If they find out I'm lying to them, it will change the way the see me, the person I am. My sisters and I weren't always close. In fact, up until a couple of years ago, I hardly saw them. I was so wrapped up in my sorry life. Now, that I have them back, I can't risk losing them."

"You won't lose them."

"How do you know?" She pushed out of the chair. The day heated up around her, stifling her breath. She needed space to think.

"Because they won't find out. We're the only two people who know the truth. I'm not planning on telling them. Maren, we can do this. We can have it all."

"No one gets to have it all." She twisted the back of her earring.

"Some people do. This arrangement doesn't have to be a prison sentence. We can have some fun." He handed her a cannoli.

An hour ago, she had been determined to end this, but now she wasn't sure what to do. She wasn't ready to admit to her family that things were over with Shane before they had begun. How foolish she would look. She needed to save some face now that the ball was rolling. A breakup later would make more sense. His career was an easy villain for their story.

She dipped her finger in the sweet cream and licked it off. Shane was right about no one knowing the truth except them. They would have to be the ones to spill. She searched his face for answers. His ice blue eyes shined in the sunlight. Could she trust him?

"We can have some fun, but I'm not sleeping with you." She didn't care what he thought. She needed to lay down that boundary.

"Why don't you want to sleep with me? Was I that bad?"

"Never mind your rankings." She turned away from him so he couldn't see the truth in her eyes. She had only ever slept with him and Dave. Dave didn't exactly measure up, but then again Shane made sure he was the best at everything.

"I'm a baseball guy. Everything is about rankings."

"We're not having sex. I don't sleep around."

"Okay. I can go three months or more without sex. Can I have some?" He took the cannoli from her.

She didn't believe for a second he could go months without taking a woman to bed. "No sleeping with other women. That's grounds for a breakup."

"I would not cheat on you. Not a good look for the image I'm trying to create, and I can't trust another woman to keep that secret. If you don't want to have sex while we're together, then we won't. There are other ways of handling things." He cocked a brow.

"Thank you." She fought the smile tugging at her lips. Images of Shane doing some of those things flashed through her mind. She would never be able to unsee them and might not want to see anything else—ever.

"But if you change your mind, I'm okay with the whole friends with benefits things." He bit into the cannoli. Cream tangled in his beard.

Her fingers moved without permission and wiped the cream away. Shane grabbed her hand like a serpent striking and licked her finger clean.

Her pulse misfired. She wanted to tell him not to do that again, but her voice stuck in her throat.

He continued to hold her hand. "I'll take that as your agreement to continue to be my fiancé."

Chapter Nine

Shane swirled the ice in his glass. The whiskey burned the back of his throat, but he needed the discomfort to remind him that this conversation would be the most difficult of any he'd had in a long time.

Evan sat beside him on Shane's back patio. The fire pit sat dark because the night air was too warm for a blaze.

"Say something." He put the whiskey on the table. This was his third. He wasn't drunk, though he wanted to be. Evan wasn't making this any easier for him.

He had second guessed his decision to involve Maren after she almost baled on him the other morning. At least she had come around. He didn't know if her decision to stick with him was because he had said something to convince her, or she changed her mind because of the dessert with her coffee.

Having his brother's support for once, would have

been nice, but Shane was the supportive brother who had been there, taking care of Evan since he was a kid.

"What I have to say isn't important. You're going to do what you want. You always do." Evan downed the rest of his drink and wiped his mouth with back of his hand.

He didn't always do what he wanted, even if Evan thought that way. Shane had often tried to help Evan through whatever crisis he had stirred up and that had meant putting his own wishes and wants aside.

Shane had taken the blame for him countless times when they were kids so their father wouldn't berate Evan or worse hit him. Shane had defended Evan in the steroid scandal that had locked its jaws on them both. Evan's career had barely taken a ding thanks to Shane. He had been the one to get kicked off the team. Securing his first coaching job had been a stroke of luck he didn't think he had coming back then.

"So, you think this is a bad idea?"

Evan leaned in. "I think you marrying Maren Russo is the worst idea you have ever had. And what makes it worse is that you're asking me to support it because we both know she's no good for you."

"For once, why can't you be happy for me?" He pushed out of the chair and circled the dormant fire pit. The source of Evan's dislike for anything Shane did, started when Shane was put on the high school varsity baseball team as a freshman. Evan was a starting junior at short stop and the team's top player until Shane stepped onto the field. Shane was faster and had a strong bat which only angered his brother instead of being glad for Shane.

"What do you see in her?" Evan pulled a cigar out of his pocket and lit it.

"Plenty." He wasn't going to explain himself. If he and Maren were in a real relationship, he wouldn't bother telling Evan that he loved the simple things about Maren. She was smart, kind, funny, sexy. He could be himself around her. She had stats a mile long, but since this relationship wasn't real, he saw no point in listing her qualities for Evan's benefit.

"She isn't in our league, Shane."

"What the hell does that mean? That she isn't rich enough for your liking? She doesn't have a big enough social media presence or business for someone like you who makes millions catching balls?"

"Oh, come on. Since when do you date the small-town girl? Do you remember your last two wives? Maren was fine when you were in school playing D1 ball. But now? You're Shane Sutherland. You could have any woman you want. You're settling."

He had thought once that he needed to have all the objects to prove he had made it. Coming from nothing and always having his old man in his head telling him wasn't enough, drove him to grab onto anything that showed he had made it.

What had that proven? He had two failed marriages under his belt, a few nice cars, an empty house with no one to come home to, and a closet full of things like clothes and watches that didn't keep him warm at night.

"Don't talk about her that way."

"Why? Because you're going to fight me? I see your clenched fists." Evan pointed with his cigar.

He shook his hands loose. "I don't want to fight with you. I asked you over here to tell you about my engagement. I hoped for once, you'd be happy for me." If he could convince Evan of this fantasy relationship, he could convince others that Maren was the reason he had changed.

"Have you ever thought about the fact, she might be using you? That guy she was married to was a loser."

"How do you know about the man she was married to?"

"I did my research before I hired her. If you hadn't suggested her—strongly—I wouldn't have hired her at all. I did her a favor."

"I don't know how we're related sometimes." He had suggested in a firm manner that Evan hire Maren because like Evan, he also kept tabs on Maren through the years. He knew she had divorced and was trying to make a name for herself. Planning Evan and Paris's wedding was another big event for her quickly growing resume.

"I filed for divorce." Evan said, dragging him back to the here and now. His brother looked up at him through hooded lids. His whiskey glass was empty again except for the ice cubes.

"It's only been a few weeks." Shane wasn't exactly surprised. He never understood Evan's attraction to Paris except for maybe the physical stuff. He only wished Evan hadn't bothered to get married.

"A few weeks too many. I have to stop being so impulsive."

Evan thinking before he leapt was a lot like him not fighting with an umpire. Without a real incentive, it wasn't going to happen.

"I'm sorry to hear things didn't work out." He truly was. All he ever wanted was for his brother to be happy and whole. Evan was his own worst enemy.

"No, you're not. You never liked Paris." Evan swirled the ice around in his glass.

"But I did want you to be happy."

"I thought I was until she hauled off and belted me in front of all of our guests," Evan said.

"I never asked. What did you say to her?"

"I told her she spent too much on that dress, and it would look better on the floor with her on top of it while I screwed her until she screamed."

"Ah. Not exactly romantic." He now had an image in his head he could never unsee. He should learn to not ask questions of Evan without being ready for the answer.

"You should hear the things that come out of her mouth." Evan continued to swirl the melting ice in his glass.

"No, thank you." He held up his hands, hoping to stop his brother in his tracks.

"Anyway, what really got her fired up was I told her I changed some of the honeymoon plans because they were too expensive. I'm a little short on cash."

Sirens went off in his head. Evan short on cash could be a disastrous thing.

"Have you been to the casinos?" He should stay away from this topic too, but the door had been opened, and he had to jump through in case he had to be prepared.

"Do you think because I'm getting a divorce already and that I told Paris my cash flow is low that I've been sitting at the blackjack table losing my shirt?" Evan poured another whiskey.

Shane put up his hands again. "Easy. I'm not accusing you of anything. I was just wondering if you were having a hard time."

"Why don't you ask it that way instead of assuming I went straight to Atlantic City and blew my entire season's salary?" Evan downed half his drink.

He had asked Evan if he was handling his stress with gambling because Evan had done that very thing before, and Shane had to bail him out then too. Evan had a sizeable salary to spend on bad habits and a gambling problem he wouldn't admit to entirely.

"I'm sorry. I should've asked you if you were stressed out." He hated to admit it, but sometimes players were big babies. He also hated to think about how much he had acted like one while he was playing.

When he became a batting coach, he saw firsthand how every player had demands they wanted their coach to listen to, fix, or applaud. The cycle never ended, and Shane had wondered if he had made the right decision to be a coach, but he loved baseball more than anything. He never wanted to be out of the game.

"Well, I am stressed. Paris is a complete bitch. I slept in my car in the garage the other night because she wouldn't stop shrieking about the curtain or the sofa or whatever the hell it was that had crawled up her panties."

"You can stay with me, if you want." Living with Evan was never easy, but the house echoed with emptiness. He would rather have Maren move in with him, but he couldn't let his brother possibly end up in trouble again.

"Tonight?" Evan's eyes filled with desperation.

"For however long, but definitely tonight. You shouldn't drive." He would help in any way he could. He and Evan only had each other.

"I'm not drunk."

"You are drunk. Sleep it off in one of the bedrooms. In the morning, I'll help you pack some stuff." He took the drink away from Evan.

"That's my house. I don't want to leave it."

"I think you should for now before she hits you with something harder than her palm. At least until the divorce is finalized."

Evan stood and swayed on his feet. "I don't need you to tell me what to do. We aren't kids anymore and you're not the one getting me ready for school. I'm going home and sleeping in my bed in my house."

"Sleep it off here. If you go home, you're only going to have a fight with Paris."

Evan tripped over the chair leg, and Shane caught him before he smacked the concrete.

"Okay. I'll sleep here. But just one night." Evan let out a whiskey burp.

"Gross." He helped his brother to bed, taking off his shoes and putting the blanket over him. Evan was out as soon as his head hit the pillow. "Yeah, just like when we were kids and there wasn't an adult around to tuck you into bed."

He would always have to take care of Evan if he didn't clean up his act. Fatigue ached deep in Shane's muscles. For the first time, he was glad the season was over for him. He needed a break.

He went back outside to clean up the glasses but stopped and grabbed his phone instead. He hadn't spoken to Maren since their little breakfast on her back deck. He had picked up the phone to call her a dozen times but always put it back down.

He hadn't expected her to dislike the ring so much. He had picked that one because it was unique. The store clerk had said the diamond was a radiant cut, just like Maren. She had always been the brightest light in the room, and he wanted her to have something almost as beautiful as she was.

He wasn't settling for Maren the way Evan had put it. He couldn't stop thinking about her. She was in his thoughts all the time and had been since he first laid sights on her during the days leading up to the wedding. That didn't count all the times he had searched her on social just to get a glimpse of her.

He missed her and wanted to hear her voice. He had put her contact information into his favorites list. He hit her button and waited for her to pick up.

"Hey," she said in a husky voice.

A foolish grin burst free on his face, and he shook his head. "Hey, yourself. Is this a bad time?"

"I was about to get in the tub with a good book. What's up?"

He really needed to stop picturing her naked, but she made it hard with that tub comment. He could imagine her sinking into a bunch of bubbles spilling onto the floor. He'd like to be there with her, helping her in and out, washing her back. He was not going to be able to go long without sex if he continued to image making love to her.

"I hadn't eaten and wondered if you want to get a bite."

"Oh. Sorry. I already ate."

He checked his disappointment along with his libido. "Maybe tomorrow night?"

"Maybe."

"I was thinking. We need to announce our engagement and there's a party this weekend. One of the guys from my old team invited me. I thought we could go and flash that ring around." He knew photographers would be there and everyone would have their phones out. Someone would post about it, but he would too. Publicity would also help grow her business.

"We promised Kassidy we'd come to dinner this weekend."

"We could stop by the party after, or they could come with us." Bringing Kassidy and Grant would add to the drama of the night. Grant was a pretty famous singer not all that long ago. He had retired from the limelight and lived a quiet life with Kassidy now, but Grant Hawkins fans were always coming around corners and would be glad to have an in-person greeting.

"Grant isn't much of a party guy. He hates big crowds. How late does the party go?"

So much for his idea of bringing Grant and Kassidy. "Probably all night. We can show up late." As long as they show. He couldn't think of a better opportunity to make a big announcement, one that Barry Solomon was bound to see.

"I don't know if I can stay up all night. I'm usually in my pajamas and on my couch by eight."

"I'll help you stay up."

"Don't you ever get tired?" Her soft laugh brushed against his skin and warmed his heart.

"Even when I do, I push through." He didn't have the time to be tired, but lately the aches and pains in his joints complained louder than ever before. He might not be playing, but the long season and the traveling could still wear him out.

"The trainings of a professional athlete."

"Something like that." His father had drilled into his head that he had to push through all of life's tough times. Stopping to complain or pay too much attention to the things that bothered him would only hold him back. Ironic, since his father had done nothing but complain about his missed opportunity and that had held him back his entire life.

"I'll go to the party, but only for an hour or two. We might as well yank this bandage off and let the whole world see us happy and in love."

Relief washed over him. She was still in the game. She held all the power, and she didn't even know it. Or maybe she did. Either way, he owed her.

"Two hours is a fair deal. So, how about tonight? Can I come over?" He wanted to see her, smell her sweet and subtle scent. He also didn't want to stay in the house any longer and had nowhere else to go.

"Why would you want to come over?"

"So I could see you in the tub."

"Shane..."

"Sorry. Over the top. Evan is here. He's passed out. The walls are closing in on me. If I come over, we could take a walk on the boardwalk."

"A midnight stroll. I wouldn't mind that."

"Two lovers who aren't lovers." That he would like to turn into lovers.

"Did you tell Evan about us?"

"I did and he's happy for us." He would never tell her the truth about Evan and his actual thoughts about Maren and their relationship. His brother had his head on backwards. Shane always hoped Evan would turn his behavior around.

Water sloshed in the background. Maren heaved a deep sigh. "This water is fabulous."

"Are there bubbles?"

"Lots and lots of bubbles. Enough for two."

"You're driving me crazy."

Her laughter burst through the phone. She was teasing him. He liked it and he hated it at the same time.

"You can come over, Shane. I'll find a way to keep you busy, so you don't have to deal with Evan."

"Really?"

"Yes, really. I'll see you in ten minutes. The front door is unlocked." She ended the call.

He tripped over himself, looking for his sneakers. He wrote a quick note to Evan in case he woke in the middle of the night because Shane had no intention of coming back before morning.

He hopped in his car. He'd be there in five.

Chapter Ten

Maren pulled the stopper on the tub and water circled the drain. She had never stepped foot in the bath but couldn't resist teasing Shane a little. Her behavior might not be completely fair. She had agreed willingly to go along with this game of make-believe, and he had offered no sex with no problem. But a part of her was tortured knowing they would never sleep together, and her body wanted him. He could be a little tortured too.

She needed to get dressed again before he arrived and opted for sweatpants and a thin long-sleeve shirt. She debated on makeup but then nixed the idea. She didn't have to impress him.

But she did wait for him on the front porch because the idea of a stroll relaxed her. She didn't want to be cooped up with him in her small house with nothing to distract her thoughts about wanting to kiss him. She wasn't sure when the first thought had popped into her head. Maybe it was when he licked the cannoli cream right off her finger and all her heat ran south. The lust in his eyes still had her panting.

At least if they walked, the fresh air would clear her mind and remind her she and Shane were not right for each other.

Wind had come in off the ocean and dropped the temperature in the night air. She would suggest they walk away from the ocean instead of toward it.

Headlights came down the street and stopped in front of the house next door. Shane unfolded from his sports car. His other car must still be in the shop. Even in the streetlight, the paint glowed. He wore a denim jacket with a white shirt underneath and a pair of baggy jeans. Her mouth dried up.

"Waiting for me outside, huh?" He jogged around the car.

"I thought we could start with that walk." She met him on the sidewalk. The wind picked up again and blew through the thin fabric of her shirt. "It's colder than I thought. Let me just run inside and get a jacket."

"You can wear mine."

She expected him to slide out of his jacket and drape it across her shoulders. The material would smell like him and that would drive her crazy.

"I can get a jacket."

He ignored her and popped the trunk. She seemed to have no choice but to give in and wait to see what he had back there.

He handed her his manager's jacket from the Titans

—the team that had fired him. The material was soft and nylon on the outside but filled with down for warmth on those cold baseball nights on the field in April and October.

"Are you sure? This is like sacred material."

"I'm sure. It's warm, and I won't wear it again. They didn't even ask for it back. I just didn't know what to do with it until now." He helped her on with the coat.

This jacket also smelled like him, rugged and refined. The sleeves came past her hands and the waist hit her at mid-thigh, but she was warm as if she had stepped inside a cabin on a winter day.

"Thank you," she said.

"It looks good on you." He raked his gaze over her.

"It's a little big, but it's doing the job."

"I like you in it."

"Let's walk." She didn't want the conversation going off the rails right from the start and led him away from the beach.

"I thought you wanted to walk on the boardwalk."

"Too windy."

"We don't have to walk at all." He stopped and gripped her arm. His bright eyes filled with need.

"I'm afraid of all of this." She hadn't meant to say that. She didn't know what she was doing here. They were supposed to be faking a relationship, but in the dark and wearing his jacket painted this picture in a sharp reality.

He backed up. "Afraid? Of me? Maren, I would never hurt you. When are you going to believe that? I thought by now you would have forgiven me for a stupid thing I did once when I was a kid."

"I didn't mean you."

"Yes, you did."

They had never discussed what had happened. She had run from the dorm after he punched a hole in the wall and when she had returned, he was gone. He had sent one postcard from the road with the words *I'm sorry* written on it, but they had never spoken again.

"Okay, fine. Maybe I don't know if I can trust you. You've spent years getting angry right in front of millions of people."

"Arguing for my players is my job." He ran a hand over his face.

"Your job is to yell at everyone who disagrees with you? Why is that your job?" Someone looked out their upstairs window at them standing on the sidewalk. She started walking.

Shane hurried after her. "I'm not going to hit anyone. Especially not you. Is that what you're worried about?"

"Your second wife said you hit her." She needed to get everything out in the open. She had read the article about his fight with his ex-wife. The incident had made all the news programs. She didn't know if the story held any truth, though.

"Maren, I would not hit a woman. I can't believe you don't know that about me."

"I don't know you at all." She wanted to know more about the man he had been in their years apart because she was dangerously close to her old feelings.

They passed dark houses on empty streets. Their footsteps against the concrete echoed in the silence between them. Leaves whispered on a breeze. Maren shivered inside Shane's coat.

"I never touched her. I swear."

"What happened between you two then?"

"When my ex and I fought, things got loud. We were never right for each other. She married me for what I could give her. Money. Cars. Access to an elite group of people. Did I get pissed off when I found out she was cheating on me with a guy half my age? You bet. Did I grab the nearest thing to me and slam it into the wall when she said I was lousy in bed and then proceeded to tell me all the sordid details of her new sex life? Yeah, I did. I'm not proud. But I did." Pain flashed in his eyes, but only for a moment. She almost missed it.

"Why are you so angry?" Maren continued to walk, if only to help keep her head clear. Guilt, fear, and warmth for this man warred within her.

"Tell me you understand. Please tell me you don't think I'm some kind of monster because if you do, I'll walk you back to your house and we can end this. I don't want you to be afraid of me."

She was afraid of her feelings, of getting hurt again. "I understand. I do."

He slid his hand into hers and she squeezed, hoping he would know she meant what she said.

"Let's go this way." He tugged on her hand and pointed to the right.

They walked past the old hotel and ended up at the

beach anyway. The moon's rays danced over the water's surface, inviting them closer. The ocean's crash and roar met them as they leaned against the cold, metal railing that kept people off the dunes.

"Can I ask you something?" She should let what she was about to say drift out to sea with the tide, but she couldn't. Even if what they were doing wasn't real, their time together was, and she needed to know every part of him if she was going to get through this.

"Anything." He kept his gaze on the water.

"Did you not have children because of baseball?"

He tossed her a sideways glance and a grimace that even in the dim light of streetlamps she could see was etched with pain.

"Pretty much. I never wanted a family I had to leave behind and when I was just starting out, playing in the minors, it was a tough life. There was always a chance I wouldn't get called up even though I'd been signed. Never having enough money, always being away from home is hard for a wife and kids to deal with. I didn't want to put anyone through that."

She wondered if that anyone had included her. Back when they were in college, she had said she wanted a family. She never hid that from him. If he had always felt the way he does, she understood in a new way why he couldn't give her what she asked for back then.

"Did you have a change of heart?"

He turned to her. "About having a family?"

"Why did you come back to campus that day?" She had wanted to ask that question for almost two decades.

When she saw him, their fight had begun almost immediately. She had never had the chance to find out why he had returned to school. She had often wondered if being on the road, alone had started to wear on him and maybe he had returned to tell her he wanted to try again for a future together, a real future.

"To see you."

"Just to see me?"

"Well, it wasn't to see Phil." Shane smirked out a laugh. "I missed you. Didn't you know that?"

"How could I have known you missed me?"

"My hitting the wall wasn't a clue?" His lips curled up, but he dropped his gaze to the ground and scratched at his jaw. "I hated being away from you so much it affected my playing. I thought if I could see you, hold you, beg you to take me back, I'd get my head on straight. I never imagined you'd be on a date when I showed up. Pretty stupid to think you'd be sitting around waiting. Hell, if I had been Phil, I would've moved in on you too."

She put a hand on his cheek. His face was warm beneath her touch. "I never realized how you were feeling in that moment. I'm sorry."

"You have nothing to be sorry about. I left to play. You were getting on with your life. It wasn't fair of me to push you away and then get mad when you found someone else to be with."

"He and I were just friends."

"I was still jealous. I'm jealous you had a whole life without me. Sometimes, I see friends with their families

138

and think you and I would have had a great family, and I would have a legacy besides baseball."

"You have plenty of people who care for you."

"I have people who want something from me, like my brother. And I have people in my life who affect my career, but I'm not sure who the last person was that really cared about me."

She cared for him, more than she should admit. But in the end this arrangement between them was just a business deal that could change his career. She needed to tread carefully with her bruised and battered heart.

"I don't believe there isn't a soul who cares for you."

"I'm hoping you do." He brushed a hair away from her face.

"I will always care about you."

"I feel the same way about you." Shane linked his hand through hers. His rough skin was warm even in the chilly wind. "Did you want more kids?"

"I did. A house full, believe it or not. But my ex-husband only wanted one. Children were expensive and he didn't want to risk not being able to pay for college." Ironic, since Dave had lost his job and now couldn't pay his alimony. All that planning and worrying and he still ended up where he didn't want to be.

Wind whipped her hair around and chilled her skin. She hunkered into Shane's jacket.

"Let's go back. You're shivering." He wrapped an arm around her shoulder and pulled her close.

"Let's stay another minute. The moon is beautiful on the ocean's surface." And she didn't want the mood between them to end. Once they were back inside her house, the magic of the ocean would return them to their neutral corners.

Shane stood behind her and wrapped his arms around her, resting his chin on her shoulder. "All this touching is strictly for warmth. There is no hidden agenda or meaning behind it. I just need you to block the wind."

"You're like a foot taller than I am. How could I possibly block the wind for you?" She wouldn't send him away, though. She melted into his large body.

"That's why I'm back here squatting. Keep me warm, Maren."

"I don't believe my keeping you warm is in the fake relationship handbook. You should keep me warm." She slipped out of his grip and tried to jump behind him, but his reflexes were still faster than sound.

He caught her wrist and pulled her against him. She bounced off his hard muscles, but he didn't let her fall. Instead, he wrapped his arms around her and held her against him. He pinned her into place with his intense gaze.

"You aren't cold. You're a furnace." She wrapped her arms around his middle and sunk into his heat. She could easily get used to being held by this man night after night. What a scary idea that was because he wasn't offering her a real lifetime. For him, this was just another play in a book of plays that would lead to his dream job. Shane may be a different man than the one who punched a hole in her wall, and he may not be, but one thing was for certain, Shane didn't give his heart away for free.

"It's the company." His bright eyes smoldered, and his lips brushed hers.

She should pull away and run straight back to her house. That would be the sane thing to do. Instead, she stood on her toes and leaned in for his kiss. If she was going to put her foot into this mess she created, then she would go in up to her neck.

He read her as well as any baseball sign out there and cupped her face. He kissed her again, long and hard until they were breathless.

She could blame her decision to kiss him on the moon, the magic of the ocean, or her glutton for punishment.

Or on the fact she wanted him—again.

Chapter Eleven

Maren dreaded walking into Bella Notte. She stood on the sidewalk, a store down from the adorable bakery on the corner, so Mr. D wouldn't see her outside the window. She hung her head, trying to muster the energy to tell him she wouldn't need his services for the rest of the calendar year. Well, except for the twenty-five pink frosted cupcakes with strawberries on top in pink and white gingham holders for a five-year-old's birthday party later today.

She should have called, given him at least twenty-four hours' notice, but every time she picked up her phone, her throat closed. The fact that Mr. D made several dozen yellow cupcakes every morning just in case of a party emergency was something Maren knew well and had taken advantage of.

The day was unseasonably cool for September. A wind traveled west from the ocean raising goose bumps on her skin. The couple seated across the street on a bench gave her strange looks. She must appear bizarre, standing in one place for so long.

Having wasted enough time, Maren took a deep breath and opened the door. A blast of cold air greeted her first. The bakery was empty at this hour. She had arrived after the morning rush on purpose, not wanting anyone overhearing about her recent demise if they didn't already know. Paris's nasty video had served Maren enough humiliation.

The doors into the back swung open. Mr. D glided through with a wide smile that twinkled in his blue eyes. His t-shirt may have once been white, but years or too many washes turned it a dingy gray. His beige cargo pants were stained.

Mr. D was in his seventies, but his forearms were still chorded with muscle even if most of the hair on his head had given up on him decades ago.

From the photos on the wall, anyone could see Mr. D had been a strapping young man when he had arrived in America with wavy dark brown thick hair and that vibrant smile that never faulted. He posed for the camera right in this very bakery when it first opened. The cases were hauled in behind him in the shot. In another, his arms draped around customers and family members. Other photos showed customers enjoying tables full of desserts. Everyone had large smiles. The people in these photos shared a world that Maren watched like an outsider she was, always envious of these Italian roots deeper than a forest of trees. Even though her last name was Russo, her family didn't behave like the stereotypical Italian family. She only had her sisters and her aunt Joanna she rarely ever saw anymore.

"Ah. *Buon Giorno*. It's Miss Maren." Mr. D threw his hands in the air to welcome her. "You're here to talk about the parties, no? *Verrai*. I'll make some espresso. You have biscottis I baked this morning. They're good."

She had no doubt how good his biscotti was. The man never baked a single bad thing. He was a legend in Serenity by the Sea. Tourists came from miles to have a chance to taste the delicious cakes and cookies.

"No espresso today, Mr. D. I have some bad news."

"Bad news? Ah. Bad news. We'll fix it. Sit." He pointed to one of the tables for two.

She did as she was told and dropped into the metal chair. The legs scraped against the pristine white and black floor. Mr. D took the seat opposite her, turning the back of the chair to the wall and stretching his legs out in front of him.

"I don't think you can fix this one."

"Tell me. How can I help?"

She told him about the video and the canceled parties. "I'm sorry. I know you planned on those cakes for business. The brides might still come to you, they'd be fools not to, but they won't be coming through me."

"You don't worry. I don't want their business if you've been fired. We stick together."

"Oh, no, thank you, but you shouldn't turn business away." She had expected him to be annoyed or disappointed in her. She had stood on the sidewalk for twenty minutes trying to find the right way to tell him and he had made her conflict easier for her. His kindness overwhelmed her.

He leaned forward with his forearms on the table. "You are like family. Family is the most important thing. What that woman did... no... not right. You'll get more parties soon. You see."

"I do have a little girl's birthday party this afternoon I need cupcakes for, and I need a cake for Kassidy's baby shower." She tried to plaster a smile on her face but wasn't sure she had managed.

"Ah. Mrs. Klein. Yes, she was in two days ago. Gave me a picture. Said you'd be by too."

"She ordered her own cupcakes after she told me to do it?" Maren didn't know if she should laugh or cry.

"*Si*. Mrs. Klein likes things... how do you say?"

"In her control?"

"I was thinking perfect." Mr. D laughed until his face turned red. She caught the humor like a kite in the wind and laughed along with him. Mr. D was the patriarch of Main Street.

"That she does. Did she come and pick them up too?"

"No. I'll get them." Mr. D pushed out of the chair. "When I come back, you can tell me what kind of cake you want for Kassidy, no?"

"*Si*."

Maren went to the window. Gray clouds had rolled in off the water and might have scared the couple on the bench away. Jemma had requested the birthday party be held outside, but no one controlled the weather. Maren feared Jemma would blame her for the demise of Jemma's plans.

She needed to get a grip. Jemma was not Paris. Or maybe, it was time for Maren to find a new career.

Maren let herself into her house and stripped out of her clothes right in the foyer. She was soaked through from the rain and shivered in her skin. Fall seemed to be in a hurry today to shove summer aside. Jersey's changing seasons could be fickle, warm one day, chilly the next.

She had less than an hour to get ready for dinner at Kassidy's. Making small talk and pretending all evening were the last things she wanted to do.

She would rather put on her favorite sweats, make macaroni and cheese for dinner, curl up under a heavy blanket, and forget about the twenty-five screaming children who were too little to follow many directions, preferred to stick their fingers into the cupcakes and up their noses than to eat neatly with a napkin nearby.

Her head hurt from all the crying and carrying on that children that age did. The best part, if she could call it that, was Jemma's friend Cassie booked Maren for her son's party in October. The event wasn't exactly a celebrity wedding, but it was money, and money was what she needed.

She had no idea what to wear to dinner at Kassidy's that would translate to a big-league party after. Upstairs in her room, she flung open her closet and grabbed the first thing she saw.

She hated every minute of the idea that she would be paraded around like a... well, a trophy. She also hated the way the pink dress gapped at her armpits and tossed it on the bed.

Her entire closet was wrong. How could she have all these clothes and nothing to wear? As soon as she had some money coming in, she would go out and buy herself a decent wardrobe—and a few new bras. When did her boobs begin to sag?

She needed to shake her grumpy mood and sent a text to Bailey. *Can I borrow some clothes for tonight?* Bailey had the best outfits and the two of them were the same size.

To wear here? Just come as you are. Nobody cares.

It's for after. She would have to explain what she wanted the clothes for and should have thought through her request before she sent it. Bailey would have a million questions, none that Maren would want to answer.

With Shane?

Who else? Bailey still hadn't come around to the idea that Maren and Shane were together. She didn't believe Bailey ever would.

He should like you in a garbage bag.

She loved her sister for always having her back. Bailey was a true ride or die. *This is for me. He's not asking. I'm nervous to meet his friends.*

No reason to be. You're gorgeous. I'll be right over.

Before Maren could hang up all the clothes she had

strewn around the room, Bailey barged in. "Maren, where are you?"

"Upstairs."

Bailey pranced into her room with outfits on hangers. She laid out several pieces across the bed before picking up an old red fitted top Maren had for decades. "Yuk. Throw this out. No one would look good in that."

"I liked that top."

"Yeah? Well, it's over." Bailey tossed it on the floor "Okay. Do you want to say hot and sexy or sophisticated?"

"Definitely sophisticated."

"I thought as much. Try this." Bailey held up a black blouse with shear sleeves and a lace see-through patterned front.

"I can't wear that. You'll see my bra." And her middle that will pop over the top of her pants. That top would not happen in this lifetime.

"You wear it without a bra, silly. This panel covers your nipples." Bailey held the shirt in front of herself so Maren could see, but she did not want to see.

"Not happening. I said sophisticated, not hoochy momma." If she had Bailey's firm middle, maybe, but the top just wasn't her. She could never be that daring.

Bailey glanced at the top with a scrunched-up face. "This isn't hoochy. This is bold and sure of yourself. Comfortable in your own skin."

"Still a big fat no."

"Suit yourself. But you'd blow Shane's mind in it and

if I were you, I'd let him get all hot and bothered then tell him he can't have any tonight."

She didn't dare say that Shane wouldn't be getting any—ever. But after that kiss the other night, when his tongue took possession of her mouth with all the skill of the pro he was, she had wanted to rip off his clothes right on the beach. And sex on the sand was never a good idea.

"What else do you have?" She needed to stop thinking about Shane without his clothes on and start thinking about her clothes—on and firmly in place.

"This might be more of what you're looking for." Bailey held up a pair of dark dressy jeans with rolled cuffs and a cream sleeveless turtleneck. "You pair it with this long camel cardigan that has the gold thread sprinkled in. That makes it classier, and you have those cute open-toed gold strappy sandals."

"You think?"

"Put it on. You'll see." Bailey shoved the clothes at her.

The fabrics were soft and smooth against her skin as if they were made for her. She felt like herself and like someone more glamorous at the same time. The pieces weren't unique, but together they gave the image Maren wanted—a woman who knew her mind and what she liked.

"What do you think?" She turned around for Bailey's approval.

Bailey tapped her chin. "The shoes make the whole outfit, but it's missing something." She snapped her fingers. "Earrings."

Bailey pulled the dangling gold leaves from her ears. "Wear these. Just enough shimmer. The gold compliments the cardigan, and you don't need any extra sparkle with that rock on your hand."

She glanced down at the ring. She would never get used to it sitting there. In fact, she had forgotten to take it off before she went to the party earlier. Jemma caught sight of it first thing and Maren had to explain about Shane. Word was out. The whole town would know soon enough. No amount of backing out could happen just yet. When they did decide it was time to end this thing, they would need a plan so she could save some face.

"Did you pick out the ring?" Bailey gathered a few of Maren's things and hung then on hangers.

"Shane did."

"He doesn't know you at all." Bailey shut the closet door with force as if punctuating her statement.

Kassidy had said the same thing. "The ring is beautiful." That was the truth even if she wouldn't have picked it for herself.

"I didn't say it wasn't. In fact, I'd love a stone so big it could be used as a weapon, but not you." Bailey slid it off Maren's hand and placed it on her ring finger. "Looks better on my hand."

Bailey laughed and handed it back.

"I hope you'll find a way to accept Shane. He's a good man and only wants the best for me." She kept her gaze on the ring.

"I don't trust him. I never did."

"You were a kid when we were together, and you only lived with us in the summers."

"Doesn't mean I wasn't right. It's his eyes. They give him away. He's angry or hurt or fearful about something. I just hope he doesn't direct it at you." Bailey hung up another top in the closet.

Maren's words froze on her tongue. Bailey had walked right up to the truth and Maren had never said a word to anyone about the last fight. Maybe some people would think nothing of the fact Shane had hit that wall, but at the time when she was young and naive, he had scared her and frightened was the last thing she ever wanted to feel around Shane.

"Wear your hair down, not in that clip. I still think you should wear the black blouse, but you'll be more comfortable during dinner and dressy enough at this party even if some of the women are wearing short skirts and flashing their hoochy hoo-has."

"Bailey, really?" She needed to get downstairs. Shane would arrive soon, and she didn't want to have him in her bedroom.

"Come on. A party filled with young eligible wealthy athletes? Lots of hoo-has will be on display for the highest bidder." Bailey flipped her curly hair.

Maren shook her head because she could imagine the scene of women wearing next to nothing draped over some of the players, but there were also men who were good and decent who wanted a real relationship with a woman who could support them and their careers and who they could love back.

"I could hook you up."

"Absolutely not in this lifetime. I don't date athletes. They're too stuck on themselves."

She didn't argue because for the most part, Bailey was right. "Thank you for the clothes."

"Don't worry about it. I'll see you at the house. I don't want to be here when Shane shows up."

"Why?"

"Because I want to lecture him and that's not my place. Besides, Kassidy told me to keep my mouth shut." Bailey threw her arms around Maren and hugged. "Love you."

"Love you." She held on for a second longer.

Bailey turned before she went out the door. "Does he set you on fire?"

"Shane?"

"Who else?"

When she was around Shane, the colors were brighter and sounds louder. Her insides warmed even now, knowing he would be there soon to pick her up. Their kiss seemed a lot like fire burning extra hot. "When I'm with him, I don't want to be with anyone else." That had been the truth all those years ago, and somehow, when she wasn't looking, it had become the truth again.

"I'm glad, but if he hurts you, breaks your heart even a little, I'm taking one of his baseball bats right upside his head."

Shane checked his watch for the third time in five minutes. Maren caught him the last time and flashed a pissed look at him. He hoped the smile on his face would soften her glare, but no such luck. She grabbed their dishes and went into the kitchen, leaving him alone at the table. They had been at Kassidy and Grant's for hours. He was ready to hit the road and get to the party. People were waiting for them. But he forced himself to stay in the chair.

"Ready for dessert?" Kassidy stuck her head around the doorway.

"I can't eat another bite." He rubbed his stomach to try and emphasize his point. "The food was great."

Maren floated back into the dining room, holding a round cake on a plate in one hand and a cutting knife in the other. "Have a little taste. It's Mr. D's yellow cake with cannoli filling." She arched her brows.

She tortured him with that cake filling. His mind went straight to the other day when he had licked that cannoli cream off her finger. Her cheeks had flushed pink and, in that moment, he wanted to take her to bed and lick that cream from every inch of her.

"I also have his sugar cookies with sprinkles," Kassidy shouted from the kitchen.

He couldn't sit still any longer and pushed out of the chair. Maren met his gaze, but he saw no sign like the other night. She was still mad about something.

"Can we please go now? It's getting late." He leaned in to whisper so no one else would hear him.

"I don't want to go to the party anymore." She placed the forks around the table without looking at him.

"We have to go. We're announcing our engagement to the public tonight."

"That's not the way I want to do it, at some party. We can have our own engagement party and do it that way."

He hadn't told Maren that some photographers from sports magazines would be at the party. They wanted to get close to Alvin Rogers who not only was hosting this event but just renewed his contract for an obscene amount of money.

Shane wanted to capitalize on the opportunity by showing off Maren and her ring. The photographers as well as some party goers would do the announcing for him. Maybe then this relationship would feel less real, because with each moment they were together the line blurred for him.

He opened his mouth to protest, but his phone buzzed in his pocket. "Hang on a second," he said, pulling out his phone.

He didn't recognize the number on the screen, but he didn't want to take a chance Barry Solomon was calling from a house number and answered.

"Shane Sutherland." He walked out onto the front porch to keep the call private. At this hour, when the streets were quiet, the soundtrack of crashing waves drifted toward him. He took a deep breath of salt air.

"Sutherland, this is Rich Charles from the Warriors." A worn-out voice with a heavy New York accent cut into the quiet.

Rich Charles was the pitching coach with a long winning streak and a longer stick up his ass. "What can I do for you, Coach?"

"For starters, you can stay away from my team." Charles was also a life-time New Yorker from the city with the attitude to prove it.

"Excuse me?"

"Don't play dumb with me, Sutherland. I know Barry Solomon has lost his mind for good this time by offering you the manager's position. He's turned the whole back-office operations on its head by going behind the GM's back to talk to you."

"I don't know what you're referring to." He would have to touch base with his agent to find out where they were in negotiations. Until the Warriors made a public statement about him coming aboard, he wasn't going to comment even though he wanted to shut Rich Charles up.

"Our team doesn't need your losing streak and bad attitude stinking things up and I won't be listening to you when we're on the field. Do everyone a favor and crawl back under your rock."

Rich Charles had a reputation for arguing against the manager's decisions. Charles was stuck in his ways. Shane wouldn't put up with a coach, arguing with him at every turn, making him look bad to the players. Once his contract was signed, he'd be firing Rich Charles.

"You're stepping out of line."

"Out of line? You haven't seen out of line, Sutherland. Do you think you scare me by the way you argue with every ump? You don't. And I promise you this, I won't have your back when you get thrown out of another game like that weasely batting coach on the Titans. I'll be the first one in the GM's office pushing for you to leave."

"That's enough."

"Enough? I'll tell when you've had enough. As long as I'm living and breathing you won't go one day in a Warriors blue. I'm going to fight you being on my team. You're not fit to wear the uniform."

Heat flushed over his body from his gut out. Sweat broke out on his skin.

"Which uniform I wear is none of your business, but when I become the manager what uniform you're wearing will be mine."

Rich Charles belted out a cracked and broken laugh. "You have no say over what I do with this team. The Solomon family will never get rid of me, and they will listen to me. I help win them games."

His hands clenched and his vision blurred. Rich Charles had helped to win plenty of games in his time. He had a gift for understanding the way each player hit. Shane had been on a long losing streak and recently, hadn't understood his players at all.

"Let me make something clear. When I get to that team, you will be finished there if I have to throw you out myself."

Barry Solomon's offer had come out of left field, but Shane had believed it was a real offer. Needed to believe it, but Rich had splintered some of Shane's confidence.

"Let me finish with this. You're gonna call Solomon tomorrow and decline his offer or I'm going to make your life a living hell until you go running and screaming for your momma." Rich Charles ended the call.

Shane stared at his phone. His body shook. Rich Charles wouldn't have the last word. He would put that guy in his place and let him know who would be in charge when he stepped into that locker room. The Warriors would be his team, and he would decide how things were done from now on. He stabbed at his phone screen to call the asshat back.

"Shane?" Someone put a hand on his arm.

He swung around, startled by Maren's appearance. His arm missed her head by an inch.

She jumped back. Horror stretched across her face.

"I'm sorry. I didn't see you there." He lunged toward her, but she backed up further. "Maren, that was an accident. I swear. I was lost in my thoughts. I didn't hear you come outside."

He willed his heart to slow. He had to make her understand.

She blinked at him a few times as if trying to get him into focus. "Okay. It was an accident. Who were you talking to then? You sounded pretty upset."

"I can't talk about it right now. Go back inside. I'll join you in a minute."

"What did you say to me?"

"I said... I didn't mean it like that. If you want to stay outside, then stay outside. But I have to make a call, and you probably won't like the sound of it."

"Figure I won't, because I don't like the sound of your tone with me right now. You know what, take your call in your car or wherever you want, but get off my sister's porch. I'm done with you this evening."

This whole night was rapidly getting out of control. "Please don't be mad at me. This was a work thing, and I just need to set something straight."

She crossed her arms over her chest and glared at him. "A work thing? Let me ask you this. Will responding to this work thing in the state you're in make things better or worse for you with the Warriors?"

Kassidy pushed open the screen door. "Is everything okay out here?"

Maren turned to her sister. "We're fine, Kass. Shane got some bad news at work. We'll be back inside in a second."

"If you're sure." Kassidy arched a brow and rubbed a hand over her belly.

He wasn't sure if he believed Maren either, but he wanted to pull her against him and whisper how thankful he was that she didn't throw him under the bus.

"I'm sure. Just a minute, okay?"

"Okay." Kassidy returned inside.

Maren turned to him. "Please answer my question. If you respond to this work thing with the anger in your eyes, will it help you or not?"

Whatever feelings had swarmed in his veins like angry hornets, had settled down because of her and the way she stood up to him. "I don't know."

"Well, I can guess it will not. Do you want to ruin your chances with the Warriors before you even begin?"

"Maren, I can't let Rich Charles get away with what he said." He needed to establish the hierarchy before he got there or Charles would think he had the last say and he would not, not when it came to Shane's players.

"I don't know who that guy is, and I don't care, but whatever he said, was it true?" She glared at him from across the porch.

"I wish you wouldn't look at me like I stole someone's dog."

A smile tipped her lips, but the weight of it wasn't enough to hold. "Stop acting like a child who can't have his way. You don't have to prove this guy is wrong if what he said about you isn't true."

"What if people believe it anyway?"

"So, let them."

He cleared the space between them and closed his hands over hers. He wanted to touch her, always and she rewarded him with a softness in her gaze that wasn't there before.

"You can't control this person or what he thinks. You're a good manager. Your players respect you. Your team was in a slump recently, and owners don't like to wait those out. That's why they let you go."

"I'm also infamous for fighting with umpires and getting tossed from games." Each year fewer and fewer management teams wanted to work with him because they blamed his losing streak on his hot-head and not the hundreds of other factors that go into a nine-inning game.

His time in the professional league was running out and he couldn't get his hands around it to hold on longer. He had no idea who he would be without baseball in his life. Maren was his last chance.

"True, you do have that reputation. But that doesn't make you a bad man, Shane. It makes you human. Now, let's go inside and have some of Mr. D's delicious cake and cookies."

"Thank you."

"For what?" This time her smile held, and the rest of his anger circled the drain.

"For being you."

She tilted he head back and laughed with a lyrical note in her voice. "You can come up with a better line than that one."

"It's not a line. You're incredible the way you see the world. I want to fight everyone, even when I try not to, and you just walk away. You're helping me let things go."

"Some things are worth fighting for and some just aren't."

He would fight for her, but he didn't think she wanted him to do any such thing. If he had been a smart young man, he would have chased her down that day she ran from him because she was afraid of him and begged her to stay in his life. He might've made better choices with her by his side. Maybe his career wouldn't be hanging by a thin thread right now.

She tugged on his hand. "Let's go inside. I don't want to keep them waiting any longer."

"What about the party at Alvin's house?" He needed

to make an appearance. He had given his friend his word and he wanted to stick to it.

"I want to skip it."

"We can't skip it. I promised we'd be there."

She deflated as if someone had pulled a pin from her back. "Fine. But this isn't the place where we announce our engagement."

"People will notice that ring."

"So, let them. I'm not making any statements, and neither are you."

"You play hard ball."

"You bet your ass, I do."

Chapter Twelve

Maren slid off her engagement ring—fake engagement ring even if it was worth more than she had made in three years combined. If she had to walk inside this party, she would not allow anyone to determine when or how she and Shane announced their engagement.

"Tonight, I'm just your date."

"Maren, please. People will see your—where's your ring?" He stopped short.

"I tucked it into my purse. I'm not going to give anyone inside this mansion a reason to snap photos or spoil our big moment. We decide when we announce us. Not whoever's inside here."

They stood on the street outside his friend's house. Except this was no house Maren had ever visited. A mansion loomed tall above them with columns and a stucco and stone façade. Warm gold light filled every window. She lost count how many windows decorated the front of the house. People dressed in clothes that screamed high-end fashion spilled out the door and all over the magazine worthy lawn like sparkly ornaments.

Shane and she followed the long driveway parked up with cars that must each cost more than Peyton's college education. A heavy beat of a bass drum pounded its way out the door and bounced at their feet.

"Have it your way. I won't say anything about our engagement, but I won't pretend to be happy about your decision." He shook his head.

She had hoped he'd be more agreeable to this, but he wasn't, and she wasn't going to change her mind. He would have to deal with his emotions around this situation. Fake and phony people didn't care about their happiness, made up or otherwise.

They would have a small engagement party in the next week or two with her family and if he insisted, Evan and Paris. They would take some nice photos on the beach, and he could post it on his social media to control some of the frenzy she wanted to avoid.

"This is some party." Maren slipped her hand into his as a peace offering. He didn't pull away. She would take that as a good sign.

"It's a celebration. Alvin just became worth a small fortune. I'll introduce you to him first." He took the wide cement steps two at a time with his long legs. She hurried to keep up in her strappy sandals.

The grand foyer opened into vast living space with the back wall made of windows. People filled these two spaces as well. Their clothes in various colors and patterns stood out against the white backdrop that decorated the inside of the house.

Sterile white washed every inch of the space from the floors to the walls and the sofa. The large man reclining on the white leather also wore white, a stark contrast to his brown skin.

Alvin unfolded his large frame when Shane and Maren approached.

"Coach Sutherland, my man, you came." Alvin shook Shane's hand.

"Congratulations, Alvin. You deserve it."

"Thanks. My agent kicked some serious ass. You should switch. You got screwed by the Titan's general manager. They never should've fired your ass the way they did."

"It's all okay. I'd like you to meet someone. This is Maren."

"Nice to meet you and welcome to my home. Is this man treating you right?" Alvin stuck out a hand for her. She slid her small grip into his larger one.

"It's nice to meet you too, and yes, he's treating me fine." She offered Shane a smile and a wink. He returned a nod, but his put his arm around her. He was doing a good job to make this look real. She hoped she was too.

"Ooh, Coach, she said you were only treating her fine. You'd better up your game, my man." Alvin laughed and slapped Shane on the shoulder.

"I'll work on it." Shane laughed too.

Alvin leaned in close to both of them. She caught a whiff of a very nice cologne. "Your brother and his wife are here too. So far, they're getting along, but if she slaps him again, I'm throwing her ass out."

"Noted. Thanks."

"Make yourselves at home." Alvin turned to a guest who called his name, ending their conversation.

"Do you want a drink?" he asked Maren.

What she wanted was to go home. She might like to plan parties of this size with this kind of crowd, but didn't want to be a guest at one. She preferred standing off to the side of the room, watching

"I'm good. Thanks."

Someone called his name. She glanced over Shane's shoulder to see a tall woman with bleach blonde hair pulled low on her neck. She wore a pink fitted top tucked into tailored black pants that went on forever. The gold necklace around her neck reflected off the lighting. Her perfectly manicured nails waved in their direction. The dome shaped gold ring took up a lot of real estate on her finger.

"Who is that?" Maren bit back the jealousy crawling across her tongue and was shocked by the unexpected emotion. She had no right to stake claim to him. She didn't even want to, at least she hadn't believed she wanted to keep him for herself.

"That's Barry Solomon's ex-wife, Rebecca." Shane waved back.

"Barry Solomon from the Warriors? Your Barry Solomon?"

"The one and only. Come on. I'll introduce you."

Maren gripped Shane's arm, unsure if she wanted to

meet this person. A month ago, she would have jumped at the chance to shake hands with Rebecca Solomon who had money and power and might want to plan a big event. But now, the shattered pieces of her career poked at her skin like a stingray's stinger.

"Why is she here?"

"She runs the team with him. They couldn't stay married, but they are quite the business duo."

The former Mrs. Barry Solomon headed their way. The choice to meet her or not slipped from Maren's hand.

"There's one more thing." Shane turned to her, blocking her view of the statuesque woman only feet from them.

"What's that?"

"She and I slept together."

Before Maren could get a word in, Rebecca Solomon stood before them in all her tall splendor.

Maren gave a glance at the outfit Bailey had helped her pick. She wished now that she had gone with the black lacy thing that showed her nipples.

"Shane Sutherland." The tall woman leaned in and kissed the air beside Shane's cheek.

"Hello, Rebecca. It's nice to see you."

"I'm sorry to hear about what happened with your team." Rebecca kept her gaze on Shane and ignored Maren.

Maren reached for the back of her earring but shoved her hand down.

"Thanks, but we were both ready to part ways. I'm excited for the next chapter of my career."

"That's wonderful. I hope you can rise to Barry's challenge. Oh, my. We're being awfully rude. Who is this lovely woman, standing beside you? I apologize for my impoliteness. I'm Rebecca Solomon." Rebecca stuck out a hand.

She slipped her hand into Rebecca's firm grip. "I'm Maren."

"It's nice to meet you."

"You as well. That's a pretty top." She stifled a groan. Of all the things to say, did she have to start with the woman's top? She could've brought up the Warriors winning streak or an interesting bit of their history.

"Why thank you. I know you don't work in baseball. We would've met by now. What do you do?"

"I... I'm in between jobs now." Her words twisted around her tongue and held it hostage.

Shane's eyes narrowed. "Maren is a party planner."

"I can never be bothered with the details of a party. Shane, there's someone I'd like to introduce you to. You don't mind if I borrow him for a minute, do you, Maren?"

"I'll just be a minute," Shane said.

"Take your time." She stepped away before anyone said another word.

Maren turned down a hallway in hopes of finding a bathroom. She needed a minute to pull herself together away from the crowd of flashy people. Her confidence had gone the way of the tides. How was she ever going to build her business back up if she couldn't say something worthwhile to a woman like Rebecca?

She found a door cracked half-open. By luck, she had stumbled upon the bathroom and pushed at the door.

The room was large for a half-bath, having two sinks instead of the usual one. A small bench covered in black velvet sat against one wall, waiting for an occupant. The white marble covered the floor and climbed the walls to the ceiling.

She plunked her purse on the counter and searched for her lip gloss. She would hide out here for about ten minutes, go find Shane, then try to remember who she was, or she wanted to be anyway.

She pretended to have her act together just as much as she pretended to be engaged to Shane. She had tried to keep a good face during the divorce because she didn't want Dave to think she was desperate for him. She wasn't, but when her ritualistic life had blown up, she still suffered from the fallout.

She had tried to be strong when Kassidy had taken her to their father's house after he died and revealed the secret Maren hadn't known he kept. She had wanted to fall apart in his living room because her father wasn't the man she had believed him to be.

Maren kept telling herself everything would be okay even after Paris ruined her, but booking children's parties hadn't been the dream and now she couldn't find the strength to look Rebecca Solomon in the eye. Nothing in her life appeared the way she thought it would by now.

The door banged against the wall. Maren spun around and groaned. She had forgotten to shut it.

"Sorry. I didn't know anyone was in here. Maren? What are you doing in the bathroom?" Paris glared at her with glassy eyes.

Paris sashayed up to her in a sparkling silver, low cut in the front and high cut up the leg, dress. Only Paris's middle was completely covered and that wasn't saying much. Her eyeshadow matched the silver dress. She held a drink in one hand.

If Maren had to guess, that wasn't drink number one. During the entire time Maren planned her wedding, Paris held a drink in her hand. If it wasn't a mimosa in the morning, then it was something blue at lunch and then two to three glasses of white wine with dinner or after dinner—or both.

"Hello, Paris."

"Evan mentioned you and Shane would be here." Paris gave her the once over. "Cute shoes, but the rest of it...."

"The rest of it what?"

"Were you at a PTA meeting before coming here?" Paris swayed on her skinny heels.

"You look as lovely as usual." Maren ignored her jab. Paris was a pill with a bad aftertaste.

"Oh, this old thing? I wanted to buy something new, but Evan wouldn't let me spend any more money during the house renovation. Where is Shane? Don't tell me you two are fighting." A twinkle passed over Paris's eyes.

Maren might have missed it because of all that silver shadow on her lids.

"I don't typically take him to the bathroom with me."

"Smart girl." Paris raised her glass in toast. "Do you have any ibuprofen? I have a raging headache."

She actually might and considered saying no, but that would make her as bad as Paris. She rummaged through her bag again. Paris stood closer. The smell of sweat and perfume rolled off her.

"Oh, my God. Is that what I think it is?" Paris reached over Maren's shoulder, forcing her to the side, and shoved her hand inside the purse.

Maren lunged for her bag, but Paris blocked her and yanked the engagement ring right out. She held it above her head.

"Is this thing real? Did Shane give it to you?"

Maren refused to answer that question. "Please give me my ring back."

"Oh, no. This is the nicest ring I've seen up close. Is it real?"

"Yes, it's real. So, please give it back because I don't want it accidentally falling into the toilet." She held out her hand. Shane would kill her if his expensive investment went into the sewer. She also planned on selling that thing when their engagement ended.

Paris glanced at the bowl as if considering tossing the ring in there then glanced back to Maren. "Did Shane give it to you?"

"Why does that matter?"

"Because I want to know why you aren't wearing it, if he did."

"Give me back the ring, Paris." Her throat tightened around the words. She had never been in a physical fight with another human, but if she had to, she would start tonight.

Maren's biggest mistake, besides taking off the ring in the first place—she understood that now—was allowing Paris to stand closer to the door.

Paris examined the ring. "It's nicer than mine."

"That's not true. Your ring is spectacular. Every woman wants to have one like it." Paris needed to hear things like other women envied her.

"I can tell yours is better. If I know Shane, he bought you the best quality ring along with the biggest one. Shane asked you to marry him. Evan told me."

Maren still didn't answer. She had wanted to show off her ring during an intimate party she had planned with every detail considered, because someone like Paris would find a way to belittle the small gathering. She did not want a nosey, rich woman who hated everyone, including herself, seeing Maren's ring for the first time in a bathroom.

"I don't know why you're all tight lipped. If I were you, I'd be shouting from the roof that Shane Sutherland was in my bed."

"Paris, please give me my ring." She held out her hand again.

"I'll be honest, I didn't understand why Shane would want to date someone like you. I get why you'd want him, though. I'd date him. He's definitely the better brother of the two, but Shane never glanced my way. Not once."

"Paris, my ring."

Paris ignored her and slid the ring on her middle finger next her own wedding set.

"I'm sorry, Maren. But there's no way I can let Evan get away with giving me an inferior ring." Paris bolted from the bathroom.

Maren tried to catch up, but her sandals slipped on the smooth floor. Paris must have gum on the bottom of her heels because she ran without effort, holding her hand in the air.

"Hey, everyone. Can I have your attention?" Paris shouted into the crowd.

Voices settled around her.

"Shane and Maren are engaged. I have the ring right here because Maren had shoved it in her purse. Can you believe it?" Paris cackled with laughter.

Maren stopped in her tracks. If she tried to get the ring back, she would appear like a fool or a child on the playground who lost her toy to the bully. If she allowed Paris to run out of steam, maybe everyone would go back to what they were doing.

"Hey, Evan. Where is Evan Sutherland?" Paris yelled some more. "Someone go get my good for nothing husband and tell him his brother out shined him again. This ring is spectacular and belongs on my hand and not the hand of the plain woman who's probably marrying Shane for his money."

Everyone held up their phones, snapping pictures or

videoing what played out in front them. Some actual photographers, Maren hadn't noticed before, pointed and clicked at her, Paris and Shane. Their engagement announcement would be all over the networks large and small in hours. She would never get another chance to control how the world found out about them. Once again, she would be the ridiculous wedding planner who made a fool of herself.

Shane reached Paris before anyone else. It appeared no one wanted to get too close, and Maren didn't blame them. He gripped Paris's arm and said something in her ear. She handed the ring to him. Her bottom lip stuck out in a pout. The cameras remained in place, documenting the entire scene.

Evan came through a doorway from the right. His shirt was half undone and his hair was a mess. Red rings rimmed his eyes. He took one look at Paris, turned and walked away.

Paris ran after him.

Shane turned to Maren. His lips moved, as if he tried to tell her something, but someone's flash blinded her. A black and red spot blocked her vision.

She didn't care what Shane had said because she had nothing to say to him.

Instead, she turned and headed for the door, pulling off her sandals as she went.

Chapter Thirteen

M aren carried the grocery bag full of ingredients to make s'mores around the back of Kassidy's house. She had called an emergency session after her engagement to Shane hit the airwaves with the echoing effect of a bomb.

She and her sisters were overdue for an evening of empty calories and a full-on sister bonding session, and she needed one. These nights at Kassidy's firepit were a huge reason why Maren returned to Serenity by the Sea. Nothing topped time with Bailey and Kassidy—when they weren't fighting.

"Oh, good you're here." Kassidy, in over over-sized sweatshirt that accented her baby belly, placed a tray of what looked like iced tea on the table by the roaring fire pit. Flames danced in the air and ash sprinkled back down to the ground.

The air smelled of woodsmoke and heat. She immediately thought of Shane and their ride home from

Alvin's party. She had barely spoken to him the whole way. Anger had burned through her veins over what Paris had done. Shane couldn't control his sister-in-law, but that didn't change the helplessness Maren experienced when dealing with Paris.

"Pregnancy looks good on you."

"Oh, please. I'm a whale. My feet are always swollen, I have the worst indigestion, and the only thing I fit in are Grant's old shirts. But thanks."

"You're wrong. Trust me. Where's Bailey?"

"She's running late. She went up to Main Street for an errand. She didn't say what that errand was." Kassidy eased into the lounge chair and propped up her feet with a sigh.

"Should we wait for her?" She pierced a marshmallow with the wood stick.

"Do you want to hear her complain that we didn't?" Kassidy's eyes twinkled with delight. They both tried to take care of Bailey since she was the baby and several years younger.

"Fair point."

"Do you want to talk about it?"

"Talk about what?" She kept her gaze on the task of poking marshmallows with a stick.

"Maren, I saw the video. Paris Sutherland screaming at her husband that her ring wasn't as nice as yours. All those people pointing and snickering. I also read some of the comments."

Maren had too and wished she hadn't. People behind their keyboards could be ruthless, not thinking they were talking about a living person. Some had said she looked horrible in her outfit. Some had claimed the whole thing was show. Others said Shane was slumming and what happened to his hot wife.

"How did she end up with your ring anyway?" Kassidy asked, pulling Maren away from the memory.

Shane had asked her the same question.

"Honestly, it had happened so fast, I didn't even realize at first. She reached into my purse and yanked the ring out."

"Why was the ring in your purse?"

"The band is too loose. I didn't want to lose it." The lie flowed like water from the river to the sea. She didn't want to admit she had been determined to announce their engagement her way.

If she had allowed Shane to make a statement, taken a few pictures, the whole ordeal would be over. Instead, she was a laughing stock again.

Paris had run to the airways telling her followers that Maren was a gold digger. What hurt the most was Paris wasn't far from the truth. Maren had willingly participated in this stunt to earn a buck.

Kassidy handed her a glass.

"Iced tea?" The drink was cool against her fingers. She placed her hand on her heated cheek. She could blame the fire, but her internal rise in temperature probably had more to do with Shane and the endless stories they weaved.

"Just the way you like it."

"You made this for me?" She made an S in the condensation and then wiped it away. "Why wouldn't I?"

"I don't know. Thank you." She forced a smile and hoped it looked real.

"Maren, are you really happy with Shane?" Kassidy leaned forward.

"Not this again." She put the glass back. "You saw us at dinner. Did I look unhappy?"

"Well, honestly, you kind of did. And you're still not wearing that ring." Kassidy fought her way out of the chair.

"Please don't get up for me. You deserve to sit there and relax."

"Stop telling me to relax. Everyone is telling me to take it easy. I'm pregnant not dying. In a few very short months, there will no taking it easy ever again."

"I'm just saying you should take extra care of yourself while you can, because you're right. Once the baby comes, nothing is the same."

"You want me to take care of myself, but are you doing the same?"

"This is ridiculous. I came here tonight to spend time with my sisters and eat s'mores like we usually do and forget about the party and Paris's constant badgering. But if every time I'm in your company you're going to grill me about marrying Shane, then I won't come anymore. I love Shane, Kass. My feelings for him are real."

She had always loved him and assumed people never got over their first love, but first loves were incapable of lasting.

Now she wondered if her feelings bordered on something more like *always meant to be*. When she was around him, logic and emotion mixed like the marshmallows and chocolate in their s'mores. He wasn't the same man he had been, but she wasn't sure she could trust the man he was now. She wasn't sure she could trust herself to make good decisions.

"Well, I believe you love him. But love and happiness don't necessarily go hand in hand."

"Tell Bailey I'm sorry I missed her, but I think I should go."

"Don't go." Kassidy gripped her hand. "Please stay. I don't want to fight with you."

"Thanks, but I'm tired anyway. I'm going to walk home along the beach. I'll see you tomorrow."

"If you go now, do you want to search for sea glass tomorrow?"

"Maybe." The pleading look in Kassidy's eyes tugged at Maren's insides. Kassidy was only trying to help and keep them connected. Not all that long ago they were more estranged than close.

But Maren couldn't keep up the pretense that everything was okay. She thought she could, by spending time with her sisters tonight, but once Kassidy had started in, all Maren wanted was to go back to her house and pull the covers over her head.

The gate door swung open. Bailey charged through, her hair bouncing behind her. "Guess what?" She bent forward and gulped in air.

"Are you okay?" Maren placed a hand on Bailey's shoulder. Heat rolled off her body.

Bailey nodded. "I ran all the way from Main Street,"

"Why would you do that in those wedges?" Kassidy pointed at Bailey's adorable but not practical shoes.

"The bookstore is closing." Bailey looked between her and Kassidy.

"That had you running?" Maren always loved the bookstore, but it had been there for decades. The owners probably wanted to retire. Someone else would buy it or another store would be in its place by next summer. Everything changed, came to an end. She knew that better than anyone.

"What will Serenity by without a bookstore?" Bailey blew her hair out of her face.

"Like every other small town that lost its bookstore. The residents will have to find the local Barnes & Noble or buy online." Kassidy handed Bailey a glass of tea.

"I don't want to see it gone." Bailey put down the glass and opted for a piece of chocolate. She popped it in her mouth.

"Buy it then," Kassidy said.

"I can't buy it. I have my life coaching business. Maren, you should buy it."

"Me? You're the reader. I wouldn't know the first thing about a bookstore." And no desire to own one.

"Well, I hate that it's going." Bailey flopped into the chair. "What were you two arguing about before I got here?"

"We weren't arguing," Kassidy said.

"I could hear you from the front walk. You're trying to mother Maren about her choice to marry Shane and you're mad because no one will support you. Same old same old. What's the funniest part is Maren is the oldest and it should be her job to mother you, especially since your mother is... well, your mother."

Their mother wasn't much of a prize and neither was Bailey's. Their father had questionable taste in women. Maybe that was why Maren was so screwed up in the relationship department—and in life.

"Maren, stay and have s'mores," Kassidy said.

"Were you leaving? We haven't done this in a month. We're supposed to get together every week." Bailey pouted.

"I'm not feeling up for chocolate and marshmallows tonight."

"Don't let Kassidy's pushy personality get to you tonight. We need time together," Bailey said.

"What about tomorrow? Do you want to look for sea glass?" Kassidy asked again.

"Yes, let's all go." Bailey's smile returned full force as she bounced in her seat.

She wanted to say no. She wasn't much in the mood.

"I'll text you in the morning." She wouldn't commit to anything else.

"Do you and Shane have some fancy event he wants to parade you around at? Is that why you can't commit to an hour at the beach with your sisters?" Kassidy said.

"Why do you hate him so much?" She couldn't imagine what Kassidy would think of him if she knew the real reason they had broken up.

"I don't hate him."

Bailey arched a brow. "Look, I'm not Shane's biggest fan either, but you don't want to let this go, Kass. No one said anything when you ran off to Chicago with what's his name."

"Bear," Kassidy said. "Bear Foster."

"Whatever. You were in love with a guy named after an animal that craps in the woods and had brains the size of walnuts. We didn't judge you." Bailey put another marshmallow in the fire.

"I wish you had. Then I wouldn't have had my heart broken and come home with tail between my legs."

Kassidy had been devastated when Bear dumped her for someone with more education and money. She had been tending bar to go to school and he had said he didn't want to be with someone who served drinks.

"But then you wouldn't have been in the right place to meet Grant and have that baby." Bailey turned her stick with a shrug as if that was the easiest of explanations.

Kassidy opened her mouth but shut it again. Bailey was right. All of Kassidy's hardships had led her to the place she was now, and Maren didn't have to ask her sister to know she wouldn't change a thing as long as she ended up with Grant.

Bailey looked at Maren. "Finally, she shut up because she knows I'm right. Maren, do whatever makes you happy. We don't have to like it or agree. He just can't hurt you. I will come for him."

"Thank you." Maybe Bailey would do nothing at all

because Maren had asked for the pain by reuniting with him, but she liked thinking her sister would.

"I'm not going to keep my mouth shut, Bailey." Kassidy turned to Maren. "He has a temper. You think I don't know what happened when you were in college, but I do. You can't keep a secret in Serenity, and you should know that. I never told you that one of your college friends let it slip because I didn't want you to be embarrassed. He has anger issues, Maren. He might haul off and hit someone during those angry rages. He's been accused of it by his ex-wives. I don't want it to be you this time."

"Stop it, Kassidy. Just stop it." Her voice echoed off the trees. "You don't know him. You never did. You were never interested in me or Shane when we were together. Now that you're in your first successful relationship, you think you have all the answers. Well, you don't. I know what I'm doing. I'm a grown woman who can make up her mind. And I've decided to spend the rest of my life with Shane Sutherland. If you don't like it, you don't have to come to the wedding. In fact, you don't have to come around at all."

She flew from the backyard. She made it past the Topside Community and to the corner of Main Street before bursting into tears. The shops were all closed now, and she was grateful for that. If this had been the heart of summer, a street full of people would see her in hysterics.

Everything was ruined, and she didn't know if she wanted out of this thing with Shane or not. She didn't want to lose her sisters, and she may have.

Her foolish heart had taken control. Maybe it couldn't tell the difference between what was real or fake. Either way, she wanted to be with Shane in spite of Kassidy's worries. That was Maren's biggest problem.

She had left her car back at her sister's and didn't have the energy to return for it. She leaned against the brick building and pulled her phone out of her back pocket. She tapped at the screen until Shane's number rang.

"Hey," he said.

She bit back a wave of fresh tears. "Can you come pick me up?"

Chapter Fourteen

"I was surprised when you called." Shane followed her up the front walk to her house. The breeze had shifted off the ocean, taking a cold bite out of her skin. He wore basketball shorts and a t-shirt, seemingly unaffected by the weather. She wondered what she had interrupted when he came to her rescue.

"I didn't have anyone else to call who might understand what I'm going through and I didn't want to walk all the way home." She had considered it, and maybe that would have been the best choice, but that heart of hers had other ideas.

She had kept quiet for the short ride to her house. He had asked what was wrong, and she had said she'd talk about it later. He had honored her request for silence but held her hand during the ride.

Just his touch had been enough to soothe her that she might tell him what happened with Kassidy. She also mulled around an idea in her head that she wanted to run past him. She wasn't sure how he would feel about it, but she needed to take control of something before she lost her mind.

"I'm glad you called. We haven't really spoken since the night of Alvin's party. I wasn't sure if we were even still an item."

"We've never been an item. Not this time, at least." She unlocked the door and let them inside. "Do you want some wine?" She went into the kitchen, dropping her keys and purse on the table along the way. She would need a little liquid courage to run her idea past him.

"Do you have beer?" He followed her into the kitchen.

"I do not. I can make coffee. If you want to stay a minute, that is." She wanted him to say if for no other reason than to hear what she was about to say, but she wanted him to stay for other reasons too. Right now, she didn't want to be alone. Lately, that was her most prominent emotion. Everywhere she turned she was alone. Having Shane here blurred that loneliness a little.

"Do you want me to stay?" A look of expectancy flashed through his ice blue eyes.

"Having some company is nice. Thank you again for the ride."

He dropped his gaze to the floor and a small smile tugged at his lips. When he looked back at her, his eyes darkened to storm clouds. She didn't think he was angry. Some other emotion had gripped him. She could guess which one.

"Are you ready to talk about what happened?" he said.

She pulled out a coffee mug and held it up. He shook his head.

"Kassidy and I had a big fight." She filled him in on the specifics. Maren never knew Kassidy was wise to the last fight with Shane. She appreciated that her sister kept that secret and when things cooled down, she would say so. But that incident had twisted Kassidy's view of Shane and lying to her wasn't going to make that view any better.

"What are you going to do?" He leaned against the counter.

She grabbed a wine glass and allowed herself a hefty pour. "Besides drink this? I have no idea."

"What about us?"

"We're in it now. The whole world thinks we're engaged thanks to Paris." She sipped the wine and relished the warm trail it left inside her.

"I'm sorry about that."

"You didn't do it. I'm the one who should be sorry. If I had listened to you, we would have controlled the narrative. Now I look like a gold digger, and you look like you've lost your taste in women."

"Hey." He closed the space between them and tilted up her chin with his finger. "Don't talk like that. You're smart, you built a business, raised a child, and have taken every ounce of heat from Paris. Do you know how sexy that is?"

He smelled rugged and strong and just like Shane.

186

She fought the urge to lift onto her toes and place her lips on his.

When she was with Shane, even now when nothing was real, hope shown a little brighter. He always saw the world as his. He believed everything would work out because it always did for him. He was the anointed one.

"We aren't real."

"What I just said is real."

"But we're using each other. That isn't who I am, someone who uses people." She compromised her values to get her child a job and to buy her time to come up with enough money to pay her bills.

"We're helping each other. There's a difference."

She wasn't so sure.

"I want my baseball career to go out on a high. I've worked hard and I earned that right. Maybe I fly off the handle too much, but I'm not the first manager to do it. I won't be the last. If I have to manipulate Barry Solomon a little until my contract is signed and I'm wearing Warriors blue and gray, so be it. He won't get hurt because of it."

"What if we get hurt?"

He brushed her hair away from her shoulder. His touch sent shivers over her skin.

"I will never hurt you." His voice dropped into a sexy whisper.

"You can't make that kind of promise." She held his gaze.

"I made a promise to myself a long time ago that if I ever got the chance to be with you again, I wouldn't hurt you. Let me prove it." He cupped the back of her neck and pulled her close.

His lips brushed hers with a soft touch. Her insides lit up like a beacon from a lighthouse, bringing her home.

She leaned into him, wanting more. He obliged by gripping her waist with his other hand and taking the kiss deeper. Her body remembered before her mind and melted at his touch. No one had ever kissed her the way Shane had—or was.

He eased away before she was ready, but she acquiesced anyway. That kiss seemed real, full of genuine emotion and just for her. Thinking he might be telling her the truth with his actions rattled her insides more than the kiss. Nothing about what happened between them was pretend for her.

"I have a lot to lose," she said.

He rested his forehead on hers. "We both do, and I'm going to do my best to make sure we both walk away from this with what we want."

She wanted him to kiss her again and could stay in his arms all night, even standing in the kitchen, but she needed to talk to him.

"Shane, I think we need to keep to the plan, and I have a way to help us."

He ran his thumb over her still throbbing bottom lip. "I want to hear this plan of yours, but know that kiss wasn't pretend, and I'm pretty sure it wasn't for you either or you're the best damn actress on the planet. No one has kissed me like that. Not either one of my wives and certainly not Rebecca Solomon."

"Are you saying you have real feelings for me?" At least her kissing had edged out the two younger models and the woman who half-owned a baseball team. She supposed money and looks didn't equate to good kisser.

"How could I not?"

"I don't know. Because we were supposed to pretend." She went into the dining room to give herself some space.

He held his palms up and shrugged. "Looks like I didn't follow the rules."

"Can we just get to the point where you contract is signed, and I pay you back and then we can talk about real feelings?" She wasn't ready to admit to anything yet. Saying out loud that her feelings for him were more than make-believe could end up snapping her in two.

"Can I kiss you like that again until that time?"

"You're impossible. You know that?" She fought the urge to smile because he would take that little gesture as a win. Not that she didn't want to kiss him, because she did.

"So I've been told." He came around the breakfast bar and stood before her. "Tell me this idea of yours and which part of the plan it pertains to; the part where we're a couple or the part where you're redeeming my image. Hopefully, both."

"Come with me to a birthday party this weekend." She wished she had thought of this sooner, but they weren't too far behind the eight ball. Shane's contract wasn't signed yet and she hadn't earned a fraction of the money she needed to pay him.

"Who's birthday?"

"Her name is Jordan and she's turning eight."

"You want me to go to an eight-year-old's birthday party? Doesn't that make me look like some kind of weirdo?" He scrunched up his adorable face which made his ears stick out further.

"I want you to come with me. I'm planning her party. She wants a baseball theme. You would be the perfect addition. We can take pictures of you tossing the ball with the kids. Lots of smiling, happy people. Maybe a few shots with the parents. It will go far for your image." And she would finally take control of some of the narrative that had become her life.

If she can show others that he's not an angry man, but a man with a soft side, then maybe her sisters will believe the image too.

He blew out a long breath. "You really think that will work?"

"I do. I have some other ideas too. Will you do it? Will you come with me?"

"Will you wear the ring?"

She glanced down at her empty fingers. "Yes. I will pretend to be the future Mrs. Sutherland for all to see if you'll show up at this party and act like it's the best thing you've ever done."

He gripped her around the waist and pulled her close. "Second best to kissing you."

And he kissed her again.

Chapter Fifteen

R ain fell from the sky in a constant mist. Clouds as gray as a naval destroyer hung low as if to say they were in town and not leaving. Ocean waves slammed against the sand in protest of the bad weather.

Shane stood on the front lawn of the Tepper's house and tossed a ball with ten eight-year-olds. Maren's insides bloomed as she snapped picture after picture. He had not protested at all about the damp weather or having to be outside with kids.

The cold had seeped into her bones. She didn't believe she'd ever be warm again but tried to follow Shane's lead. He had played in the rain his entire life. A little mist wasn't going to set him off. The weather had set off Whitney Tepper and all her plans for her child's big day.

As Maren suspected, his appearance at this child's birthday went over well. His presence allowed Whitney to save face with the adults who were impressed. The kids were in awe of Shane Sutherland. The afternoon should have been an ego boost for him too.

He had never said, and he wouldn't, but she knew what getting fired had done to that very delicate ego. Even though he now had the opportunity to play with his dream team, his agent hadn't managed to get the contract signed yet. She hoped the posts about today would speed up the negotiations for his sake and hers.

That kiss the other night had swept over her and shaken her to the core. She had wanted him to press his lips other places and had to control herself from saying so or they would've ended up in her bed.

She needed to stay focused. Once today's photos hit his social account, she would send a few to Kassidy and Bailey. Maren hadn't spoken to her sisters all week. These photos could break the ice a little.

The Teppers hired a professional photographer to take some pictures of the day as well. The short man with glossy black hair had run around after the kids until he was out of breath.

"Come on in for cupcakes." Whitney Tepper leaned over the porch railing and rang a school bell.

Whitney wore designer cropped jeans with the knees cut out. She probably paid extra for those holes. Her sea foam green ribbed sweater draped over her torso, but the topper of the whole outfit were the white dress loafers. Whitney looked like she belonged on a fashion magazine for chic moms.

Maren tried not to roll her eyes at the bell. If it wasn't

for women like Whitney with highlights that were good enough to pass as natural and who thought their children should have elaborate birthday parties, Maren would not have made enough money to make a payment to Shane. She didn't want this loan hanging over her head longer than it had to be there.

The children ran to the porch, screaming for sugary treats and forgetting about Shane and baseball. Whitney ushered everyone inside. Maren should join them because it was her job to coordinate the event, but Whitney also enjoyed being in charge. Maren wasn't going to argue.

"Maren, let's take some shots of you and Shane while Miss Thing hands out her sugar in a paper cup to the little munchkins. You can use them as engagement photos, and I can photograph something other than children rolling around in the mud." Gerald waved his hand in the air as if conducting an orchestra.

"I really should get inside." She wasn't dressed for engagement photos. She had even put on Shane's huge baseball jacket again to ward off the cold, and the damp air wreaked havoc on her hair. Today's goal was shots of Shane. Not her.

Shane slid beside her. "Just a couple. You look adorable in my jacket and I'm tired of entertaining the younger crowd."

She glanced toward the front door already closed against them and the weather. One or two might not hurt.

"Face each other. Shane pull her closer. Can you dip her like you're about to kiss her? Great. Now give her a look like you're ready to ravish her. Like that. Hold it." Gerald put his camera down.

"Maren, doll, can you relax? You look like you'd rather die than have that gorgeous hunk of a man holding you."

"Sorry."

"Don't be sorry to me. I'm not the one in the photo."

Gerald took a few more photos before Whitney popped back out on the porch. "Maren, I need some help inside please. Gerard, you had better not charge me for those pictures of Maren and Shane. I'm not paying for the help to have a personal photo shoot."

"Hey, now, that isn't fair. I asked her to take pictures with me." Shane stepped in front of her.

"Shane." She hissed his name between her lips, but Shane either didn't hear her or ignored her.

"Shane, that's very kind of you, but this is an important day for Jordan and her friends. Maren is here to work, unlike you. You can use Gerard as long as you'd like."

"Gee, thanks. Go ahead and parcel me out." Gerard raised his thick eyebrows. Whitney didn't acknowledge his sarcastic dig.

Maren tried not to laugh.

"I'm only here because of Maren," Shane said.

"I don't care that you two are engaged. I hired Maren. She needs to perform her duties."

"I think this arrangement is over," Shane said.

Maren gripped his arm and pulled him back. "Whitney, I'll be right inside. If you can give me just a second with Shane."

"You're in for it now," Gerard said to Shane. "Maren, gorgeous, I'll see you inside. But hurry. Those munchkins might eat me alive."

"Why did you stop me?" Shane said after Gerard closed the front door.

She was tired of standing in the mist and shivering in her clothes. She wanted this day to be over with, but she needed to get sone thing clear first.

"I appreciate you trying to stand up for me, but this is my livelihood and when you're gone from my life, I will still need to make a living. Women like Whitney know other people who have too much money in their wallets. I can't have you going all Shane Sutherland on her. Got it?"

"I didn't like the way she spoke to you. She had no right."

"She didn't. But we're not all you. You snap your fingers and people jump. You're the coach, the manager, the man who decides if a dream goes up in flames. I'm just a woman who's starting over again for the third time and I need this gig."

He placed a warm hand on her cheek. "You're more than that. People treat you the way you let them treat you."

"None of this matters, anyway. Today was about changing your image and I think we did that. I'll post these pictures on your account later. I need to get inside. Are you staying?"

He glanced at the door then back at her. "I've done all I can do here."

"Barry Solomon is going to see your pictures and sign your deal. You'll see."

"I hope so." He placed a kiss on her lips. "Whitney is watching out the window. Go inside. I'll talk to you later."

"Don't forget tomorrow I have another idea for your image. Be at my house in the morning."

"Are you going to tell me what that idea is?"

"Not on your life. You might not show up."

"I'll be there. It can't be any worse than playing with a bunch of kids."

"You loved playing with those kids. Don't deny it."

"I did. Thank you for inviting me and giving me a chance to remember why I loved baseball so much. I think I forget sometimes." He crossed the street to his car. She waited until he slipped inside before turning toward the house. Whitney stood at the window, arms crossed over her chest and a scowl slapped across her face.

Maren brushed her tongue over the hint of Shane's taste still staining her lips. She had meant what she said about needing this gig, but maybe Shane was right too about how she allowed people to treat her. She pulled his jacket tighter and went inside.

The kids were ready for their craft and Gerard needed saving. But she needed to remember she was more than a place for someone like Whitney to wipe her fancy shoes.

Chapter Sixteen

"Why are we going to the University?" Shane navigated around the cars on Route 35. The traffic was heavy for the early morning, but he shouldn't expect anything less. Monmouth County was the home to beach towns and a straight shot to New York City, making it a very desirable place to live.

Maren turned to him with a smile. She wore a striped top and fitted dark blue pants that showed off her sexy ankles. He had to force his gaze back on the road and not on the way the material hugged her thighs.

"You'll see. It's a surprise."

"Is it another birthday party?" He hit his blinker and turned onto Deal Road.

Maren had pulled off a great party in a short amount of time, not that he knew anything about kids' parties, but the birthday girl and her friends were entertained the whole time he was there. Maren had found baseball decorations and used the blue and gray color scheme of The Warriors for balloons and plates and things like that. The adults seemed content and were happy to shake his hand and ask for photos and autographs.

Whitney Tepper needed to know how lucky she was to have hired Maren. That was why he had tried to defend her. He hadn't meant to cause trouble or get Maren annoyed with him.

"No parties. For now. When we get there, park near the new sports center."

"What did you do?" He hadn't spoken to Dillon Lynch, the athletic director, since he had called to get Peyton her job. As far as he knew, Peyton was doing well and none the wiser about his paying her tuition for the semester. He wanted to keep it that way. Maren already didn't like being indebted to him and reminded him when she had given him her first loan payment.

He had shoved that check in drawer. He had no intention of taking her money.

"I didn't do anything. Well... I did a little something. I made a couple of calls. I hope you don't mind. The team is waiting to practice with you."

"What?" He almost veered off the road and onto someone's lawn.

"I spoke with the athletic director. Dillon Lynch."

"I know Dillon."

"You do? Great. I told him you need a photo opportunity for social media. I said I was your new PR person." She practically bounced in the seat.

"Did you tell him you're also my fiancé?"

"Fake fiancé. But I didn't have to say anything. When he heard my name, he guessed. He's been following you on your socials."

Of course, he was. "Maren, I can't practice with the team. It's not my place. I don't know the players. I don't want anyone getting injured because of me."

"Hate to break it to you, hot stuff, but Dillon disagrees. He said the team would be thrilled. You don't have to do it for long. Just to get some more footage. A few videos and still shots. An hour tops."

Shane would have to remind Dillon about their little secret, if he could get Dillon away from Maren long enough.

He turned onto the college's west parking lot for the athletics building, stadium and student center. She had an ability to see the big picture and make the situation better. She did that for her parties and now she did it for him. She was good, and he was grateful.

"Thank you for setting this up. I never thought to call in a favor from a friend." He kept his gaze straight ahead when he said that. He had called in a huge favor to this very friend and he didn't want Maren to know about it.

"You're doing them the favor. There's a spot." She pointed ahead. "Oh, and two more things."

"What's that?" At this point he would agree to anything.

"We're having lunch with Peyton. She's been asking to meet you. I couldn't hold her off any longer. I think we should also ask Dillon, and Gerard is coming to take your photos."

He put the car in park and turned to her. "You're not taking the shots?"

"Nope. Gerard is great. He's going to take those action photos I could never get with my phone." She slipped out of the car before he could say another word.

He hurried to catch up and slid his hand into hers before they reached the building. She didn't pull away as Dillon crossed the lawn and met them.

"Sutherland, you ready to step up to the plate?" Dillon said.

"Bring it on."

"That's a wrap, people. Let's get out of here." Gerard waved his arm in the air. He turned to Maren. "I don't think I can look at these young baseball players another second. Their bodies slick with sweat are perfect, but I'm so old now I can't relate to a thing they're saying."

"I get that," Maren said. She didn't understand their slang or pop culture references. She would have to ask Peyton to fill her in with the latest.

The players ran off the field. A couple of the young men stopped to shake Shane's hand and say a few words. His smile had stayed plastered in place the entire hour he stood on that field and coached.

The team had listened and taken his suggestions. Some of the players faces were wrapped in awe the entire time. They had grown up watching Shane and now he was standing on their field giving them advice. In addition to Gerard's photos and videos, the boys had taken some of their own. She was certain many would make their way to social media. If this morning didn't help Shane's image, she wasn't sure what would.

"Did you get some good shots?" She turned back to Gerard.

"Sweetheart, is that a real question?" Gerard packed his fancy camera into its bag.

A laugh escaped through her nose. "Sorry. I forgot who I was talking to."

"I'll get them to you later today. When are you getting back on the wedding scene?" He flung his bag over his shoulder and arched a perfectly shaped brow.

"I'm not sure. I haven't been able to book any weddings lately." She had tried to email a few of the brides who had canceled on her, but they had all replied with a big fat no.

"When you do, I'd like to tag along if that works for you. And if a bride comes my way, I'll recommend you."

"Thank you. I really appreciate that. And if a bride decides to trust me again, you will be the first photographer I call." She would only call Gerard. Even the photographers she had worked with in the past had snubbed her after Paris' viral video. No one wanted to be near Maren and possibly catch her disease.

"If those brides aren't smart enough to know what they have with you, it's their loss. You're a smart lady. You'll come back from Paris' nasty borage."

"I hope you're right." Only time would tell. At least she had a couple more birthday parties lined up and she had Kassidy's shower if her sister was still speaking to her.

"I'm starving. Lunch?"

"Join us. Shane and I are having lunch with Dillon and my daughter Peyton." Maren checked her phone. Peyton had sent a text saying she was on the way but hadn't arrived yet.

"We're not eating in the Student Center, are we?"

"Does something on the Long Branch boardwalk work?"

"Better. I'll meet you there. I need to make a stop first." Gerard sauntered off.

Shane and Dillon joined her by the backstop.

"So, Maren, what do you think of your man?" Dillon tipped his chin in Shane's direction.

"I think he's very good at what he does." She met his gaze. His ice blue eyes warmed over.

"I tend to agree. He's a good man. Way more decent than anyone gives him credit for." Dillon gripped Shane's shoulder and gave him a little shake.

"Okay, Dillon, you can stop laying it on thick. She already said yes." Shane glanced at her again. Heat passed between them.

"No, man. I mean it. Not everyone is a stand-up guy like you. Paying for Peyton's—" Dillon's eyes went wide.

"Paying for Peyton's what?" She glanced between the two men.

"Nothing," Shane shot a look at Dillon. "Dillon doesn't know what he's talking about."

"I think he might. What did you pay for, Shane?" She wasn't going to be so easily convinced. She knew Shane well enough to read his facial expressions.

"Just tell her, man. It's a good thing what you did."

Shane looked at the ground then up at her. His lips thinned out. "I paid for Peyton's tuition for the semester. Dillon didn't have a job for her work study program."

"You did what?"

"I paid for—"

"I heard you. How could you?" Any warmth in her veins turned to water.

"I'm going to take a rain check on lunch and give you two a minute. Thanks again, Shane. The team really enjoyed having you. I wish I had thought of bringing you by myself. Maren, you're terrific." Dillon jogged off the field toward the building.

She couldn't stand still any longer. The rush of confused emotions propelled her forward. Her feet pounded the ground and sent vibrations up to her teeth. Shane hurried after her, and with those long legs caught up to her seconds.

"Please let me explain."

"What's to explain? You lied to me about the work study job." She halted in her tracks.

"Does Peyton know?" Where was she, anyhow?

"Dillon wasn't going to say anything to her, but with that big mouth of his I'm not sure."

Peyton hadn't mentioned anything. Maren suspected

if Peyton had found out, she would've told. Maren weaved through the cars in the parking lot. Shane followed.

"You needed a way for Peyton to stay in school. I had a way. She still has the job. She's meeting her responsibilities."

"But now I owe you." She stopped again by Shane's car. This whole thing was hard enough with her owing him money for the taxes. Most of the time she could forget about the loan hanging over her head while they played house together, but at the end of the day theirs was a business relationship. Nothing more. She didn't want to have to pay him back for Peyton's tuition too.

If she was pretending to be anyone else's life-partner, she could get through it, but this was Shane and each and every day she was with him made the inevitable end that much harder.

Her feelings for this man had never gone away. She had only pushed them to the side, but not far enough. Standing before him, she wanted to throw her arms around his neck and thank him for the kind gesture. If she didn't love him before, she would have reason to now. Loving him wasn't going to do her any good. She couldn't trust this thing between them.

"You don't owe me anything. I called Dillon because I could."

"You called Dillon because you wanted me to save your image." Nothing in her life was real. She didn't have enough of her own money to call her bank account real. What should be the most important relationship in anyone's life was fake for her. Her business wasn't real any longer either—if it ever was.

"I called him because I wanted to help your daughter. I would've made that call even if we didn't have this strange arrangement. I care about you. Can't you see that?"

"Would you have called me if you hadn't crashed your car outside of town?"

He opened his mouth but shut it without answering. He leaned against the hood of the car and crossed his ankles.

"I didn't think so. What you care about is managing The Warriors. What you care about is your image. I understand that. I do. I care about keeping my home, my daughter in school, and maybe finally at this late stage of my life, carving out a career for myself. Something that is truly mine. For real. Something I can put my hands around." She didn't blame Shane for approaching her with this idea to pretend to be engaged. She may have done the very same thing. But when he walked away, she wanted something left for her. Because she was ready to say goodbye to love forever.

"Those things do matter to me. But I also care about you. Maybe the circumstances that led us together were unplanned at best and bizarre at worst, but my feelings for you are real. I've never stopped loving you."

"Oh, please don't say that. The idea hurts too much. You off living your life all these years and still having feelings for me. The thought is too much to bear." Because then she would have to think about the wasted time, the time they could've been together.

"What about you? Are you saying you don't have any real feelings for me?" He pushed away from the car and stood inches from her.

She could tell him the truth. Or she could tell him what he needed to hear.

She wasn't sure which one was which.

Chapter Seventeen

Shane stood on the second-floor balcony of his rental and shoved his phone in his pocket. The long day had leaked out of the sky, and evening spilled into its place. The rain had drifted off to sea. Now stars dotted their inky backdrop accompanied by the soundtrack of crashing waves. Salt seasoned the air, and he sucked in a large gulp.

His social media account blew up with positive comments about him tossing a ball around with the kids from the birthday party and the players from the university.

Maren had been right about all of it. He wished Barry Solomon would call and tell him when to show up for work. As far as Shane's agent knew, the contract was moving from desk to desk with no end in sight.

From his vantage point, he could see the ocean, but not the beach. If the house was for sale, it would be priced in the millions and if it were on the market, maybe he would buy it.

With a view like this, sunrises in the morning, the moon's glow on the water at night, the house was worth every penny. Maren belonged in a house with this much to offer, an open floor plan with an up-to-date kitchen and large family room right off it instead of that strange set-up where her large eating area and small kitchen were pretty much the same room, and the living space divided from it by the foyer.

But she would never take this house if it came from him. She would rather live in her car than take what could be misunderstood as charity.

He had wanted to shake Dillon when he spilled about Peyton's tuition. Shane had insisted Maren didn't have to pay him back.

Instead of answering his question about whether or not her feelings for him were real, she had transferred to him a hundred-dollar payment. As soon as he could, he'd give that money back or give it to Peyton. He didn't want her damn money. He wanted her hands on his body and her lying beneath him in his bed. Every single day.

Shane went back inside and downstairs to the empty living room and flicked on the television. A game had to be on one of these channels. He needed something to get Maren and the lack of a signed contract off his mind.

His phone buzzed in his pocket. He hoped for a call from Maren, but it was a number he didn't often see. He hesitated unsure of why Timothy Stone, the CEO of TS

Watches, would be calling him now. His sponsorship with them ended when he got fired.

"Sutherland."

"Hello, Shane. It's Timothy Stone. Did I catch you a bad time?" For all his smarts, Timothy Stone didn't realize his name came up when he called.

"Not at all. What can I do for you?"

Stone was the third generation to run TS Watches. His grandfather had started out crafting watch faces before the war. Stone's father, Timothy Stone the second, took what his father had created and made an empire on deluxe watches. The Stones were a right-winged, conservative family with very traditional values. They had built their company on those values and were proud of it.

"I was sorry to hear the Titans let you go."

"It's business." Losing his job stung just the same. The Titans hadn't focused on what he had brought to the team or how hard he had worked to get the team performing their best. Management needed someone to blame when a team lost, and Shane had given them more than enough reasons. Being the manager was reason enough, but his hot head had only put the nail in his proverbial coffin.

He would be glad to make the announcement about his new contract with The Warriors and stick his middle finger up at his old management. He'd also like to get involved with the signing of some new players so he could have a say as to who would be on his field, but he might not be there in time.

"I'm calling with something personal."

He couldn't imagine what that could be and wasn't sure he wanted to know.

"I'm not sure I can help."

"I believe you can. My youngest, Dakota, is getting married. She wants a beach wedding in New Jersey. For the love of me, I can't figure out why, but I learned a long time ago not to argue with my daughters or my wife." Stone snorted a chuckle.

Shane had never really learned the art of not arguing with his wives. But for some reason, one he didn't want to poke too hard, he never wanted to fight with Maren. He hated the idea of her being mad at him, and she was pissed about his paying for Peyton's school.

"Anyway, my wife, Irene, you remember her, saw your recent post on social media playing ball at that birthday party. She's always been a fan of yours and thought it was a fit that your fiancé is a wedding planner in the very place our Dakota wants to get married. She also thinks you were unfairly judged by the Titans. What I'm trying to say is, we'd like to hire her, if she's available. And if she isn't, ask her what price she needs to become available. Dakota and Irene will be impossible to live with if I can't make this happen. You understand."

Shane had better understand, which he did. Timothy wanted to keep his family happy, and Shane now had a chance to make good on the last part of the deal with Maren. If a wedding for Dakota Stone went well, and it would, it had to, Maren would be booked for a decade.

Then she could stop being pissed and maybe kiss him again.

"I don't know her schedule, but I can have her call you." He might be desperate for this union, but he couldn't show it.

"Have her call Irene tomorrow. We're on our way out at the moment. Irene will conference Dakota in. The three women can talk lace, flowers, and how to spend my money." Stone had himself a good laugh at that one. "Do you have a pen? I'll give you Irene's number."

"I'm ready." What he had was his Notes app, but he doubted Timothy used his phone for anything except calls. Shane didn't care if Stone wrote with a quill. As long as his money was green and he wanted Maren to throw it around, he would write Irene's number in blood.

They said their goodbyes. Shane wanted to tell Maren the good news in person so he could see her face when reality sunk in. He was going to swing for the fences with this one.

His phone buzzed in his hand. Barry Solomon's name scrolled across the screen. Shane accepted the call.

"Shane Sutherland."

"Shane, my boy. Barry Solomon here."

"Hey, Barry. How's it going?"

"Looks like it's going well for you. I've seen those videos of you recently. Playing ball with a bunch of elementary school girls and helping out those young men. You've shown a responsible side we haven't witnessed from you lately. Brilliant. Your fiancé has turned you around. You're smart to hold onto her."

"Lucky is what I am." His words were complete truth.

"I have your contract on my desk. You'll have it signed and back to your agent in a few days. After that, we'll schedule some meetings and get you up to speed. We have games to win next season. I hope you're ready."

More ready than he had ever been.

Maren climbed the steps from the sand to the boardwalk with the single piece of sea glass. She had walked the surf for an hour, back and forth, as the sun left the sky and the lights from the boardwalk turned on their warm glow. She found only two other pieces. Those pieces weren't fully smoothed and smokey the way sea glass should be. She had tossed them back into the ocean so it could work its magic and some lucky person years from now, on another shore, would find them. Luck hadn't been on her side lately.

Sea glass made her think of her sisters. She missed them. They hadn't spoken since their last argument and their absence ate at Maren's insides. She needed to come clean about this arrangement with Shane. She would swear them to secrecy, and he would have to understand. She couldn't continue this lie without having them by her side because she would be all alone when he left. At least by telling the truth to Kassidy and Bailey, they would give her their shoulders to lean on while her heart broke.

She sent a group text to them and included some pictures. The first one was of her, Peyton, Shane and Gerard at lunch. Peyton had shown up in the parking lot at school and gave her an excuse to avoid Shane's questions about the realness of Maren's feelings. Lunch had been tense, but the waiter had insisted on taking their picture and everyone at least looked as if they had a good time. Gerard had bristled, but in the end had caved and had the largest smile of all of them.

Maren also included one of Shane playing catch from Jordan's birthday party to prove he was a good guy and then finally her lonely piece of sea glass with the caption *not as good at finding as you.* She followed that with *I'm sorry.*

Bailey responded with a heart emoji. Kassidy didn't respond at all. With a weight in her soul and heaving sigh, Maren shoved her phone in her back pocket. Time to head home to her empty house.

She rinsed her feet under the public faucet designed for exactly that task. She wanted to curl up on the couch and watch a good movie. Lately, that was all she had the energy for. She used to be able to stay up late and work on one project or another, but now she was no longer willing to dig deep enough to muster the effort.

She headed down Main Street. Most of the stores were shut for the night. With the summer crowd gone, it made little sense to keep businesses open past six. But the bookstore still had a light on, and she peered in the window.

Bailey spoke with a man behind the counter. Her arms moved about as if she were conducting an orchestra. The man, maybe around Maren's age with some gray salting his hair, beamed at her sister.

Bailey responded with her hands on her hips and a turn on her heel. She charged for the door. Maren had to jump out of the way to avoid being hit.

"Oh. What are you doing here?" Bailey came up short.

"I was walking home and saw you in the window. What was that all about?"

Bailey looked over her shoulder and back at Maren. "That man is so frustrating. He's the owner's grandson and he's determined to sell this wonderful store. He claims no one reads books and if they do they buy them online."

"The online part is true."

"I don't care. If we all roll over and play dead, then the major corporations win." Bailey glanced over her shoulder again at the store. The owner paid them no attention and Bailey snarled.

Maren admired Bailey's determination to make the world a better place. Maren had always been so busy trying to keep her head above water she sometimes struggled to find the strength to contribute in a larger way.

"What are you going to do?"

"I don't know yet. But there has to be something. Anyway, where were you?" Bailey gave her the once over. "You just sent me a text."

"Down at the beach looking for sea glass."

"Got it. Do you want to keep walking? I want to move away from the store."

They walked a little but stopped again as they neared Kassidy's street.

"This is where we part ways," Maren said.

"Do you want to come over? We can have s'mores. I need a chocolate fix after dealing with Sterling Brillinger." The crease between Bailey's brows deepened.

"Is that the bookstore owner's name?" If she thought about it, he did kind of look like someone with that kind of name.

"Stuffy, right? Just like him. So, s'mores?"

"I don't think Kassidy wants me over." She checked her phone again. Still no text from Kassidy.

"She'll get over it. Come over."

Maren debated on telling Bailey the truth. She would be betraying Shane if she did. He had held up his end of the bargain as much as he could. He kept Peyton in school and even though he had hidden his involvement from her, Peyton was thriving at college. Maren had Shane to thank for that. He had graciously loaned her the thousands of dollars to pay her property taxes. She would need years to pay him back and he hadn't complained.

But she was alone and tired.

"I think I'll pass. I don't want to discuss Shane again. When she's ready to accept that he and I are getting married, then I'll come back."

"Can I ask you something?" Bailey picked at her cuticles.

"Not if it's about Shane."

"Did he ever hit you?" Bailey dropped her hands to her hips and held Maren's gaze.

The whole time they had been together these weeks; he hadn't raised his voice or had a fight with anyone. She wasn't sure if her sisters judged him by who he was today or who he had been.

After they had broken up last time, she had sought information about abusive relationships. Shane had never tried to control her. He never tried to cut her off from her friends or family. He never judged her or invaded her privacy. When he had hit that wall, he had been a young man dealing with his own demons in a way that hadn't served him.

Everyone deserved a chance to be judged by who they were in the present moment and not by the mistakes they had made in the past. She chose to believe him when he said he had never raised a hand to either of his wives. He was gentle and kind. When she was with him, she was safe.

"I'm going to head home. I'll see you soon." She pulled Bailey into a hug and inhaled her sweet smell.

"You didn't answer my question." Bailey gripped her shoulders.

"I'm not hiding anything about my relationship with Shane. If you can be kind to him, spend time with us. You'll see what he's really like." She glanced away so Bailey couldn't see that she wasn't telling the entire truth.

"Is that a real invitation?"

"It is if you want it to be. And the same goes for

Kassidy. Let me know." She walked away without looking back.

As she headed home, cool air whisked her hair around and soothed the heat in her face. She couldn't tell them after all. She would have to keep her secret to the end because she loved Shane. However things ended up between the two of them, that much was the truth.

Chapter Eighteen

S hane sat on her front steps. Her insides tingled at the sight of him, and she reprimanded her traitorous body. Even in a sweatshirt and jeans he was the most handsome man she had ever seen. The fabric of his shirt molded over his arms and the jeans creased in all the right places.

"What are you doing here?" she said.

He stood and met her halfway. "I have some great news, and I couldn't wait to tell you."

"You could've called."

He backed up a step. "You don't want to see me?"

"What? I didn't mean it like that. I'm just surprised to see you." All her thoughts of him this evening had conjured him. She wasn't expecting to find him at her door and now that he was, she wasn't sure what to do about it.

"Are you okay?" Shane's brows creased.

"Why wouldn't I be? It's not as if my sisters are mad

at me. Or maybe it's because I'm mad at them still. I don't even know which. Do I appear like a woman who can't take care of herself?"

"I think you're very good at taking care of yourself considering what you had planned for me recently and the fact that you're navigating our secret like a pro. Nothing stops you when you get your mind made up."

"Thank you. I don't understand why they think they can't trust my decision to be with you." Or why she cared so much since this wasn't even real. Maybe it was because she wanted her sisters to support her no matter what her choices were.

Maren hadn't bothered to call her mother to tell her about any of this because her mother would tell her what a bad idea it was to get married again. She would go on and on about her own failed marriages and Maren didn't want to hear it. Maren expected her mother to withhold support because that was what that woman did. But her sisters... she had higher expectations. Expecting them to support her was too big an ask.

"They love you. And I hate to admit this, but they think I'm not a good choice for you. They think we're being hasty getting married. Marriage is a commitment, and they believe once you're tied to me, you won't be able to get free."

Joke was on her. She didn't want to be free from this man.

"What did you want to tell me? Wait. You didn't get into an argument with someone and undo all I worked to create, did you?"

A darkness passed over his bright eyes. "You have no faith in me. No matter what I say to you."

"That isn't true, and you know it. I agreed to this hair brain idea, didn't I?" She brushed past him to get inside.

"But you think I'll fail."

"I'm not your father, Shane. I don't expect the worst from you. Not anymore, at least." He gripped her wrist. "You remember what my father was like?"

"Just because we haven't been together in two decades doesn't mean I've forgotten our relationship or the one you had with your father. He was hard on you and Evan, unnecessarily. My dad wasn't perfect, but he never pushed us just to see if he could make us break."

His father had wanted superstars because he had failed at being one and didn't stop until he had exactly that. Both Sutherland boys may have made it to the big leagues, but Shane had trouble controlling his temper and Evan, the more sensitive of the two, had taken his father's harsh words harder, resulting in problems with drinking, gambling and women.

Standing inside her foyer, Shane tugged her closer and she went without hesitation. Heat rolled off his strong body and she wanted to wrap herself in him. Tangling with frayed desire could find her inches from the danger zone.

"What else do you remember?" His voice dropped into a husky whisper. His eyes filled with unmistakable lust.

She could stop what would surely happen, if she allowed this moment to continue. All she had to do was lie and say she remembered nothing else, or she could pull from his grasp. He would leave her alone.

She didn't want to walk away from him, but jumping into the ocean from the jetty would be less risky than giving into the sizzle beneath her skin. These past months had left her lonely too and it had been years since a man looked at her the way Shane did now. She wasn't sure Dave ever looked at her that way. But she had to remember that Shane may be pretending.

"I remember everything." Foolish words on her dry lips. She couldn't take them back or fix them to sound rational. She could close her eyes and transport back to the moment he walked toward her for the first time or to the last time his voice came across the phone line, saying they were over.

A low growl escaped from his lips. "I like the sound of that."

"What do you remember?"

"The first time you allowed me to make love to you."

Shane had been her first. The night had been far from perfect. They had to find a place to go because they both had roommates in small dorm rooms. They had parked down by the beach on a quiet street with no houses, just a small apartment building that faced the other way.

Shane had a sports car at the time. They had dropped the passenger seat as far as it would go, but it still wasn't enough room for his tall frame. They had fumbled through most of it, laughed in parts, but in the end—a very quick end—they held each other's sweaty bodies that had steamed up the windows, giving them as much privacy as they could get.

She wouldn't change a thing about that night.

"That was a lifetime ago. I barely remember that girl." Maren had been filled with hope and dreams like so many young people with their lives stretched out in front of them. She had believed she and Shane would stay together, and they would build a life that gave them everything they wanted.

"Yeah? Well, I remember her just fine. I'd never felt anything like that for another person before."

"You were young and still impressionable. I'm sure you've felt plenty since then." She moved away from his grasp and went into the kitchen. All her feelings back then were amped up on the extremes that come with that time in one's life. Everything with Shane had glowed from the inside with a light and warmth that couldn't be measured. That kind of love wasn't any more real than their engagement now.

He was quick on her heels and slipped between her and the sink. "Hey, hang on a second. What we had meant something to me back then."

"Sometimes, as we get older, those fleeting memories begin to mean even more." She wondered if they had for her. Memories had helped her through some of her more difficult moments as a mother and a wife.

"Are you saying I didn't have feelings for you?"

"Of course, you did." She placed a hand on his cheek.

He turned his face and kissed her palm. "Why are you acting like I was some jerk to you? I know things ended badly, and that was on me. But the rest of it was good, wasn't it?"

"Shane, I don't want to relive the past. Let's leave it where it belongs, okay? What did you come to tell me?" Most of their time together had filled her with excitement because everything was new and crisp. But as their relationship went on, and Shane was courted by baseball teams, that crispness dulled. Their paths had separated and when he ached for the familiar, he had come to find her. Much like that night in Sea Glass. When he couldn't have what he wanted, he had become angry.

"That can wait a second. Please tell me you know how much you meant to me."

"I have no idea how much I meant to you. You said things that didn't match up to your actions. Back then, I didn't always know what to believe. I know what I wanted to believe, but in the end you left anyway. What difference does it make now, whether or not we cared for each other a hundred years ago?"

He stepped closer and tilted up her chin with his finger. "Do you regret our relationship?"

She glanced away unsure how to answer. The view out the window of lights strung on her neighbor's fence, was easier to look at than him.

"Maren?"

She glanced back. "I've regretted a lot of the dumb things I've done in my life; I even regret the things I wasn't brave enough to do, but I don't regret you."

"I'm repeating what I said to you at the university.

I've never stopped loving you, Maren. I just didn't know it until you agreed to pretend to be my wife."

"How can you be sure of your feelings now if you didn't realize you even had them until a few weeks ago? We've been over longer than we were together."

"I trust my gut. It's never wrong on the field and when I don't listen to it is when we lose. I'm trusting it now. This is where I want to be, with you, if you'll have me."

"You're talking for real. No more pretend?" She couldn't wrap her mind around what he said. He loved her, always had. He wanted to take this thing from phony to for real, but did she?

"There is nothing fake about how I feel for you. Being with you these past few weeks has shown me that. I know this is a lot to throw at you. We're supposed to be pretending, but I'm not anymore. We can take our time to get to know each other all over again."

"What will we tell everyone? The engagement is off, but we're dating now?"

"We don't have to end the engagement. We just don't have to rush to set a date."

"This seems a little backwards, don't you think?"

"I didn't get to where I am because I used conventional thinking. Barry Solomon called me earlier. He's signing my contract as we speak because he saw those videos. We did it." His smile burst open.

She threw her arms around his neck. He smelled warm and familiar. "Shane, that's wonderful news."

"It's because of you." He set her on her feet but kept his hands on her hips. His touch grounded her.

"I didn't do anything."

"You set the whole thing up. You gave me the opportunity to show another side of myself."

"Barry Solomon knew he wanted you. He probably had to make his whole offer look like an ultimatum."

"Even so, I don't think I would've even thought of those ideas if it wasn't for you. I'm the one who came up with the crazy idea to lie to everyone. You're a better person than I am."

"That isn't true." Shane was a good man. He was flawed like everyone, including her.

"I have more good news for you. Do you know who Timothy Stone is?"

She didn't. Shane told her about his other phone call today and what that meant for her. She would plan a large wedding for a wealthy and connected young woman.

"You need to call Irene Stone in the morning and set up a meeting." Shane typed the number into her phone. "You've hit a homerun with this one."

"Thank you." She reached for her phone. His hand closed over hers. Heat radiated from her center.

Shane had made this incredible opportunity happen for her. She had a chance to rebuild her business and make a name for herself. After all her hard work, she might actually survive the hit her career took. She had Shane to thank and would do so in a way she wanted to, but until now had shied away from.

She stood on her toes and pressed her lips to his. He tasted salty and sweet at the same time. She yielded to him and his tongue swept the inside of her mouth. Her hands gripped his shoulders, sending her phone tumbling to the floor. She didn't care.

All she cared about was Shane kissing her and his hands sliding under her shirt. A frenzy raced through her with the need to connect to him in the most intimate way. If she didn't slow down and anchor herself, she would be swept out to sea.

He eased back from the kiss, his lips a little red and puffy. "Are you sure about this?"

She took his hand without a word and led him through the dining area. He stayed close as they ascended the winding staircase, the wood creaking under their heavy steps.

She paused outside her door. He pressed against her from behind, evidence of his arousal obvious. His heat burned through the fabric of her clothes. She sunk against the warmth, wanting only to be in that exact place. A weighted sigh escaped her lips. She was safe and at home.

The only light in her room came from the moon's glow through her gauze curtains swaying in the quiet breeze. Plenty of light to see Shane as she turned to him.

"I've never been more certain about anything." And showed him just how certain she was.

Chapter Nineteen

S hane held Maren while she slept. The ocean breeze floating through the window kept the room cool. She had one arm over his middle and her cheek pressed against his chest. He tangled his fingers in her soft hair.

Her deep breathing relaxed him. He could stay that way all night with her heat searing his skin. He never wanted to get out of this bed. Based on their conversation earlier, he may never have to leave.

Part of him still couldn't fathom that he and Maren had made love. He had never expected them to end up in bed when he had first approached her in Sea Glass. He had hoped somewhere along the way but never expected. She was too good for him.

With his free hand, he reached for his watch on the side table. The hours had slipped away. It was the middle of the night. He didn't think sleep would come for him. That was okay. He could sleep when he was dead. He didn't want to miss a minute with Maren. He had a lot to make up for with her. He would spend every day for the rest of his life, proving to her how much he loved her and would never hurt her. He would never argue with another umpire, and he would never throw another punch.

He wanted to marry her for real and would ask her again in a way she deserved and not like the way he had when they were pretending.

His phone vibrated against the table. He should ignore it. The call was probably spam at this hour. As soon as the ringing stopped, it started again.

Maren shifted against him. "Is that your phone?"

"I'm sorry. I'll silence it." He eased out their embrace. The screen read *Evan*. Evan calling now could only mean trouble. He hesitated for a second. "I'm sorry, Maren. I have to get this."

He didn't wait for her to answer and stepped out into the hallway, closing the door behind him. Hopefully, she would fall right back to sleep.

"Evan, what's going on?" He saw no point in opening with useless pleasantries.

"Shane, man, I need your help."

"What is it now?" A weariness passed over him. He had lost count of the times Evan had started a conversation with *I need help*.

"I screwed up. Big time. I'm so sorry." Evan's voice cracked against his words.

Shane waited for him to continue, but only Evan's

heavy breathing came across the line. Shane couldn't be sure, but Evan might be crying.

"Evan, what are you sorry for?" He didn't want to think the worst, but his mind took off like a hundred mile an hour fast ball. Every possible worst-case scenario flashed before him.

"I shouldn't have come down here, but I had to get away from Paris. She's such a bitch." Evan drew in a mucus filled breath.

"Evan, get to the point."

"I'm in Atlantic City. I lost... lost... please come." Evan broke down. "I know I screwed up. I swear I'll never do it again. It's just. Oh, God. What am I going to do? Please, Shane. I think they're going to kill me."

Shane slumped against the wall. He stood in Maren's hallway, butt naked, debating on getting in the car and driving over an hour to help his brother or leave him to drown in his mess. Evan had found himself in gambling debt more times than Shane cared to think about.

He had promised himself the last time he would not help Evan again. But Evan had never said before tonight, that anyone had wanted to kill him. Beat him senseless maybe.

"Who do you owe?"

"Some scary guys. Can you bring money? I swear I'll pay you back. I'll forward my entire salary next year straight to you."

"Where are you?"

Evan gave him the casino and the location of his hiding place—a janitor's closet on the third floor.

"This is the last time." He ended the call in the middle of Evan's profession of thanks.

Shane eased back into the bedroom. He would have to wake Maren and tell her. He would never leave without saying goodbye.

Except he didn't have to wake Maren. She stood by the window. She had slipped on a fuzzy robe that grazed her ankles.

"I like the robe. You had it on the first time I slept here."

"This thing is old."

"Maybe so, but you are so damn adorable in it." He went to her unable to keep his hands to himself and drew her to him.

"I have some bad news." He rested his forehead on hers.

"Is everything okay?"

"Evan is in trouble. I have to go to Atlantic City and help him out of a bind." With regret, he pulled away and collected his clothes.

"Do you want me to come for the ride?"

"I would like nothing more, but he may have gotten himself into something he can't get out of. I don't want you getting hurt in the crossfire."

"What kind of trouble is he in? Do you need the police?"

"That's the last thing we need. I'm sure whoever he owes money to this time are not fans of public servants. And I don't want to take a chance any of this leaking out. If the Warriors get wind of me in AC and involved with gambling, my contract will disappear."

"Then why go?"

"He's my brother."

"You can't save him from himself."

"I can try." He placed a kiss on her soft lips. "I'll be back tomorrow. Don't forget to call Irene."

"As if I'd forget that." She gave him a playful shove. "Shane, be careful. I don't want you to get hurt. I can't lose you now that I have you back."

"You won't lose me." He paused at the bedroom door. "I love you, Maren."

"I love you too."

He hurried from the house to his car. His heart was full. Maren loved him. Her words would keep him company on the ride south.

Shane moved through hotel lobby. The open space was decorated with blown glass fixtures in all different colors, shapes and sizes. Even though it was the early hours of the morning, people moved about everywhere. Some checked in at the expansive front desk backlight with white light. Others hurried to their destination, either the casino that never slept or the bar that was still open. Or maybe they'd had enough of losing their shirts and were retreating to the safety of their room. Shane guessed no one was like Evan—hiding in a janitor's closet.

He followed Evan's direction to the third floor of the

hotel, down a labyrinth of hallways where his footsteps were muffled by the thick carpet. He stopped at a door with a sign that read *housekeeping*.

He knocked, using their prescribed code. Two quick knocks, a pause then three more. The door opened on a slow swing. Evan motioned for him inside and closed the door behind him.

Evan's hair stuck out straight from the sides of his head. His left eye was red and swollen. His bottom lip was split, and blood had dried on his chin. Some had dripped onto his dress shirt.

Shane wasn't surprised that someone had popped him. Evan had often found himself in over his head with his gambling problems and at the receiving end of that person's angry fists.

The closet was bigger than he had imagined. Shelves lined three walls filled with cleaning supplies and small toiletries offered to the guests in their bathrooms. On the back wall was a porcelain slop sink stained from years of use. Brooms and mops propped up the corner. The space smelled like bleach and vinegar.

"Nice digs."

"Shut up. I paid the janitor a hundred bucks to let me stay here until you came. I've been sitting on a crate for the past two hours. My legs are numb." Evan pointed to the milk crate he had turned upside down to create a makeshift chair.

"I don't care about your legs. How much do you owe?"

"I can handle the full amount. I just didn't have

enough cash on me tonight to show them I'm good for it. The poker game got away from me is all. If I'd had a few more bucks, I would've won it all back and then some."

Shane had heard that a hundred times, and the few bucks Evan referred to was thousands. Their father also had a problem with gambling, but Dad liked the horses. With Monmouth Park Racetrack practically in their backyard, their dad spent a lot of time betting the ponies.

"How much, Evan? I could only get five thousand from the ATM. Is that enough to keep them from breaking your legs?"

"We can talk about it more when we get out of here." Evan reached for the door.

"Wait. I thought you wanted to give them the money you owe them." That was why he had jumped out of Maren's bed and raced down the Parkway.

"I want to get the hell out of here. I'm not going back into that room. They'll shoot me."

"If all you had to do was make a run for it, why did you call me?"

"Keep your voice down. I lost my car." Evan's face bloomed red. He dropped his gaze to the floor and tugged on his hair.

"I'm sorry. I don't understand. How did you lose your car?" He tried to speak lower, but he wasn't sure he managed.

"I bet it." Evan's face crumpled. Tears poured down his face.

"You bet your Temerario?" That car was worth over four hundred thousand dollars. Shane didn't even an own a car worth that much. This was the worst thing Evan had ever done.

"I didn't have enough money to stay in the game. I thought my luck had to turn around. I was due."

"And when you lost your car, you didn't get up and walk away?" They were in over their heads here. Whoever Evan owed wouldn't go quietly. They had to get out of the casino before anyone noticed or they might both end up dead. He had never run from a fight before.

Not from the first time when he was fourteen and an upperclassman declared a fight because Shane had accidentally taken his seat in class. That time Shane had pounded that kid for all he could because if that senior had a chance to lay his mitts on Shane, he would've been dirt.

Now he saw the benefit in taking another stance.

"Can we just get out of here? If they find me, they'll kill me."

"Evan, this shit doesn't happen in real life." Shane couldn't believe this night had turned into a scene from a thriller movie.

"It happens more often than you think. Gambling is as common disease."

"Let's go." He no longer wished to stand in the janitor's closet, discussing Evan's disease as if it were a common cold. His brother always refused to get any help for his addiction, and now Shane was tangled in his mess —again. Only this time things were much worse.

Evan checked the hallway. "It's clear."

They retraced Shane's steps into the lobby. Evan stopped behind one of the blown glass fixtures.

"Why are you stopping? Keep going." They had no time to waste.

"I'm making sure no one is looking for me."

"Let's get out of here." He gave Evan a shove.

They made it to the parking garage, and he allowed his teeth to unclench, and his shoulders to drop. The open air gave him a false sense of security.

"Where did you park?" Evan said from behind him.

"In the next aisle, near the back."

He looked over his shoulder at Evan. Two large men in black suits charged toward them. His breath left his lungs. His mind yelled, but he couldn't form the words to tell Evan.

Evan must've noticed the look on Shane's face and turned around. "Oh, shit. Run."

"I'm not running." Running never solved the problem. Standing and fighting for what was right changed the outcome. If he ran now, those men would only catch them, and Evan would never be out from under this night. If they stood and fought, then Evan would have a chance to fix his life. Shane would see to it this time.

"What?" Evan skid to a stop but didn't return.

Shane would have to handle this alone. Like he always did when it came to Evan. He had promised Maren no more fights. He had sworn to Barry Solomon he was a changed man, but this time they would have to understand. This time was different than the arguments on the field.

Shane took a fighting stance. He said a silent prayer these men didn't have guns, that their only goal was to send a message to Evan to pay up.

The first man ran past him toward Evan. Shane couldn't turn to see if Evan ran away or not. The second man, bald and with hatred in his eyes, lunged for him.

Shane reacted much the way he had that day outside the school. He pounced and fought for all he was worth. He was bigger now and stronger, but his body was stiff and slower. He blocked and threw until the skin over his knuckles burst open. Blood flew in different directions. He didn't know if it was his or his opponents. He didn't let up until the man, on the ground, beneath him, finally lost consciousness.

He struggled to his feet, out of breath. Sweat ran into his eyes. He wiped it away with the back of his bloodied hand. He needed to find Evan. Shane turned. Evan was bent at the waist, farther down the lane, hands on his knees, gasping for air. The other man lay on the ground, not moving.

They needed to get out of there before someone found them or those men woke. He and Evan got lucky this time. If the people Evan owed money to came for them again, they would be the ones on the ground. Shane had no doubt.

They'd have to figure out a plan for Evan and him to stay safe. But for now, they needed to get back to Serenity. He couldn't go to Maren's and risk her safety. Maybe they should drive north and all the way to his home in New York. In the morning, Evan could hire an attorney or a bodyguard.

Shane fumbled with his keys. Before he could press the key fob, he saw his hope fade away.

Two people, a man and a woman, huddled behind a nearby car. The man used his phone like a camera. The woman used hers like a phone.

Sirens screamed in the distance.

He was screwed.

Chapter Twenty

"Mr. Sutherland, you're free to go."

Shane's neck cramped as he held the guard's gaze. He tried not to wince, but didn't do a good job of it.

He and Evan had been arrested in the parking garage, along with the two goons they had fought, and brought to the city jail.

The place smelled of vomit and piss. Some old guy in clothes covered in enough dirt and grime that they could snap off his body was passed out on the only bench in the cell. Shane and Evan had taken spots on the floor away from the old guy. Shane had no idea where the two they fought were. Maybe the hospital.

"Which one?" Shane said. Every part of his body ached. His right hand had swollen. He wanted to get out of there, grab a shower and find Maren. The officers had taken his phone when they booked him. He couldn't reach her. He had promised Maren he'd return to her house. She was either worried or angry. He didn't want her to worry, but he didn't want her mad at him more.

"You. The coach. Your bail cleared." The officer, a short stocky guy with pock marked skin, slid open the cell door.

Shane peeled himself off the floor with the effort of a man twice his age. His knees popped and groaned until he was at his full height.

"What about me?" Evan stared up with fear on his face.

"I didn't have enough money to bail us both out. You'll have to sit tight."

"Until when?"

"Until you can post bail." He was done saving Evan. Shane wasn't foolish enough to think that couple didn't post their video of Shane being arrested all over the internet. The man had called out to him by name. By now, everyone, including the woman he loved would have seen that fight. He needed to explain to Maren what really happened and how he was done saving Evan.

"Wait. You're not going to bail me out?" Evan jumped to his feet and stood inches from Shane. The stench of shame rolled off his brother, but Shane wasn't cleaning him up anymore.

The guard stepped into the cell. "Mr. Sutherland, you need to go now." The guard pointed a finger at Evan. "You need to sit down and shut up."

"You almost got me killed tonight. I'm tired of getting tangled up in your messes. No more. I can't save you from yourself. I always knew that. I should've stopped trying years ago, but... I don't know what to say, Evan. Get your life in order. Call Paris to come get you."

"She won't help me. You have to fix this for me. Just this once. I promise I'll go straight to a rehab for gamblers. I won't do this anymore. I can't stay in jail." Evan's eyes filled with tears.

Shane fought the guilt. Every time Evan had ever shed tears, as a boy until now, Shane believed he had to save his brother because no one had ever saved him.

"I'm sorry, Evan. You're going to have to clean this one up yourself." Shane turned his back and forced himself forward as his brother screamed for him to come back.

Shane stepped out into the late afternoon's light. He blinked against the horizontal glare bouncing off a windshield and adjusted his watch. The day promised to be warm for the end of summer. Serenity's beach was probably already filling up with the most committed dwellers. He was never one for sitting still on the sand. He preferred a game of frisbee, volleyball, or a swim in the surf, but right now he would trade almost anything to sit in the sun's heat.

He needed to call a ride service for a lift back to his car. The second call would be to Maren to explain what happened.

He opened his phone to find several text messages and a few voicemails. He hesitated but played the first message from Barry Solomon.

"Shane, if I had signed your contract, I'd fire you. But since I never actually put the pen on paper, I'll just say your behavior was disgraceful. I saw those videos of you fighting like a hoodlum plastered everywhere. You have no place on my team. You're through in this business. The Titans were right to set you free. I am a foolish old man to think you had something worth salvaging. Don't bother to call back."

The next message was from Matt, his old batting coach with the Titans. He hadn't spoken to Matt since the night Shane was fired.

"Shane, are you okay? I saw the videos. Call me if you're out of jail and need anything. I know a good lawyer, if you don't."

Shane howled at the sky. He pulled up a search engine and typed in his name. Post after post populated about him and along with the video of him beating the crap out of that guy lying on the ground. Some of the local new sources grabbed sound bites and click bait. He was ruined for good. He'd never manage again.

He needed to talk to Maren. Nothing else mattered except what she thought. He couldn't lose her too.

He called her, but the call went straight to voicemail.

Maren walked along the surf's edge. White foam swirled around her ankles as her feet sunk into the cool wet sand with each step. She needed the cold slap of water against her skin to keep her focused. She had called Irene Stone first thing in the morning. The woman had insisted Maren meet with her and her daughter later that day.

She wanted more time to be prepared, but she couldn't blow this opportunity. She might not get another one.

She hoped Dakota wasn't as bad as Paris had been. Part of Maren feared she didn't want to continue to plan weddings for the rich and famous. They had too much power to destroy her hard work because people who didn't know them in real life believed what they always said to be true. Fans often followed blindly. Maren was at risk each time she agreed to be responsible for the outcome of a wedding. Had she taken on more than she was ever capable of? Maybe kids' parties and baby showers were more her speed. Kassidy's shower was next week. Maren didn't even know if Kassidy still wanted her there. They were still not speaking.

She wished she could talk to Shane, but he wasn't answering all day. She hoped he found Evan last night and everything was all right. But after all this time, her insides frazzled with uncertainty. Something must be wrong. He wouldn't avoid her after last night. At least she hoped he wouldn't.

Instead of talking to Shane, she had attempted to calm her nerves by searching for sea glass. But again, she had come up empty today. She did not have Kassidy's luck in this area. *Kassidy*. Families were complicated at best and destructive at worst. But Maren wanted hers around her.

She tapped at her phone.

Thinking of you. Hope you're having a great day. She hit send on the text for Peyton. She missed her daughter but had wanted to give Peyton the space she needed to settle into college. Even with the university close by, she never wanted to invade Peyton's new life. Her daughter needed to find her way. A way that wouldn't always include Maren.

Thanks mom. Want to have lunch on Thur?

Which was translation for Peyton wanted to go shopping for something. Maren smiled. She would take any excuse to spend time with her.

Sounds good. Noon?

Peyton sent back a smiling emoji and heart emoji. Maren loved the message. With her spirits lifted a little, she tried Shane again.

She stepped on something hard and pointy in the sand. Pain shot up her leg. She stumbled and dropped her phone into a crashing wave.

Foam swallowed up her device. The wave receded from the sand, hiding the phone like a pickpocket and rushing back out to sea. Maren jumped into the water, slapping the surface to find the phone. She lunged at a reflection moving in the water, but her hand only curled around water. A strong current swiped her legs out from under her. She tumbled beneath the surface. Her clothes pulled and tugged against her. The wave pushed her toward the beach.

Her feet sought purchase until she could stand. Her phone was nowhere. She turned in circles, hoping to see it wash to shore beside her. Her whole life was in that phone. She bit down on her trembling lip to keep from bursting into tears.

Defeated, she dragged her waterlogged self up to the boardwalk. Sand stuck to her skin. She would find the grains everywhere on her for days no matter how much she scrubbed. She needed to get home and cleaned up before she was late. She turned with one more look at the unforgiving ocean. Talking to Shane would have to wait. Talking or texting anyone would have to wait.

She hoped her client meeting went better than her morning had so far.

Chapter Twenty-One

Maren twirled her engagement ring around her finger. The motion eased her nerves as she weaved her way around the tables of The Wave House restaurant toward Irene and Dakota Stone.

She should be focused on this meeting, but her thoughts drifted to Shane. Where was he? Was he looking for her? He wouldn't know where to find her.

She had tried to send a quick text from her computer before she had left but hadn't had the time to wait and see if he responded.

Irene and Dakota sat by the wall of windows that stretched from floor to ceiling. The scope of the ocean from the dining area was why everyone came to The Wave House. The boardwalk was across the street and every window seat had an unencumbered view.

Irene saw her first and waved. Mrs. Stone had to be about twenty years older than Maren but didn't look it.

Her hair was still jet black and from the looks of it—
natural. Unless she had the very best hairdresser on the
east coast, which could be the case. She wore it in a
simple bob to her chin. Her makeup was natural, not a
line on her face. Maren would need to ask her about her
skin care routine at a later date.

Dakota was the picture of young and beautiful. She
had long, flowing sun-streaked hair. Her cheeks were still
filled with the benefits of collagen. Her eyes were as
bright as the setting sun dipping through the side
windows.

Each woman had a drink in front of them.

"Thank you for coming on such short notice." Irene
shook hands.

"My pleasure. It's nice to meet you both." She settled
in and tucked her notebook to her side in the chair.
"Have you ordered?"

"We waited. We thought we'd start with some picky
foods so we could get right down to discussing the plans.
Dakota has lots of ideas and we wanted to hear what you
had to say as well." Irene sipped from her glass.

Maren wondered if the drink was a simple iced tea or
cocktail. She made a mental mote to pay attention to Mrs.
Stone's drinking habits, as well as Dakota's. She would
not miss a thing this time.

"Maybe I should tell you a little about me and my
business." She usually started a meeting with a brief over-
view of what she offered.

"That's okay. I did my research on you. You've
planned some amazing weddings," Irene said.

"Thank you. Typically, what I like to do in at first is get a feel for what you're looking for on your special day and whether or not we're a good fit for each other. If we both want to move forward, then we can talk payments." She had no business implying she wouldn't want this job, but she couldn't come off desperate either.

"Money isn't a problem." Irene pulled her wallet from her designer handbag and retrieved a check. "I'll write you whatever you need today. Dakota wants to work with you. You will be a great addition to our planning."

"And I have a lot of ideas already. I've been planning this day since I was little." Dakota giggled and produced a large binder from under her chair.

The binder was covered in white lace with a picture of Dakota and her fiancé on the cover. Papers stuck from every direction as if it were a gourmet sandwich losing all its toppings. If Dakota had been thinking about this day her entire life, there would be very little room for suggestions on how to make her day unique. With that giant binder bursting at the seams, Maren didn't think Dakota needed a wedding planner at all.

She forced her mind to stay quiet. She could not assume Dakota and Paris were anything alike, but Paris had had many ideas as well.

"Great. Let's talk about your vision."

The server took their order. Maren's stomach twisted like boat lines. Eating was out of the question. She sipped on her diet soda instead. The bubbles settled her nervous belly.

After their food order was underway, they returned to the decorated pages of Dakota's binder. She had many ideas, all right. She had every idea from the past thirty years and then a few from the time of World War II.

Maren wished she could check her phone for a sign of Shane or even check the time. Not knowing was turning her insides out. She missed the days when not everything revolved around her phone and the expectation of instant gratification.

She made a few attempts to glance at Dakota's phone, but without luck. All she had to go by was the lengthening shadows through the windows and the emptying tables around them.

The conversation swung from dress ideas to centerpieces to what should go into the ladies' room in case the guest needed any personal items. Maren fought the sea sickness sloshing around in her stomach.

"Why don't we pick one area to focus on at a time. The first thing we should decide on is the venue and the date." She opened her notebook.

"I hope you don't mind me saying," Irene placed a hand on Maren's arm. "But your engagement ring is simply stunning. Did you pick it out yourself?"

Maren glanced at Irene's hand then back at the woman's face. The ring was a conversation starter, and she wore it today as a way to stay connected to Shane and show the world how real their feelings were. She was glad to wear the ring even if she hadn't picked it. He had chosen it because he wanted her to have something special.

"Thank you. Shane picked it out." She turned to Dakota, needing to end the conversation about Shane at least until she knew if he was okay. "So, Dakota. What venues were you thinking about? I think we should visit at least three."

"I love the place on the beach in Serenity by the Sea. You know the one... where Paris and Evan Sutherland were married." Dakota's eyes lit up with a dreamy quality.

Maren tried not to groan. Of all the places in the state, the young woman had to say that one. "Have you considered some of the places in Red Bank on the river?"

"No. I want the one in Serenity. That outdoor patio area that leads down to the beach... I love it. I must have my photos taken out there. I can picture the whole thing. The ocean will be in the background. My hair and veil will blow in the wind like something from a romance movie."

Maren didn't have the heart to tell her that the wind would probably rip her veil from her head if the direction was wrong. "I'll set up an appointment."

The server brought their food, interrupting the flow of conversation.

"Speaking of Shane," Irene said. "How is he?"

"He's fine. Thank you." At least she hoped he was.

"Even after last night?" Irene's brows bent together.

Maren kept her face still. She had no idea what Irene was talking about. Something must've happened in Atlantic City and was now all over the internet. If he got himself into trouble for Evan and ruined the work she had done for him, she would kill him.

"He's fine."

"That's not what I saw online." Dakota shook her head.

If she had her phone, she would excuse herself to the ladies' room and search for herself.

"I must ask you, Maren." Irene pushed her food around on the plate. "You seem like a very smart woman who knows what she's doing. But can you explain to me what everyone sees in Shane? My husband thinks he's the cat's meow. Sure, he's easy on the eyes, but he's a volcano ready to blow. I would be concerned about being married to him. Don't you have a young daughter?"

Maren's body shook. She didn't know how to reply.

"Mom, you shouldn't ask that." Dakota hunched into her shoulders. A pink blush crept up her cheeks.

At least Dakota had the decency to appear embarrassed.

"Irene, I'm not sure what you're referring to where Shane is concerned." She tried to keep her voice light and her gaze on her plate.

"Oh, please. His fight and arrest were all over the news. I would've assumed you were the one to bail him out of jail."

"Jail?" The word burst out. How had Shane ended up in jail? She had a million questions and needed to get out of there to find him.

"You didn't know? I'm so sorry you heard it from me. But one look at any social media site would show you."

Irene tapped at her phone screen then turned it for Maren to see.

Someone had videoed Shane committing assault. Maren gripped the table to keep from falling out of her chair.

"You're going to dump him, aren't you?" Irene said.

"There must be some mistake." Videos could be doctored. Shane would never hurt someone in that way. She had to believe that.

"Doesn't look like any mistake to me. If I were you, I'd give back that ring. You deserve better than some hoodlum lowlife. I could take you places with Dakota's wedding. Don't let yourself be tied to a man like Shane." Irene pressed her lips into a thin line.

"Mom, you really need to stop."

"Hush, Dakota. I'm not saying anything Maren's own mother would say to her. A violent man is unsafe."

Maren pushed out of the chair on wobbly legs. She spun her engagement ring around her finger. All she cared about was knowing Shane was all right.

She didn't have to take the crumbs thrown at her by women like Irene Stone and Paris Sutherland to prove she was good at her job. She'd find another way to succeed.

"Irene, Dakota, thank you for your time, but I'm not the right wedding planner for you. I love Shane and even though that video puts him in a questionable light, I'm certain there's more to the story. I can't work with anyone who would disparage my future husband. Best of luck."

She hurried to her car without a look back. She needed to find Shane.

Chapter Twenty-Two

Shane knocked on Maren's front door. He had called her all the way from Atlantic City, but each time the call went to voicemail. He had been up for close to thirty-six hours. Every part of his body ached including his eyelids, but he had to talk to her.

She must've seen the video and decided to dump him. He needed to explain what had happened, and if she still wanted to leave him, he would walk away. He had already lost his career. He didn't want to bring her down with him. She deserved better than a man with his reputation.

Her car was not parked on the street outside her house, but that didn't stop him from going to the back-door and knocking there.

"Maren, if you're in there, open up. Please." He behaved like a fool, begging her through a locked door.

"She isn't home." An older woman in the yard behind

Maren's placed a potted plant on a picnic table. She wore a wide dress with flowers and swirls in red and purple that swung by her ankles. Her white hair sat on her head like a bunch of cotton balls.

"Are you sure?"

"Saw her leave a few hours ago. She was dressed like she had somewhere important to be. I waved to her, but she didn't see me in her hurry. Are you her boyfriend?"

"I'm just a friend. Thank you."

Defeat tasted like dirt. He hated losing and he had lost in a big way. He would go back to his rental house, back up his gear, and get the hell out of Serenity by the Sea.

"Oh, I wasn't expecting to see you. I thought you were still in jail." Kassidy appeared in the backyard out of nowhere. Her eyes were wide, but a pained look pressed on her brows. Her swollen belly stretched the fabric of her shirt. One hand rested on her bump.

He ignored her dig. "If you're looking for Maren, she isn't home." He jogged down the steps but kept his distance. He wasn't in the mood to deal with her hatred or her misconception of what she had seen online.

He had almost ruined Maren's relationship with her sisters with his dumb idea for them to pretend to be married. At least he could give her back a relationship with her sisters. He would never have to see Kassidy's sneer again either.

"Where is she? I've been trying to reach her all day, but she isn't answering her phone." Kassidy looked around the yard as if Maren would appear from under the flowerbed.

"I've been trying her too."

"Does she know what you did?" She spit the words at him.

"Kassidy, I'm exhausted. I don't have the energy to argue with you. If I hear from Maren, I'll let her know you're looking for her."

"So, you're saying her disappearance has nothing to do with you then." She folded her arms over her chest.

"Her disappearance? What do you think I did? Hide her body someplace?" He laughed at the absurdity of Kassidy's comment.

"That isn't funny, Shane." Her hand circled her belly.

"What you said is out of line. I would never hurt Maren."

"I want to know if you said or did something to her before you found yourself in a fight and thrown in jail." Her brows furrowed more. Sweat beaded her upper lip, but it wasn't that hot out now that twilight was upon them.

He would like to tell Kassidy that he had made love to Maren the last time he saw her, that she had looked up at him with love in her eyes and had wrapped her body around his completely satisfied before Evan called and blew everything out of the water, but he would not tarnish what he had shared with Maren.

"Your sister is a grown woman who can make her own choices." She had chosen him, and he blew it. He would understand if Maren never forgave him for what he did last night.

"I know what I saw. You standing over some guy, pummeling him unconscious. I don't want you near my sister. You're no good for her."

He couldn't argue with that. "I need to go."

She flattened her palm on his chest. "You're not going anywhere until I have my say. I know what you did when the two of you broke up. I know you punched the wall near her head. You only missed her by inches."

"That was a long time ago." He wasn't the same man, but after last night maybe he was exactly that person. He had used the field as an excuse to let out his anger, but he had often wanted to fight back against the wrongs in his life.

"I'm glad you didn't stay together because you would've hit her eventually. When she told me you two were going to get married, I couldn't bear the idea that she would live alone with you. What if this time you hit her? Or Peyton? You'd hit your other wives—"

"I never hit my wives." That untruth would follow him around until his death bed.

"That's not what the news said." Her hand circled her belly again. A darkness passed over her eyes.

"The news lies." When he had been called up to the majors, he had thought his dream had come true. It had in more ways than he could have imagined, but he could never have known what being well-known to the public would do to his life and how news outlets would twist the truth until it snapped just to get a headline.

Kassidy regarded him. "If you were a good man, you'd walk away from my sister and let her find the happiness she deserves with someone who won't hurt her."

What Kassidy said was true, but his insides burned from the judgement she threw at him. He didn't have to be around for decades to know Kassidy had made mistakes of her own, probably ones she didn't want to be judged for.

"If Maren wants me in her life, that's her decision."

"I hope she doesn't."

"Good thing you don't get to decide."

"Why, Shane? Why did you start up with Maren again?"

"Because I missed her." That was the truth. He didn't know how much he missed her until he saw her during the days before Evan's wedding. After that, he couldn't think of anything except her. He had wanted a chance to try again. The car accident had given him one, and getting fired from The Titans.

"I don't believe you."

"Believe whatever you want. I have to go." He side-stepped her.

"She never mentioned you. Not in years." Kassidy followed him onto the sidewalk. "After she and Dave split, she talked about putting herself first finally. She wanted

companionship but she never said she wanted to be married again. Those were her words. Then you come along out of nowhere and you're engaged. It never made any sense to me."

"Our relationship doesn't have to make sense to you."

"I know my sister. She wouldn't make a crazy decision like marrying you out of the blue. What did you do to her?"

"Do to her?" He couldn't help but laugh. "You really think I'm some kind of monster."

"Are you? Have you blackmailed her? Do you have something to do with what Paris did to her? That retched woman is your sister-in-law."

"You don't know what you're talking about." He wasn't going to say it out loud, but he wondered if those pregnancy hormones had affected her brain. He remembered Kassidy as the most levelheaded of the three sisters.

"Tell me, Shane. Tell me what you have on my sister that she would jeopardize her safety by being with you, that she would put a wedge between us for you? I spent too long without a close relationship with Maren and Bailey. I won't let you come along and rip it apart. Tell me, damn it."

"I made her a deal, all right?" He threw his hands in the air, unsure of what to do with all the raw nerve endings under his skin.

"A deal?" Kassidy stepped back.

"I asked her to pretend to be engaged to me and in turn I would help her with a couple of things." He stopped at what those things were. He wouldn't embarrass Maren by talking about her money problems. That was for her to say.

"I knew it. I knew something was up. I never liked you." Kassidy pointed a finger in his face.

"Whatever." He pushed past her.

"Oh no."

He wanted to keep going and not be drawn back by her declaration as if he had no right to leave. But instead of getting in his car, he turned to find Kassidy bent over, holding her stomach.

"Are you okay?" He reached out to help her but pulled his hand back unsure if she would want him to touch her.

"My water just broke." She looked up at him with fear deep in her eyes and groaned low and long. A puddle formed between her feet on the concrete.

"Should I call Grant? Do you want me to take you home?" He had no idea what the protocol was. When a player was injured, he called for the trainer.

"I think I'd better go to the hospital and meet Grant there. All this pain can't be right." She yelled again.

Shane hoped the neighbors didn't hear and think he was harming her. "I'll call an ambulance."

"No." She gripped his arm and dug her nails into his skin. He tried to pull away, but she held on like a vice. "No ambulance. You have to drive me. It will be faster."

"Me?"

"Do you see anyone else here? Oh, baby, that's a big one." She leaned her weight into him as she gritted her teeth and moaned.

"Can you walk?"

"I think so."

He helped her into his car and drove out of Serenity by the Sea like a hurricane traveling up the coast. Out on Route 33, he drove without concern for the speed limit. Kassidy called Grant on the way.

"He's in the city. He's hailing a cab to drive him all the way down. Oh, my God." She gripped the doorhandle. Her knuckles turned white.

"He'll still be an hour away." He would wait around until Grant or someone showed up for Kassidy. Shane wouldn't leave her alone, but he wished Maren were there.

"Ya think, Magellan? Of course he's an hour away. I can't believe the one day he goes into the city to record." Kassidy writhed in the seat.

"Did you know the baby was coming?" He raced the yellow light and said a silent prayer that he didn't get pulled over. Or maybe that would be better, and they'd get an escort to the hospital.

"Besides at the nine month mark?" She shot him a death glare.

"I meant now. Are you due now?"

"I'm not due for over two weeks. I thought we had time. And no one delivers their first baby early." She wrapped her arms around her middle as if to hold the baby in.

"Is the baby coming right now? This minute? In the car?" He stole a quick glance hoping she wasn't getting ready to pop the baby out in his front seat. Relieved that she wasn't trying to pull off her shorts, he glanced back at the road and passed a car moving too slowly in the exact spot he had his accident a few weeks ago. That night seemed like a lifetime ago.

"Not this second."

"Is there anyone else you can call?" The car was too hot even with the air conditioner on full blast.

"I've sent a text to Bailey, Maren, Peyton, and my Aunt Joanna. Bailey said she'd meet us at the hospital."

"What about Maren?"

"Nothing yet. She wouldn't miss the birth of my baby because she's mad at me, would she?" For the first time since she showed up at Maren's, Kassidy's face softened. Worry filled her eyes, and a tear slipped free.

"Not a chance." He hoped the smile on his face told her all she needed to hear. Maren might be annoyed at her sister, but it would take a tidal wave to keep her from the birth of this child.

Kassidy gave him a watery smile. She grimaced against another pain then started panting. "I think you'd better hurry."

He tore into the hospital's driveway. The car bounced over the dip in the road, rattling his teeth. He stole another glance at Kassidy. She squeezed her eyes shut.

"Do you want me to drop you off at the emergency room?"

"You're going to leave me?" Her eyes flew open, and her eyebrows shot up to her sweaty hairline.

"What? No. I wasn't sure if you could walk from the parking lot." He had no idea what to do here. Babies and world championships weren't exactly the same thing.

He threw the car in park outside the emergency room doors then ran around to help Kassidy out of the car. She leaned into him as he walked with her inside. She smelled like sweat and soap or maybe that was him. He hoped Grant was making good time. The whole situation was out of Shane's league.

A woman with wine colored hair sat behind a low desk. She looked up as they approached. "Oh boy. Looks like we're having a baby." She jumped from her seat and grabbed a wheelchair.

"Let's go up to the third floor. Dad, when we get up there, we'll get mom settled and you can fill out the paperwork." They stepped onto the elevator.

"He's not the dad. My husband is on his way, but he might not be here for an hour. Oh, baby." Kassidy gripped his arm again. He would have a baseball size bruise when this was done.

"Looks like this baby might've started without him." The woman turned to Shane. "Are you the birthing coach?"

"No," he and Kassidy said at the same time with the same definitive expression.

"I'm getting the impression the two of you don't like each other very much." The woman, who wore a hospital badge around her neck that read Holly Burton, shook her head.

"He's engaged to my sister." Kassidy glared at him.

"Say no more." The elevator doors dinged open. The hallway opened to two metal doors. Holly slid her badge over a sensor and the doors swung open. "This is where I leave you. Good luck."

Another woman dressed in pink scrubs escorted them to a hospital room and helped Kassidy change in the bathroom. He paced the room, trying to call Maren. The room was decorated like a regular bedroom with a cherry wood headboard behind the bed, a matching dresser, curtains on the window and a rocking chair with a blanket draped over the back.

"Please call me back. Your sister is at the hospital having this baby. I'm here with her. Where are you? She needs you. I need you too." He shoved the phone in his back pocket.

Kassidy limped over to the bed and with care swung her legs up. Pain etched lines in her face. Sweat damped her hair against her forehead. He wished Grant would walk through that door.

"Any word from Maren?" Kassidy held out her arm while the nurse took her blood pressure.

"Not yet. I'm sure she'll call back." He didn't believe the words and doubted Kassidy did either.

He checked his watch. Had Maren met with the Stones? Had it gone wrong? He paced the space along the bed. Where was Kassidy's family?

"You're making me nervous with all that back and forth," Kassidy said.

"Sorry."

"Thank you for taking me here."

"No problem. You're doing great, by the way."

"I'm scared out of my mind. Please stay until

someone gets here. I don't want to be alone when I have to bring this baby into the world." A softness coated her words that hadn't been there before. She probably was frightened. He didn't blame her. He would be terrified if he was the one about to give birth.

"Nothing to be afraid of. Women have babies every day. This is just a jog around the diamond."

"Easy for you to say. You don't have to push a beach-ball out of a hole the size of a shot glass."

"Women are champions in this department."

"I'm sorry, Shane."

"For what?" He stopped pacing.

"Yelling at you. Saying I didn't like you. Accusing you of hurting Maren. You have been nothing but kind to me this whole time."

"Let's forget it, okay?"

"I do like you. Maren does too. I can tell by the way she looks at you. Whatever agreement you two came up with, it's real for her."

He couldn't think about that now that he had blown it. "Seriously, Kassidy. Let's focus on the game plan. What happens now?"

Kassidy's face scrunched up. She gripped the side rail and came up off the bed. "Oh my God. I have to push. Now."

The nurse's eyes went wide. Shane's stomach turned in on itself. If the nurse was freaked out what did that mean?

"Let's check," the nurse said.

Shane turned away from Kassidy and the nurse.

Through the window, the beach was only a block away. A few beach goers speckled the sand in what was left of the dying sunlight.

"I have to push."

"Hold on. I'll get the doctor." The nurse hurried from the room.

In a flurry of chaos, the doctor returned wearing scrubs and beat up sneakers. The original nurse stood on one side of the doctor and a new nurse stood on the other.

"Okay, Kassidy, on the next contraction you're going to push." The doctor smiled wide as if this was nothing more than batting practice.

"But Grant's not here." Tears filled her eyes.

"Your baby has her own timeline," the doc said.

"Please, I want to wait for him. We've practiced the breathing together." Kassidy took short and hurried breaths as if to prove they had indeed practiced.

"Gotta push for me," the doc said.

"Shane, can you try Maren again?"

He would be happy to try Maren again, but even if he reached her, unless she walked through that door right now, she might not get here in time. Whether he liked it or not, he was all Kassidy had.

"You can do this. You're strong and resilient. You've accomplished so many great things. Right now, the situation might seem hard but remember why you're here. You and Grant wanted a family. I know he's hurrying to you, but you're the one on the mound facing the hardest hitter in the league. You have to take the team to victory. I'm right here helping from the dugout. You've got this."

"Are you a motivational speaker or something?" The doc's brows creased.

"He's my brother-in-law." Kassidy reached for him. He took her hot, sweaty hand.

Kassidy groaned against another contraction and crushed his fingers at the same time. Maybe his speech wasn't so good.

The doc smiled. "Here we go, Mom and Uncle."

He stayed positioned by Kassidy's shoulder as she worked to bring a new life into the world. She gritted her teeth and yelled with every push then flop against the bed, panting for breath.

The hands on the clock on the wall moved with a painful slowness. He glanced at the door every few seconds, hoping for Kassidy's sake one of her family members arrived before the end. She didn't want him to be the only one in the room. She couldn't possibly even if she had called him her brother-in-law.

His heart swelled at the idea of being a part of Maren's family, but he needed to figure out his next move and be the kind of man she deserved.

"I can't push anymore."

"A few more times. We're almost there. Do you want the mirror to see?" The doc's voice was calm and soothing.

The door burst open. Grant barreled through, almost tripping on his boots. His hair was a mess, as if his hands had raked through every piece. His gaze searched the room, landing on his wife. A smile burst wide on his face.

"I'm here. Is it too late?" He hurried to Kassidy.

"Grant." Kassidy sat up with more fire in her eyes than had been there the last thirty minutes.

Grant cupped Kassidy's face. She burst out into tears. Their gazes locked. Everyone else in the room could easily be an intruder in their moment. He could think of a thousand other places he'd prefer to be.

"I'm here, baby. Are you okay?" Grant smoothed Kassidy's hair from her face.

"I am now." She groaned again. "This baby wants out."

"I'll leave you to it." He patted Kassidy on the shoulder.

"Thank you, man." Grant stuck out his hand.

Shane shook. "No thanks necessary. I'm glad I could help." He was glad to be here for part of this, but he didn't belong.

"Shane, please wait in the waiting room. You have to be here when the baby arrives." Kassidy's smile was more genuine for him than it had ever been.

He agreed and went out to wait.

Chapter Twenty-Three

Maren changed out of her work clothes into her favorite soft old sweatshirt and jeans. After the day she had, all she wanted was to be surrounded by everything that made her comfortable.

She popped a frozen pizza into the microwave and grabbed a diet soda out of the fridge. After she stuffed her face full of carbs and carbonated chemicals, she would muster the energy to drive out to the phone store and get a new one. If it weren't for the possibility—slim as it may be—that Peyton might need her, she would wait until tomorrow to get a new phone. The quiet was a welcome guest after her meeting today.

Her career was completely in the toilet now. If she had any chance of building it back, she had ruined that by walking out on Irene and Dakota Stone. They had probably told everyone they knew that Maren was off her rocker.

The microwaved dinged. She dropped the small pizza on a plate and took it to her long dining table with her soda.

She searched her heart and her gut for some sign of remorse for walking out of that meeting, but nothing appeared. She would do it again because they had no right to talk about Shane that way. They didn't know him.

Neither did she, really, but she wanted the chance to find out. She wished he would show up at her door, frustrated by her lack of response, assuming he was trying to reach her.

She flipped open her laptop sitting next to her and searched for this video that the Smiths had mentioned.

"Maren, are you here?" Bailey burst through the front door, banging it against the wall. "Maren?"

"I'm in here. Why are you yelling and breaking down my door?"

Bailey raced toward her. Her curly hair was pulled back in a silk scarf. Her oversized gray sweatshirt hung off one shoulder and tucked into the band of her denim shorts. She grabbed Maren by the hand and tugged her out of the chair.

"Come on. We have to go."

"What is going on? I'm having dinner."

Bailey fisted her hands on her hips. "Why aren't you answering your texts or calls?"

"My phone fell in the ocean."

Bailey scrunched up her nose. "What? Never mind. We're missing the whole thing."

"What thing?"

"Kassidy is having the baby." Bailey screeched.

"Now? How can that be? We haven't had the shower yet." The shower wasn't until next week. She had told Kassidy not to have it too close to her due date, but she had wanted Grant there and they had to work around his recording schedule. Kassidy had also wanted to wait until after the summer season ended because Sea Glass was packed every day in the summer.

"You'll be rescheduling that. Come on."

Maren grabbed her purse, and they hurried to Bailey's car. Maren couldn't believe her sister was about to be a mother. Her heart swelled for a new little person to love and this miracle addition to their family.

"I have to tell Peyton." She reached for her phone, then remembered. "Ugh. I can't believe I lost my phone."

"You can use mine, but Peyton knows. Kassidy sent texts to me and Aunt Joanna. She mentioned she couldn't reach you. I sent Peyton a text. She's on her way to the hospital too."

"Thank you."

"For what?"

"For being the best, quirky sister, I could ever ask for."

"Am I quirky?" Bailey snuck a glance at her.

"You're wearing cowboy boots with those shorty shorts. I could fly an airplane through those hoops dangling from your ears. And you eat too much chocolate." But she wouldn't trade Bailey for all the sisters in the world.

Bailey burst out laughing. "The boots were closest to the door when I left. They're Kassidy's. Grant's were too big."

"Are you going to keep living there now?" So much had changed these past few weeks. She had always resisted change and that might have been why Dave had left her. She couldn't blame him really. Even since her return to Serenity by the Sea, she had challenged some of the changes life had thrown her. She needed to stop being so stubborn. Change came whether she liked it or not.

"I need to get my own place. I don't want to intrude. They need time to be a family."

"You can stay with me."

"Thanks. But I found a cute apartment. It's a winter rental."

"Where?"

"Above the bookshop." Bailey turned into the hospital parking lot and found the first available spot and parked.

They ran.

The elevators opened. Maren and Bailey hurried down the hall. She passed the waiting area, but didn't bother to look. She had to get to her sister.

"Should we knock?" Bailey stopped at the door to Kassidy's room. Maren almost banged into her.

"Maybe." The receptionist in the lobby told them

Kassidy had the baby and she'd been moved onto the maternity floor.

Bailey knocked and opened the door at the same time. "Is everyone decent?"

The room was full of visitors. Peyton and Aunt Joana stood by the window. Dana from Sea Glass sat in a chair, and Shane huddled in the corner, but Maren went straight to Kassidy lying in the bed holding a bundle of love. Grant perched on the edge of the bed near his wife and new baby with a smile as vibrant as the afternoon sun. Hellos were quick.

"Oh, my God, can I see?" She held out her arms. All she wanted was to have a warm baby snuggled against her and breathe in that amazing sweet baby scent.

Kassidy's face lit up. The deep patches of purple under her eyes told a story that would most likely include a lot of hard labor, and Maren would ask all about that when they were alone.

"You came," Kassidy said.

"Why wouldn't I come?"

Kassidy held out her hand. "Maren, Bailey, I want you to meet your new niece. This is Emma. We named her for Grant's brother Emmet."

Maren lifted baby Emma into her arms and held her close. Bailey leaned over Maren's shoulder.

"Welcome to the world little Emma. I'm your Auntie Maren."

"And I'm your Auntie Bailey. I'll be your favorite. Tell her, Peyton."

The room pulsed with laughter. She glanced at

Shane. Their gazes held. He gave her the slightest of nods. She wondered what a child with Shane would have been like. She wasn't as brave as Kassidy to have a baby late in life. Maren would never know what it was like to create a child with the one man she had loved more than any other.

"May I hold her again?" Aunt Joanna stepped around the bed.

Her aunt was still beautiful in her sixties with her silver hair and bohemian sense. She and Bailey had their style in common. Maren always loved her aunt who tried to forge her own life by her own rules, but Maren wondered if she was happy now that she was mostly alone.

With some regret, she handed over the baby. Maren did want a chance to talk to Shane though. She didn't understand how it was he stood in Kassidy's room. He appeared as if he'd also had a rough night in the clothes he had left her in the night before. His lip was swollen, and he had a gash on his cheek from the fight.

She couldn't believe he had allowed himself to fight again. All the hard work to change his image was for nothing now.

"Can I talk to you a minute?" she said to Shane. She turned back to Kassidy. "We'll only be a minute. Then I want to come back and spend as much time with you and the baby as you'll let me."

"Maren, I'm sorry," Kassidy said.

"Me too. We can talk later. Right now is about Emma." She kissed Kassidy's cheek. "Shane?"

All eyes were on them. But they pushed into the hallway without a comment to the crowd.

"Do you mind if we get some fresh air?" Shane said.

"The parking lot?" She couldn't think of another place.

"That will do. I just need to be outside."

The night air held a chill. Summer was only days away from handing the calendar to autumn. She missed the fiery season already. The shorter days and brisk air would scurry them like rabbits on the run into the holidays. She wasn't ready for that. But she did love the beach in the fall when the miles of sand were free from tourists.

They found a spot away from the hospital doors with a flower bed of mums and a bench, but neither of them sat. She wished she'd brought a jacket but leaned into Shane for warmth. He offered her a thin smile and disentangled himself from her embrace. Her stunned heart lurched.

"Are you okay after last night?" She brushed her fingers over his hairline. She wanted to touch him all over, climb back into bed with him and shut the world out, but something was going on with him.

"You heard?" He shoved his hands in his pockets.

"I did. What happened with Evan?"

"It's a long story, and I'm exhausted. I'll tell you about it later." He kicked the ground with the tip of his shoe.

She hadn't noticed the pale tint of his skin or the dark bruises under his eyes. His beard was unkept. He must've had a terrible night. She wanted to make things better for him, but he seemed ready to shut her out.

"You don't want to talk about the fight." Just like he hadn't wanted to talk about what he saw all those years ago on the college quad. He had acted first and that seemed to be what he had done with Evan.

"Not now."

"Where did you go after the fight?" She wanted to reach for him, but she didn't want him to push her away again.

"To jail."

"Jail? Is someone pressing charges?"

"I don't know. Considering who came after us, I doubt it. I tried to call you and tell you, but you've ignored me all day."

"I wasn't ignoring you. I dropped my phone in the ocean this afternoon." She had a hard time believing that event was only hours ago. "Who came after you?"

"I promise I'll tell you everything. I want to go home, take a hot shower and sleep. There is something you need to know though."

"What's that?"

"Kassidy and I had a fight. When I couldn't get a hold of you, I went to your house to find you. Kassidy showed up. We argued. She went into labor."

"She went into labor right outside my house? This whole day is a comedy of errors."

"I was even the birthing coach for a while."

"Now, I would have paid good money to see that one. Shane Sutherland major league baseball manager by day, baby coach at night. You are a man of many talents." She hoped her joke would make him smile or take her in his arms, but he did neither. "Please tell me what's going on with you. After last night, I thought we had moved forward."

"I told Kassidy about us." He scratched the back of his neck.

"You did?"

"It might've been the thing that sent her into labor. She's okay with us now. I guess after I helped her, she didn't see the point in staying angry."

She couldn't believe he would tell Kassidy. "Why would you reveal our secret without talking to me first?"

"I hadn't planned on it. We were arguing. She said she didn't like me. I don't know. It was stupid. But none of it matters. I got fired from the Warriors. You're free to go. You don't have to stay with me."

"I'm sorry. Barry Solomon got wind of what happened, then?"

"He did."

"I'm not looking to end our relationship. You meant what you said last night, didn't you?" Lying in bed with him tangled together had been the most real thing she'd experienced in a very long time.

"I'm no good for you. I've worked my whole life to be the best damn player and manager. I've screwed it all up because I've never learned to let Evan work his shit out. My life doesn't make sense to me without baseball. How can I bring you into a relationship when I don't know what I want right now?"

His words slapped her. She stepped back. "You don't want me?"

"I can't have this conversation right now. I spent the night sitting on the floor of a jail cell. I haven't eaten a thing all day. As amazing as it was to be a part of Emma's birth, I'm wiped out. I should go. I'll call you tomorrow." He turned.

"Shane, wait."

"Go spend time with your family. I need some space." He weaved through the parking lot.

She stood there until the darkness swallowed him, wondering how had things gone from bad to worse faster than the changing tides?

Shane had left her—again.

Chapter Twenty-Four

The fire did nothing to warm her insides. Maren sat curled in her lawn chair with Aunt Joanna sipping her wine in the chair opposite her. As the flames trembled in the breeze, Maren's thoughts matched their dance. They fluctuated between Shane and her precious new niece.

Aunt Joanna and she had returned to Maren's after the hospital. Peyton returned to school and Maren already missed her. Watching a newborn, made her want to hold her own, grown child close, but Peyton had other ideas—as she should.

Grant had swept them all from the room when Kassidy's heavy lids could no longer stay open. He had wanted his two ladies to rest.

Maren envied Kassidy the new life she had built. Maren had wanted some of that for herself. Not the baby part, but a man who gazed at her as if she had painted every star in the sky just for him.

"You okay, darling?" Aunt Joanna waved her arm, startling Maren from her thoughts.

Her aunt was an amazing woman with a full life. She had been married, had children, traveled, worked. She never complained and always saw life as the gift it was.

"Just tired."

"I noticed you came back to Kassidy's room without Shane." Aunt Joanna eyed her over the rim of the glass.

"He wanted to go home and get some sleep." She didn't know if her aunt knew about Shane's brush with the law, but Maren wouldn't highlight his worst moment.

"Quite the day, he'd had, waking up in a jail cell." Aunt Joanna untwisted her hair from the clip and let it fall to her shoulders.

"The whole world knows, doesn't it?" She had never thought about how hard it must be for Shane to have his worst moments televised. Fame truly came with a price; one she didn't want to pay. She loved her life in Serenity by the Sea, her small simple life. She had come too close to the hells of celebrity when Paris destroyed her business. No one should wield that much power. Even the person who had videoed Shane had no business using that fight to further themselves. Which she suspected was exactly why they had put the video up on the internet.

She wanted to help him, but he had closed down the same way he had all those years ago and walked away. He hadn't come to her to work through what had happened. He hadn't shared his fears or sorrows with her. He had become confused and frightened and ran. He was doing it again. She didn't want to leave him, but maybe they truly were better apart.

"He didn't want to talk about it."

"Men seldom do. They bottle up all their emotions as best they can and pretend they don't have any. Except in the dark. Then they have plenty of emotions." Her aunt chuckled.

"Do you ever miss being married?"

Joanna hesitated. Her gaze drifted away. "No. I'm happy on my own. I have everything I could want, friends, family, even companionship. But married? Once was enough for me."

"I miss Dad."

"Me too, darling. I wish my little brother was still here to see that brand new baby and all the wonderful things his daughters and granddaughter are doing. He would just lose it over how you changed his ugly little tavern."

"You didn't like it?"

"Did you?" Aunt Joanna arched a brow.

"Fair enough."

"Knock knock." Bailey barreled through the back door. She had pulled back her hair into a ponytail of corkscrews that bounced with each step. She swapped her shorts for a pair of relaxed sweatpants. "I brought s'mores." She held up a tray of her treasures.

"Isn't it a little late for dessert?" Maren checked the time on her new phone, secretly hoping Shane had sent a text.

"Nonsense. It's never too late for chocolate." Aunt

Joanna unfolded from the chair and helped Bailey prepare the marshmallows.

Bailey pulled a chair close to the fire and shoved her marshmallow into the flames. "I should be mad at you for lying to us, but since I have a beautiful new niece, I'll forgive you."

"What's this all about?" Aunt Joanna looked between them.

Maren took a deep breath.

"She and Shane were pretending to be engaged so he could get a job," Bailey blurted before she could speak.

"That's not the whole story," she said.

"Wait one second. I was only in your company a few minutes, but I know when a man is completely in love with a woman. That man focused on you when you walked in the room and never looked at another person or thing. No one is that good of an actor." Joanna pressed her marshmallow into the sandwich of chocolate and graham crackers.

"Like I said, it's not the whole story. I'm sorry I lied. I didn't want to hurt anyone, but we needed people to believe we were a real couple getting married."

"You two aren't a couple?" Aunt Joanna said.

"Not anymore. At least I don't think we are. Nothing makes sense to me right now. We did pretend at first. I didn't even like him in the beginning. That's not entirely true either. I was afraid to like him again." But then she fell hard.

"So what made you do it?" Bailey licked the chocolate off her fingers.

"He needed help and so did I." She might as well come clean about her money problems. Keeping secrets never helped anything. She should know that by now.

"What kind of help?" Bailey bit into her s'more.

"I was behind on my property taxes. Way behind, in fact. And Peyton needed money for school. Dave stopped paying my alimony. Everything happened at once. Shane lent me the money if I agreed to be his fiancé." She needed to make another payment to him, but without the Stone wedding, she wasn't sure how she would do that. She wasn't booked for anymore birthday parties.

"Why didn't you come to me?" Aunt Joanna said.

"Aunt Jo, are you kidding? Maren ask for help? Not a chance." Bailey handed Maren a marshmallow on a stick. "You need one of these."

"You were always so independent. Like me. Darling, if you need money, I can lend it to you. I have plenty."

"Thank you. I might take you up on it so I can pay back Shane and then make payments to you instead. I don't think I can bear to keep dealing with him if we're through." She would walk out on the Stones again, if she had the chance to do it all over. She didn't want to work for people who sat in their thrones and judged everyone below them, especially people she loved.

She doubted Irene Stone knew what it was to struggle and if she ever had, must've forgotten. Maren would take a good guess that Dakota had been protected her whole life from any hardships. They weren't better than anyone else.

"Don't you have a say in whether or not your relationship is over?" Bailey said.

"I can't make the man stay with me if he doesn't want to." She hadn't been the one to end her marriage. Dave had come to her and said he wasn't happy any longer. He wanted a new start. She wasn't given a say as to whether or not she agreed. He had packed his things and left. Funny part was deep down she had wanted the relationship to end too. But this time with Shane was different. She had wanted a chance with him.

"One of my nieces would never beg man to stay with her. You have too much self-worth for that." Aunt Joanna turned to her, placing a hand on Maren's knee. "But my sweet niece, give the man a few days to get his feet under him. He's taken quite a blow. That ego of his is fragile. I'm not judging him. He can't help it. He's been on a pedestal his entire life. He must struggle with his flaws. After seeing that video, his worst quality was on full view. Anyone would struggle with that. I miss the way things were in the old days. Your worst moments were documented forever and for everyone. I wouldn't want to have to repeat mine."

"Tell us some of the things you did in your youth," Bailey grabbed Aunt Joanna's wine and took a sip.

"That's for another time, girls. Right now, I'm going to take a soak in Maren's tub and read a good book. I love you both, madly. And Maren, tell Shane what you did for him today. He needs to hear it." Aunt Joanna kissed them both and disappeared into the house.

"What did you do for Shane?"

"I'll tell you later. Let me have a piece of chocolate."

"You know Aunt Jo has some crazy stories." Bailey handed over the package.

Maren glanced at the door. "She had a boyfriend once that might have been the love of her life."

"Not Uncle Joe?"

"She loved him. At least for a little while. But no, there was someone else. Someone who I think she still wonders about. She'll get this far off look sometimes when she talks about relationships."

"I wonder who that could be." Bailey practically bounced in her seat.

"With Dad gone, we'll never find out unless she tells us."

"We can forget it then. That woman keeps secrets better than any hoarder."

Maren gasped.

"Too soon?"

"It will always be too soon, Bailey."

"My bad. Here, take a marshmallow."

Chapter Twenty-Five

Shane pushed through the door of Bella Notte. Several customers sat at the few tables along the wall even at the early hour of the morning. The sun had cleared the horizon but sat heavy and low in the sky.

Mario Lanza piped through the speakers mounted to the wall. A small line of people waited at the pastry case as Mr. D helped each one decide.

Shane's car was parked outside and packed with his few belongings. He was ready to head back to New York before the rush hour traffic became heavy. But first he wanted to grab a cup of coffee to shake the fog from his brain. He hadn't slept well in a couple of nights. He also wanted a few cinnamon buns from Mr. D for the road. Shane didn't know if or when he'd be back in Serenity by the Sea.

He hadn't spoken to Maren. He had promised to call her that day at the hospital, but every time he started to, he stopped. He knew on some level he was being a fool for pushing her away, but he needed to put his life back in order before he could commit to her. She deserved a man whose head wasn't up his own ass.

Before he could promise himself to her, he needed to figure out what he wanted to do with his life. His agent had suggested sportscasting. But he never loved sitting down and talking sports. He wanted to play.

"*Buongiorno*. What can I do for you?" Mr. D waved him over to the counter. All the years that Shane had seen Mr. D in this bakery his smile never wavered. He wondered if the man was every angry or upset or disappointed with himself.

"Good morning, Mr. D. Can I get a few of those buns to go and a large coffee please?"

"*Si*. You are up with the birds today."

"I'm getting a head start." He was running away. He had never been one to avoid a problem, but after this last humiliation the energy to confront his problems seeped out of him.

"Ah. Are you traveling somewhere?"

"Going home." Home to an empty house and an emptier life. He hadn't spoken to Evan either. His brother had called him and sent texts several times, but Shane ignored them all. Evan had to take care of himself and fix his own problems. Shane should have made that clear a long time ago.

"This is your home, no?"

He had wanted it to be. He hadn't known that until he had taken up space in that rental and could see Maren every day. But he was finally realizing he couldn't have everything he wanted. He couldn't believe how long it took him to finally figure that out.

"I was here only for a few weeks."

Mr. D handed him the coffee. "*Aspetta.* I don't understand. You and Maren are to be married. Why would you leave town? Is she moving too?"

"She's not going anywhere. In fact, I think she'll be stopping by to discuss another wedding with you. She just booked a big client." At least he assumed she had. They hadn't spoken about it, but he had no reason to believe that meeting hadn't ended with a signed contract.

She didn't need him now. After Dakota Stone's wedding, Maren would be back in the game. He didn't want her to repay him either. At some point he would have to face her and tell her goodbye. From the road. He'd call her from the road.

"Good for her. I'll get the espresso and biscotti ready." Mr. D beamed and handed him a white box filled with the buns. "You don't look so happy. You don't want her to plan this wedding?"

"I want her to plan whatever party she wants." He had wanted her to plan their wedding too.

"So what has you down then?"

He didn't realize his unhappiness was obvious. "Work troubles."

"Ah, work." Mr. D swiped the air with his hand. "What is work if we don't have someone to come home to and share it with? I wouldn't bake so much if my wife wasn't waiting for me."

"Did you always want to be a baker?"

"I wanted to be a singer." He pointed to the ceiling where Mario Lanza had switched to Luciano Pavarotti. "But I had to find a way to make a living. Baking was easy."

"Do you ever regret not chasing that dream?"

"Regret does no good. I wouldn't have my family if I hadn't met my wife and that wouldn't have happened if I wasn't in Asbury Park the same time as she was. Instead of music, I made baking my art. It tastes better." Mr. D winked.

"You're very good at it. We're all lucky to have your store here." He should take a page out of Mr. D's playbook. If the man had a dream, but could find the silver lining in the pivot, maybe Shane could too.

"It's a good life. I live by the water like my old country. It's not always warm here, but I am used to the cold now. I have my friends and my family even if my sons don't work with me like I hoped. Will I see you coaching a team again? I watch you on tv, you know."

"I don't think so. Time for me to retire."

"What's next?"

Shane glanced out the window toward the ocean. He had no idea what was next for him, but suddenly his rush to leave wasn't as urgent. He could sit on the sand for a while and drink his coffee. He had no one to rush hone to and nothing calling his name. He could take all the time in the world. Maybe for once, he could slow down.

"For now, a walk on the beach."

Mr. D bid him goodbye, and Shane stepped out into

the salt air. Clouds rolled in from the west. A breeze picked up. He crossed the street and took the stairs to sand.

He sat near the surf, but far enough away the water wouldn't get him until the tide changed. He would get up then and make his way north. Or maybe he'd stop by Maren's and apologize for being a coward and wish her well.

His phone vibrated in his pocket. He hesitated to answer it. He wanted to enjoy the peace that the crashing waves brought him. He'd forgotten that too in his absence from Serenity. He'd forgotten how much the ocean, the smell of the salt in the air, the sand, all brought him a comfort he couldn't find anywhere else. He missed his hometown.

But that call could be Maren and he wanted to talk to her in the worst way. He dug out his phone to see Dillon Lynch's name on the screen. His curiosity fought against the urge to send the call to voicemail, and he answered.

"Hey, Dillon."

"Shane, I wasn't sure if you were going to answer. I'm glad you did. I have something I want to talk to you about. You got a minute?"

"Do you need me to come give another motivational speech to the team?" Maybe he could be a motivational speaker. He had given many to his teams over the years and he had helped Kassidy find the strength to keep going during labor. That had to count for something. He had always thought about writing a book about his career when it was all over. He could combine the old stories with ways to stay motivated.

"I do want you to come back and talk to the team." A door closing echoed in the background.

"Sure. What about?" The sun's rays sparkled against the ocean's surface. He sipped his hot coffee. Staying a little longer was the right thing to do.

"About what time to be at practice, who's playing what position, funding."

"I'm not following."

"I'm leaving the university," Dillon said.

"Really? Why?"

"I've been asked to coach at Rutgers."

"The State University, big ten and Division I. Congratulations." Rutgers University was the largest state school in New Jersey and had an impressive sports program. Any college level coach would be honored to work there.

"Thanks. My position is open, and I'd like to offer it to you."

"I—"

"Before you turn me down, hear me out."

"It might be time for me to hang up my hat for good."

"This sport still needs you."

"I'm not sure, Dillon." Going from a professional manager to a college coach seemed like a far drop. He shouldn't be arrogant, but grateful instead.

"I know college ball doesn't pay what you're used to, or has the prestige of professional ball, but this school could use you. It's still DI. It's your alma mater. You could help raise more money for the program. Hell, they'd let you teach a class if you wanted. You could ask for anything here and you'd get it. What do you think?"

He thought his head might spin off his neck. "You've given me a lot to consider. I appreciate the offer. Can I get back to you in a few days?"

"Take your time. This is a good fit, Shane. Unless you want to go into broadcasting. No other team will touch you right now."

"Then why are you doing this for me?"

"Because we go back a long time, and I know who you are. I know you aren't that person who was videoed fighting. I also know your brother has a lot of problems and you've covered for him before. If I was a betting man, I'd say you did it again. Think about it. I've got to run."

Shane stared at the phone after Dillon ended the call. Coach a college team? A small team that didn't win all that often. He didn't know what to do.

He did want to talk to Maren.

Chapter Twenty-Six

Maren handed Mr. D her card. She had stopped at the bakery before heading over to Kassidy's to see her sister and Emma. Kassidy was feeling overwhelmed in her new role as mother and Maren was more than willing to be the perfect aunt and help out. She didn't have anything else to do anyway.

"Tell your sister I said *brava!* Bringing a new baby into the world is an accomplishment. These cookies are on the house. I included two of my large chocolate chip special for Kassidy. She loves them most." Mr. D handed Maren a heavy pastry box.

"Thank you. I will. I'll bring in some pictures next time."

"Wonderful. We have espresso and biscotti and discuss your new wedding event."

"Wedding event?"

"*Si.* Shane said you have a new client."

"You spoke with Shane?"

"This morning. Maybe thirty minutes." Mr. D pointed to the clock on the wall.

Shane hadn't spoken with her since the day Emma was born. Maren hadn't called or reached out either. She had been too worried he would reject her again. But she hadn't forgotten what Aunt Joanna had said about allowing Shane to figure himself out. If she gave him enough time, maybe he would realize they could be good together. Or he'd go running because she was a grown woman with no job.

"I'm sorry I missed him."

"Is everything all right between you two?"

She glanced at her left hand. Shane's ring was absent from her finger and tucked away in a drawer in her bedroom. She would return the ring.

"We broke up." She hadn't said that out loud yet. Now that she had, the breakup was real.

"Ah. I'm sorry. Love is hard."

"You are right about that. *Arrivederci*, Mr. D."

"*Arrivederci.*"

Maren pushed out into the late morning sun. She blinked against the glare from the nearby cars' windshield and wished she had remembered her sunglasses. She hadn't noticed before, but Shane's car was parked between the bakery and the music store.

She searched Main Street, but didn't see him walking up or down. Someone sat on the beach. A few others walked along the sand. Could that person sitting be

Shane? Would she be that lucky? She hadn't been lucky so far.

Aunt Joanna's words chimed in Maren's head, but so did Bailey's. She couldn't wait any longer to talk to him. She had a right to say whether or not she wanted this thing between them to end. She wouldn't beg him. If he was determined to leave, to end what they had, then she would allow him to go without a fight. But she would say her peace.

She crossed the street with some hesitation. She could turn back, and he'd never know she was there and spare herself some embarrassment. Or she could straighten her shoulders, put her big girl panties on, and march over to the man she loved and demand he have a grownup conversation with her.

She kicked off her shoes and carried them in her free hand. The sand was cool between her toes. Shane's back was straight and his shoulders square. With each step, words jumbled in her head. She wasn't sure how to start.

"Do you mind if I sit a minute?" She stood above him. He had to turn his head to see her. He shielded his eyes as he looked up.

"Someone reminded me once that it's a public beach." He moved his coffee cup as if to make room for her. He wore jeans and a white button-down shirt. His watch glittered in the sun.

She sat beside him warmed by his comment. She had said that very thing to him the night of Paris and Evan's wedding. "Cookie?"

He chuckled. "I'm good. Thanks. What brings you down here?"

"I saw you."

"I've been meaning to call you." He kept his gaze on the sand.

"No, you haven't."

"I have." He looked at her.

"Listen, Shane, I'd appreciate it if you wouldn't try to blow smoke up my skirt. I know you getting fired from the Warriors before you could even begin was a crushing blow. I'm sorry that happened to you. But shutting me out too was hurtful. I didn't deserve that."

"I needed some time."

"Well, you've had it. What have you figured out?"

"I don't know."

"I don't understand you. We told each other how we really felt. How has that changed?"

"I'm a man who can't control himself. I'm also a man who asked you to lie for him to the people you cared about the most. You were the one who always questioned what we were doing. You have the moral compass."

"Why did you get into that fight?" She had to know the real reason behind it. Shane wasn't a violent man. That truth burned in her gut.

"Evan got tangled up with some dicey people. They came after him. And then me too. The one guy had a knife. I had to fight back. I kept thinking I had to get back to you."

"Self-defense isn't a bad thing. Why didn't you say that especially to Barry Solomon?"

"I couldn't. I think in the end I was just tired."

"Tired of what?" She ran her fingers in the sand.

"Tired of all of it. Tired of trying to prove I could take a team all the way to the championship. Tired of being the manager with an anger issue. Tired of taking care of Evan. Suddenly, baseball meant something different for me."

"You don't want to be a manager anymore?" She never thought she'd hear him say that.

"I don't know. Dillon Lynch offered me a job at the university."

"That's wonderful. I mean, if you want it." He would be local. They might have a chance.

"What if I want to do something else?"

"So, do something else." A wave drew back and revealed a small pile of shells.

"Do you really think it's that simple?"

"No. But it can be done. I've done it. And I'm going to have to do it again. I turned down the Stone wedding." She walked over to the pile of shells. The water circled her ankles before drawing out to sea and covering her feet in sand.

"You did what?" Shane followed her.

She told him about the meeting. "I don't want to work for someone who would disparage you in that way."

"You did that for me?" He brushed her hair off her shoulder.

"I did because you're worth it. I don't know if I want to be a wedding planner for the rich and famous and that's okay. I'm lucky to be able to make my own choices.

I don't think I realized that before. I was mad at Paris for taking my business from me, but I get to decide my worth. Not her or anyone."

The water swirled around her feet again. The foam slipped back to sea.

"You shouldn't give up what you love."

"Neither should you. You can have baseball if you don't mind it looking different than it has."

"I'll think about Dillon's offer."

"That's good. The school will be lucky to have you. I need you to think about something else too."

"What's that?"

"Us. I never finished loving you. I didn't even know that until you walked back into my life. I'm not ready to let you go. I want a chance to try again, a chance to build something solid this time. These past weeks, I wasn't pretending at all. I could make everyone believe I loved you because I did. I do."

"I want to be the kind of man you deserve. How can I be that if I don't know who I am or where I'm going?"

"You are the kind of man who protects those you love. You help out kids who need guidance. You become the birthing coach for a woman who gave you a hard time because her husband was racing down the Turnpike. I know who you are. I've known you since I was a young girl. I've loved you since then too."

"I can't promise I won't get angry, but I will promise I'll never hurt you." He pulled her close.

"I'll make that same promise." The water continued to float in and out around her ankles. She could stand there all day with Shane and the comfort of the ocean beside her.

"I'll love you through the hard times if you can put up with me when the world frustrates me."

"We'll figure out our journey together. We're going to make mistakes. I just need to know you won't run away when times get hard." Something blue stuck out of the sand.

"No more running. I'm sticking. Right here with you. I didn't want to lose you. I just didn't know if I was enough."

"Why? Because you might not have that giant career anymore?" She squatted down and pushed the sand away, but the foam came in and covered it up again.

"I guess." He sat on his haunches too and held her gaze.

"I don't care about that career. I'm not those other women in your past. I care about waking up beside you every morning with the sun streaming in our window and the salt in the air floating through our curtains. I want to spend every minute I can with you."

"I love you, Maren. I was a fool to jeopardize what we have."

"Nobody's perfect." She placed a kiss on his warm lips.

"What are you looking for?"

She yanked the blue piece out of the sand and held it up. "Sea glass. I have been searching for sea glass since the night of Evan's wedding and haven't been able to find any. Now I find one. Can you believe it?"

"I can see you're very excited." He helped her stand.

She rested the sea glass in her open palm. "The night of that wedding I thought I was broken like the glass thrown into the ocean. But I'm not."

"No, babe, you're not." He held her chin between his fingers.

"I'm like sea glass. And so are you. Better for the experiences. Older, wiser and still new. Will you take Dillon's offer?" She put the sea glass in her pocket. Later when she was alone, she'd make something with it. She'd ask Peyton to help her.

"Maybe. We can talk about it some more."

"Are you going back to New York?" She moved away from the water. Shane followed.

"I'll need to put my house on the market. Pack up my stuff if I'm going to stay in Serenity."

"Will you stay with me?"

"In that small townhouse? Not a chance, lady. I'll go back to my rental where I can move around some. Then we'll find a place together." He kissed her nose.

She wrapped her arms around his neck. "How about we go back to my place now."

"Who were the cookies for?" He nodded in the direction of the box.

"I'm making a move on you and that's what you want to know?"

"I'm not dumb enough to reject your move. I just figured you must've been heading somewhere else when you saw me and probably have to get there soon. I don't plan on rushing when I get you into bed." He kissed her.

"I was going to Kassidy's. I promised to give her a few hours off. I should go there." But she wanted to stay with Shane.

"Kassidy needs you. I can meet you later." He eased out of her embrace.

"Is that a promise?"

"A forever promise."

"I like the sound of that." Her new phone vibrated in her pocket. "Who could be calling me?"

"You should look." He grabbed his coffee.

She didn't recognize the number on the screen and couldn't imagine who it might be. "Hello?"

"Maren? It's Gerard."

"Hey, Gerard. This is a surprise." The call could've been from Irene Stone. Maren was grateful it was not.

Shane gave her a quizzical look. She held up her palm and shrugged.

"Are you at the beach?"

"How did you know?"

"I can hear the ocean, darling. Seriously." Gerard dragged out the last word. Maren could imagine him shaking his head.

She laughed. "How can I help you?"

"Well, I just booked a wedding. She wants my biggest package and didn't even blink at the price."

"That's great." She wasn't sure why he was telling her, but she was happy for him. He did a great job with the photos he took of both events and her and Shane. Gerard had emailed them to her.

"Look, we said we'd find a way to bring each other

some business. My bride is looking for a wedding planner. I thought of you."

"That's very nice." Her pride appreciated the thought. She mouthed to Shane that Gerard had recommended her. Shane gave her a thumbs up.

"I think you and I make a good team. We could combine our services and be a one-stop shop."

That idea had a certain amount of appeal. Her calendar was wide open. She liked Gerard. They did work well together. Having a partner in the mix might make the work easier on the hard days, someone to unite with, laugh with. She slipped her hand into her pocket and gripped her new piece of sea glass.

"What's the bride like?"

"She's a bitch on wheels. Will you do it?"

But wait, there's more! Take a sneak peek at book three in the Serenity Series.

Sea Glass Out of Balance

Chapter One

Bailey Russo hid behind the bookshelf in Tea and Tales. Cowardly, really, but she couldn't help herself. The Under the Lilacs book club met every Tuesday night to discuss one thing Louisa May Alcott or another and if they saw Bailey amongst the rare book section, they would invite her to join.

Even though *Little Women* was her favorite book since she was a girl and her sister Maren had read it to her, the last thing Bailey wanted was to sit down with these women as they sipped tea from dainty China cups and giggled over the antics of the March sisters.

These octogenarians were adorable with their gray hair, comfortable clothes, and sensible shoes. Well, except for Cara—who was still adorable—but didn't wear sensible shoes and wouldn't give up her heels. These women were warm and welcoming to all. But Bailey didn't belong in this book club.

She didn't belong anywhere. She wasn't sure she ever would.

The door to the upstairs apartment was positioned right by the book club. She couldn't go that way. She'd have to go out the front of the store onto Main Street and scurry around the back. But those old buzzards—who didn't miss a trick—would notice her running out the door and try to call her back.

She had joined them in the early months of living above the bookstore as they talked about Louisa May Alcott's books and stories. She had even helped with the preliminary planning of the Summer Afternoon of Tea and History event set to happen at the end of this month, but as the days added up, the boarders of Bailey's world closed in on her. She had never stayed long in one place, and it was time for her fly again before she ended up like Beth, Cara, Sophia and Josey—trapped in Serenity by the Sea.

Bailey weaved back toward the Mystery section then tiptoed through Romance until she was at the front of the store. The door opened and a blast of sticky, humid air assaulted her. This summer was unusually hot. As was the man who had entered, but Bailey had never liked spending time with Sterling Billinger the third or the fourth or maybe he was the fifth. She didn't know. Sterling was Beth's grandson, his only redeeming quality.

"Hello, Bailey." Sterling addressed her with his restrained voice. He pushed his wire-rimmed glasses up his nose then tugged the hem of his collared shirt into place. He had a rower's body, tall and lean. He oozed of prep school alumnus and blue ribbons.

"Sterling, hello. I was just heading out. Your grandmother is in the back with her club."

He rolled his eyes. "How many more times can they talk about the same author?"

"Forever. They're delightful. Leave them alone." She

wanted to tell him to pull that giant stick out of his backside, but now wasn't the time to take up another disagreement with him. He was an additional reason she was ready to move on from this place. He was always here, pestering his grandmother about selling her store.

"I'm not bothering them. Am I?" His eyes widened behind his glasses.

"You show up every other Tuesday, checking on your grandmother as if she can't take care of herself."

"She can. It's just..."

"Just what? Oh, never mind. If you'll excuse me. I have to get upstairs." She brushed past him without waiting for his reply. She ignored the aquatic and refreshing smell, drifting off him.

Outside, the July evening showed no sign of cooling down. Sweat broke out on her neck as she took her first few steps.

Tea and Tales sat on the corner of Main Street and Spring Street. It was the last building before the small bungalows began. Tourists and residents meandered up and down the sidewalk. The echoes of their laughter followed her as she ran around the back of the store, past the patio table, and up the outdoor wooden stairs to her apartment. She had moved in nine months ago as a winter rental never expecting to stay after Memorial Day, but the Fourth of July was upon them, and she was still in town.

She let herself in to her tiny place. She had stayed longer than she had anticipated. But now...

The space was hotter than hellfire. She checked the

thermostat which read eighty-five degrees. The central air didn't seem to be working. She threw open a couple of windows, but the apartment didn't face the right direction for a cross-breeze from the ocean. She would suffocate up here.

Just another reason to pack her bags and get out.

She would have to tell her sisters of her latest plan to leave town. They would say they figured she would run for the hills eventually. They would be disappointed in her again, but she didn't have a choice really. Her life coaching business had dried up months ago and she hadn't told a soul. She'd been living off her savings and that was almost gone. She needed a new direction, a new dream, a new vision. Serenity by the Sea had no opportunities for her.

She grabbed her beat up suitcase covered in stickers and a large duffel out of the closet.

Sweat dripped down her back and between her boobs. By the time she had her things thrown together, she would be drenched. Even if she wasn't planning on being at the Jersey state line in an hour or so, she would have to stay with one of her sister's tonight. Someone could die from all this heat.

She wasn't like her sisters who were rooted in this town. Bailey preferred to have the wind at her back and in her hair. They would have to understand. Bailey would miss them, especially her beautiful niece Emma who was nine months old and always happy to see her. Once Bailey found a place to settle or a job that would settle her, she'd reach out to Maren and Kassidy and let them know where she was.

She placed the bags by the door. She'd leave Beth a note to explain about her leaving. Bailey hoped Beth would not give in to her grandson and sell, but whatever Beth did was out of Bailey's control. She would also leave a check for August's rent. She wouldn't dream of stiffing Beth.

A knock interrupted her. She couldn't imagine who would be at the door at this hour and in this heat. She opened it to find Beth outside holding a tall, iced tea.

"It's dead," Beth said.

"What is?"

"The air conditioner. It's dead. I knew it would die eventually. I had hoped it would make it through the summer, but this year is just too hot. Anyway, I brought you a cold drink and wanted to tell you to come stay with me tonight." Beth handed her the cup with a straw sticking out of the lid.

"Thank you for the drink, but I can't stay with you." She accepted the offering and took a long sip. The beverage left a cold trail down her throat.

"Of course you can. You can't stay here. I won't allow it. You'll stay with me tonight. It's getting late. I don't want you to bother your sisters at this hour. I have plenty of room."

"No, thank you. I couldn't impose." The plan she devised tonight while hiding in the bookshelves was to leave. She hated goodbyes and explanations. Usually because she didn't know herself half the time why she made some of her own choices. She could blame her flightiness on her mother who was always moving from one place to the next.

"You're not imposing. Oh, look. You already packed your bags." Beth clapped her hands together. "You're a psychic. I always knew that."

Beth grabbed the big duffel and disappeared into the dark night.

Bailey stood there with her mouth grazing the floor. What had just happened?

Beth poked her head back inside. "Are you coming?"

READ MORE

Acknowledgments

~

As always, I cannot get to this point in a book without the help of some very important people.

Please give a round of applause to:

Lisa Olech - critique partner and friend. She keeps me laughing through the whole process. It's a good thing we don't pay for phone calls by the minute any longer.

Robin Rottner - Content Editor. She catches all my missteps and drops everything to read for me. Thank you!

Joanne Gelderblom - Backend Organizer. She needs a better title than that, but I can't pull off the stuff you guys don't see without her. She is the reason we have the Epic Book Box. Thank you is never enough. How's *merci beaucoup*?

I need to give a big thank you to The Coffee King. He has supported me from day one on this long and winding journey. He is the calm to my storm, my best friend. (And for those of you who don't know, he's also my husband.)

Last, but never least, thank you to my readers. I'm honored that you choose to take this journey with me over and over.

Read On!

xo

Stacey

Also by Stacey Wilk

The Brotherhood Protectors World

Winter's Last Chance

The Last Betrayal

Her Last Word

The Last Days of Christmas

Seduced by Denial

Chill in the Air

Fighting for Tessa

Nash's Promise

Cruz's Watch

Harlan Unleashed

Big Sky Country Series

Time Won't Erase

Stay Awhile

Love Never Ends

Dare to Tell (coming 2025)

About the Author

From an early age, best-selling and award-winning author, Stacey Wilk, told tales as a way to escape. At six she wrote short stories in composition notebooks, at twelve she wrote a novel on a typewriter, in high school biology she wrote rock star romances in her binder instead of paying attention.

But it wasn't until many years later, inspired by her children and a looming birthday, that she finally took her story-telling seriously. And published her first novel in 2013. Since then, she's gone on to publish thirty more so women everywhere can indulge in books that hook them heart and soul.

She isn't done telling stories. Not by a long shot. If you want to read her emotional and honest books about family, romance, and second chances, visit her at www.staceywilk.com

To see what she writes next, follow her Facebook

group for her amazing readers – Stacey's Novel Family
https://bit.ly/2FK8Lae

Or join her newsletter - https://bit.ly/2AojEFk